"If thou gaze long into an abyss, the abyss will also gaze into thee."

—Nietzsche

"Abyss: The primeval chaos. The bottomless pit; hell. An unfathomable or immeasurable depth or void."
—*The American Heritage Dictionary*

You're holding in your hands one of the first in a new line of books of dark fiction called Abyss. Abyss is horror unlike anything you've ever read before. It's not about haunted houses or evil children or ancient Indian burial grounds. We've all read those books, and we all know their plots by heart.

Abyss is for the seeker of truth, no matter how disturbing or twisted it may be. It's about people, and the darkness we all carry within us. Abyss is the new horror from the dark frontier. And in that place, where we come face-to-face with terror, what we find is ourselves. The darkness illuminates us, revealing our flaws, our secret fears, our desires and ambitions longing to break free. And we never see ourselves or our world in the same way again.

descent

RON
DEE

A DELL BOOK

Published by
Dell Publishing
a division of
Bantam Doubleday Dell Publishing Group, Inc.
666 Fifth Avenue
New York, New York 10103

The events in this story are fictitious. References to any real people have been drawn only from reported and accepted histories.
Any other similarities to real persons, places, or events are entirely
coincidental.

ISBN: 0-440-20708-8

Printed in the United States of America

Published simultaneously in Canada

October 1991

10 9 8 7 6 5 4 3 2 1

RAD

*This is for Johanna for the gift of the bones,
and for Davi, for her invaluable help
in sewing together the flesh.*

Wherefore, she who lives in self-indulgence
is dead while she lives.

1 Timothy 5:6

Back to Hell, where I belong,
Back to Hell to keep me strong—
Burn the babies,
Kill your folks
Do any damn thing that provokes!

Rape your girl to be real cool,
Waste the animals and use your tool—
Death awaits us anyway,
So let's revel in its play!

Back to hell is where we'll go,
Back to hell to burn real slow. . . .
Use life now and stake your claim
Do what feels good—
And take no blame!

Excerpt from his hit song "Back to Hell," by Aliester C., title track of Inferno Records *Descent* by Aliester C. (Used by permission.)

1

"Suck away my death and bring me alive. Lose your self and I arrive."

The crowd screamed as the blue lights became orange and flashed psychedelic splendor over the ancient stadium's north bleachers and the autumn trees beyond, then swept back to the hastily built frame stage in the center of the unkempt football field. A bare-chested figure in faded jeans flipped long black hair around his stony face as the wind blew harder, strutting into the glare like a psychopathic fullback. He hopped in front of the glittering drums as he scratched his square chin, his chest curls wet with red fluorescent liquid. The color glowed hot against his brown skin . . . against the green and yellow splatters spray-painted all over it. His face blazed in more of the green tint, evil mirth outlined by heavy greasepaint and clown-white makeup that was as bright as his glimmering teeth.

"I'm the dead, back from the grave—eat me raw and I'll sell what you crave." He shrieked, raising a thick arm high over his head, taking a wrestler's stance and displaying the bulging biceps as the spectator's voices rose again, their cries echoing the shrill song.

"Dead . . . dead . . . dead!" chanted the voices, a mixture from deep bass to shrill falsetto, becoming a part of his song, an unwritten chorus.

And it fit. He masked a smile and walked ahead stiffly, raking his tongue over the sour wet-metal taste of the microphone. He shuffled and bent, sliding his hand over the gritty floorboards until his fingers gripped the fluorescent pink-and-orange hair belonging to the stunt actress he threw there moments before. His voice rose and fell: "I am Death . . . back for my greed"—he cackled, listening to his evil reverberation through the screams and cheers—"and I will take your life . . . and hear you *bleed.*"

Under the black sky, the brilliant colors exploded and blazed over him until he had to close his eyes. But that was okay; he no longer needed sight for this well-rehearsed choreography. He sniffed the brisk September air and let his hand slide slowly across his jeans and over the machete knife hung to his belt, not clamping his knuckles around its handle until the wild screams became more furious. He winked, raising it and touching the blade to his tongue, then to the long-faced woman's pulsing throat, facing the stands that were only half filled by his cheering fans for the full effect and exaggerating each action precisely. With unshown amusement he waited out the drumroll. Then, as silence spiraled down, he sliced cleanly through her bulging flesh, and the cymbal crashed. She came back to sudden life and curled trembling fingers around his wrists with panic. He jerked her close by her hair. He laughed while she spit up thick blood, timed perfectly as the knife sawed the flesh-toned bag around her neck. More of the red, oozy liquid squirted out on his fingers. "I'll have what I want . . . and what I *need.*"

The lights blasted on full force, backed by the guitar's endless electronic blast, and the dry-ice fog billowed up behind him. Laughing louder in trademark insanity, he dragged her deliciously curved body into its camouflage and heard the actress snicker while she tried to stay limp. *"What you need!"* he shrieked.

The false fog was all around him.

"You almost had *me* scared that time," she breathed in his ear.

"Aliester! Aliester!" the loud cries chanted.

He dropped the knife and took a moment to wipe slimy palms on his jeans, then rubbed his sweating forehead. "Yeah . . . well, it's old, now. All the gags are *old.* They know what to expect."

"They love it."

"They *want* to love it," he grumbled, "but it ain't anything Cooper didn't already do."

"But there's nothing else—what more is there?"

He took a glass of water from a skinny stage-hand who crept out of nowhere and watched him disappear behind the huge speakers. The actress went with him. Aliester watched her leave the stage and sighed, drinking as fast as he could—before the night's uncontrollable brisk breeze blew back the wispy fog. "Shh," he hissed, squeezing her nearest tit and walking powerfully past the drummer. He tossed the empty glass behind, hearing it roll but not shatter; held his hand high as the remainder of the gooey redness dripped around his feet.

"More gore!" screeched a girl at the edge of the stage, her eyes wide and vacant as she ripped off her red-and-white Aliester C. T-shirt and threw it at him. Her tongue lolled and she licked her lips, her dripping spit shiny in the glare. "More!" She jiggled flopping, big-nippled breasts. "Seance song!"

Aliester grinned, expecting it.

"Seance song!" howled another girl, running

from the front row of the bleachers and opening her shirt too. "Do it to us with the seance song! *Do it to us.*" She squeezed her smaller breasts together and held them out, offering them, her cry rising above the other yells. "Do it to *me!*"

He nodded at the lead guitarist breathlessly, and got to his knees.

"Seance . . . seance . . ."

"Ghosts and devils dance in the night," Aliester screamed, bringing the mike close and licking it suggestively as the bright lights dimmed, "bringing us unearthly fright! They come to us in our dreams . . . holding us close and . . . *craving* our screams!"

Slowly, like a rising corpse in *Night of the Living Dead*, he struggled back up, sweeping his free hand through the misty air while the guitar vibrated evil chords. "They take our life and give us death . . . but we return as they do . . . throwing off our funeral wreath!"

The girl in front was trying to take off her faded jeans now as other spectators pushed forward to join her, ignoring the uniformed deputies that finally came to life and grabbed at their arms, trying to turn them back. Aliester smiled secretly, not missing a beat:

"Come to us, dead spirits—now! Take us from our Christian vow . . . bring us your death and return—and how—"

The cymbals clashed into the drum's rolling pace. The stripping girls danced with it, and all of the enthusiastic mob was out of their seats now, pushing past the officers, who were now just trying to get out of the way. Aliester smirked: it was almost like a tent evangelist's altar call. He bellowed:

"Come back from your shadowy grave . . . come, let us be your willing slave! Death on earth, death's will over men! Show us how to steal and sin—"

"Bring us back to life again!" howled the audience, finishing for him, and he relished the mad squeals and frenzy, tickled at the same moment by a cold galvanic rush up his back that made his wild black hair prickle and stand.

Silence.

Even the crowd—

Aliester turned to the fat drummer with a frown.

"Death will be, but not for *free,*" sang out a high voice behind him, startling him with its unexpected, biting flair.

Aliester wheeled around, and dropped his jaw at the beautiful black-robed woman right behind him, her hair long and red against a face that shone green, wanton with lust.

"Fuck the dead for eternal bliss. . . . Fuck the Father, His Ghost and Son . . . to piss!"

The lights winked as she slid out of her robe-like covering, glowing in the momentary moon-light. Her long fingernails stabbed both breasts, making them bleed freely.

Aliester's eyes were round. He saw her per-fect nakedness and gulped, even harder as he saw her purpose: the sharp nails tore slowly down from the base of her rib cage to her pubic hair with a wet, tearing scream, flaunting her ghastly white bones and pink organs as they peeked out and shimmered with her giggle. *"Fuck off with life—and fuck with DEATH!"*

He cringed from her thick droplets as they spewed onto him with the stench of bitter vomit. He backed a step, trying to remember that it wasn't real—no matter how good it looked . . . *and how bad it smelled.*

She vanished.

Aliester clutched at the empty air and bent feebly to the stage where she had stood—hardly conscious of the frenetic cheers resounding through the stadium.

No blood.

There was nothing there. No one.

He bumped into the drum set with shaking knees and retched.

The audience was deafening, and the sound finally made him regain himself enough to raise his arms in uncertain triumph, but his tremble was real like the sour puke of his breath, and her

filthy gut odor still stank in his nostrils. "God
. . . God damn," he whined, tormented by the
sickness loosening his bowels.

The audience roared.

2

"H-how did you do it?" Aliester C. picked up a perspiring bottle and sat on a metal chair with his back to the empty, moldy lockers, raising the bottle to wet his lips with the taste of cold beer. He glanced back at the teenaged woman rubbing his shoulders, trying to ignore her firm breasts and flat stomach. Though he wanted the toned cheerleader's body that fit in with these lackluster surroundings, he wanted her secret more. He wanted the way she had killed herself so realistically on the stage.

Sighing softly, he could not help but remember the promoter's warning that his violent show would become commonplace as the shocks wore into familiarity. And so they had. He had once drawn crowds five times as large as this one tonight, performing his show in acoustically perfect auditoriums on *real* stages in decent-sized *cities,* resting in first-class dressing rooms instead of long-unused locker areas like this one. He had been bolting to the top.

But now he only drew rebellious teenagers who wanted someplace to party in small college towns like this one, or who came because the local churches had managed to get him banned from playing inside the city limits, delegating him to sites like this crumbling, deserted football stadium used only for practice by local high-school teams.

Until tonight.

This girl had changed everything with her sudden appearance, her act, and her even more incredible disappearance. It was so real, even as close as he was to her. But when he managed to calm himself enough to look for her, he found that she really *had* disappeared. Not even his manager knew who she was or where she came from, or how she got into the show.

But he didn't give a damn about where she was from or *who* she was, only that she had managed to invigorate his audience more than he had in months. His graphic enthusiasm had shell-shocked fans for two years, promising more each time, and now there was nothing left but lackluster repetition and the loud songs— and the dismal surroundings he performed in now proved the music wasn't good enough to make up for the show. His rise from barroom sets to cutting records was due more to his enterprising horror effects than any real talent in music, and with the groupies becoming scarce, he knew his days as a star were fading.

Until now.

Yes. How she broke in on his act made no difference. He wanted her because her bizarre, realistic suicide gave his show power and new meaning. In this one night she had stopped his slow ebb into obscurity. Like a heavy-metal Christ her show death had given his show *life!*

And she was waiting for him in this locker room that still smelled of old, sweaty jockstraps.

"How in the hell did you do it?"

"I"—her tongue slithered over her thick lower lip and she smiled, pinching her slender face into an eerie grimace under the single incandescent bulb above them—"fucked *death.*"

He frowned, raising his feet onto the rickety dressing table someone had brought in, then moved a finger slyly through his long hair. "Right." He cleared his throat and leaned closer. "Can you teach me how you do that?"

"I might." She put a finger into his mouth and circled his saliva around her nipple. "I might if *you* fuck *me.*"

His right foot pushed a well-used hairbrush. "Want to compare me with death?" He yawned.

"You're close enough already." She smiled.

Chuckling brusquely, he patted her taut ass. "Where did you learn it?"

"Death."

"Besides death, then," he asked. "Who do you know? How—"

"Why don't you just ask who else I've been with?"

He had to force an equal humor, holding in frustration. She had something he wanted. "Okay . . . who have you had in your life?"

Her full red lips parted in a smile. "You name them."

"Cooper?"

She frowned, listening to the hollow echo of his voice as she considered the name. "Not him. I had the Beatles, though."

"John Lennon and McCartney?" Aliester laughed, gazing at a face only beginning to be ravaged by her senseless life-style. "Like hell."

Her laughter mingled with his. "No. It wasn't bad at all. I screwed 'em right here in this locker room when the Baptists banned them from town because of what John said about Jesus."

The unqualified seriousness in her made him stare more acutely, bringing back long-past headlines. He knotted his eyebrows together, then sneered. "That was 1966, darlin'. What'd you do, fuck them when you were ten?" Aliester laughed unpleasantly, and took another chug of his beer.

She smiled. "I was seventeen. Ringo wasn't bad either."

Aliester furrowed his brow and curled his lips. She looked seventeen now, far younger than that experience would make her.

She sighed. "I never could get to George, though. He was on some kind of faithfulness kick to Krishna." Her eyes became distant. "But there's still time, isn't there? Maybe I will yet." Then she raised her arms over her head and did a practiced cartwheel on the dirty floor, bouncing back to her feet beside a long plank bench and winking. "You're the first rocker that's come here since then, bub. They closed this place down right after that concert, when one of the football players raped and strangled a cheerleader for balling the Beatles." She giggled and winked again.

Aliester shook his head at her rambling words —the words of a stoned, teeny-boppin' slut who'd discovered the once-Fab Four and created a doped-out fantasy world she had never taken part in. "Shit," he said, "they've been broke up five years." He remembered McCartney's song and chuckled to himself sarcastically. "They're *yesterday.*"

She giggled with him, dropping her hands to the floor and doing another cartwheel.

"Did you have them all at the same time too?" Aliester sneered.

A vague anticipation tagged her eyebrows. "That might have been different." She brushed the dirt off her hands and touched her wet lips to his neck. "All in the same night, though. It's easier to compare that way."

"I suppose you had Mick Jagger, too, and the Stones?"

"I would have if they'd come to this place." She smiled.

"Right," he muttered, curling his lips again. The ridiculous meandering was irritating, but he listened because what she'd pulled off fascinated him. He counted to ten and rubbed his thumb over the smooth skin of her hip, thinking of the ranting crowd he left.

She nibbled at his earlobe, lifting the sweat-damp shirt up his chest at the same time.

"Come on, how did you do that little trick, darlin'?"

"Business," she mumbled, tonguing his curly chest hair. "That's for later, okay? Let's talk about fucking."

He sighed. "Right," he muttered, rolling his eyes through the shadows. "So you had the Beatles. How about Buddy Holly?"

"Buddy Holly?" She snorted, sliding her cold fingers down into his jeans. "How the hell old do I look?" She squeezed playfully.

"Ow!"

"Buddy Holly was way before my time."

She let go, shifting onto his lap with a quiver in her thighs that made him hard. "I figured that much." He grunted, lowering his half-full bottle to the concrete floor.

"Now you're talking." She scooted back and got on her knees, unbuckled his belt and pants, and tugged them down his thighs to expose his hairy, naked growth. Slowly, she lowered her face, teasing deftly. "Do you want me, hot man?"

He bit his tongue, and gulped as he managed to nod. "Yes . . . I suppose . . . I . . . want you. . . ."

"I've had the best. I've fucked life." The groupie giggled. "I've fucked death. And now I can stay with you if you want me. I can teach you things you only dream." She batted her eyelashes in a mockery of innocence, then bent back down to his arching hips.

"When?"

Her tongue flicked and prodded for several seconds, and she pulled back with leisure. "Soon. You're nearly ready."

"I'm ready *now.*" He groaned and closed his eyelids as she devoured him hungrily, pushing him without mercy to a gasping and sudden finale. He held on to the chair weakly, staggered by her ability and the feeling she put in him as she almost seemed to suck away his insides. He stroked his hands appreciatively through her long hair.

"Quick-Draw McGraw," she said wetly, pulling away. "Shit, you're as bad as Jimi Hendrix."

"I . . ."

"Let's try it again, big guy." Her mouth closed around him once more and he tried to control himself against her, and against the chill that heightened when he realized what she'd said.

Jimi Hendrix.

3

Aliester awoke, choking for breath. His lips were cracked, and he knew by the echo of his lone breaths that she was gone. The cold floor of the musty locker room impelled its chill through his naked flesh. He blinked, dazed, far removed from time and anything else.

Aching arms forced him up to his knees. A face, a body, rose through shadows into his memory. A girl . . . a *slut* . . . He opened his eyes wide, seeing last night, seeing the groupie who had empowered his show.

But she was gone. Except for the waiting lockers and sagging table and chair, the room was empty under the single dim light bulb. And she had told him *nothing*.

Trembling, Aliester pushed himself to his feet. He didn't even know her name.

She was gone.

"Son-of-a-bitch!" he choked, weakly picking up his embroidered jeans from the plywood bench. "Damn it to hell!" His head throbbed and his guts were empty of anything but disappointment. He felt sick from exertion and hunger.

But sickest because she was gone, and he hadn't learned how she'd done it.

"Bitch," he muttered, angrily pulling on the jeans and his stained tank top. She was gone, and though he'd fucked her, it was almost as though he had no choice in it—*as though she'd fucked him!*

As though she'd used *him.*

Someone knocked at the door.

"Yeah?" he gasped sullenly, but turned with hopeful anticipation.

Richard Waterman walked in, scuffing his bell-bottom jeans together in a cloud of gray dust. "Hell of a party?"

Aliester put his hands to his face and pushed damp hair out of his eyes. "Shit." He groaned with disappointment. *"Shit."*

"You must've been doing something besides just jacking off."

"What the hell time is it?"

"Show's in an hour. What, you stay cooped up with that juicy twat in here since last night? We were starting to get worried until Buzz remembered you never left. Until then we thought we'd have to do the show without you."

"Screw off, Dick."

He smirked, and patted his trousers. "They named me that for a reason, Garcia." He walked to the black metal chair and sat down. "Where is she, man?"

Aliester rubbed his hairy stomach. "I dunno. She must've left. Shit, we were at it all night. I—" He shook his head. "Can you get me some food?"

Richard nodded. "I'll send some in. She used you, huh? Wish you knew who she was. With her we could get back to the top in nothing flat. Word is that we're going to have a helluva crowd tonight because of her."

"I told her I wanted her to be part of the act."

Waterman raised an eyebrow. "Wasn't interested?"

"Maybe she went out for a while." He shuddered with the strange sick feeling of emptiness, of being used, like Waterman said. "Maybe she'll come back."

"Think so?"

He shrugged, then snarled, "I think I'm hungry. Get me some food."

When he stepped onto the stage that evening, the stadium was packed with an audience like those from two years before, even spilling into the south bleachers behind the platform; most were kids and all were frenzied with expectation.

But Aliester barely noticed as he went through his standards with boredom, gyrating halfheartedly. He needed the girl—the weird groupie—back.

"Seance song!" screamed the throng of students and hippies as he finished the final stanza of "Babies in Black." "Seance song!"

A crowd had already gathered on the grass nearest the stage. They hopped up and down with wild shouts, but he barely saw or heard them.

"Seance song!"

Aliester glanced wearily at the guitarist and lay on the uneven planks, feeling like the corpse he pretended to be. He rose stiffly. "Ghosts and devils dance in the night. . . ." He sang hoarsely, contesting the greeting cheers, but it was without his usual power—the chill of frustration tore away his vitality.

She was gone—

But he had to sing on.

The cymbals shattered the screams and the fervent cries hushed expectantly.

"Come back from your shadowy grave. . . ." Aliester nearly missed his cue. "Come, let us be your willing slave! Death on earth, death's will over men! Show us how to steal and sin."

"Bring us back to life again!" cut in a shrill, unearthly voice right behind him, and he felt the chill breath linger over him . . . like last night.

"Death will be, *but not for free,"* she sang as he spun around in the night's suddenly chilling air, almost in tears of relief. Her familiar body, once more hidden by black robes, the high cheekbones of her lovely face, full of need, haunted him. He limped to her on hollow legs, nearly stumbling.

"With me, Aliester. *Sing with me,"* she whispered. "Remember the words?"

He reached for her cold hand and gripped it with a returning strength that pulsed in her nearness. He nodded, dry mouthed.

"Now!"

In a tuneless duet he joined her: "Fuck the dead for eternal bliss. . . . Fuck the Father, His ghost and Son . . . to piss!"

The lights trembled and she danced against him, then turned to the ranting teenagers pushing onto the field from their seats in the bleachers. *"Everyone!"* she bellowed.

"Fuck the dead . . . for eternal bliss! Fuck the Father, His ghost and Son . . . *to piss!"*

Hysterical giggles sprang out of her mouth and she dropped the loose cloak to her feet, repeating her act of self-abuse as he intently watched. She was slicing the long nails into the soft flesh of her breasts to make them run with blood, deep into her stomach with sickening liquid rips, splattering the wet and cold gore on his own skin, covering him, showing again the insides of her body as she unveiled them in the spotlights and deafening howls.

"Yucky, huh?" she whispered coyly. "Look at them, A.C. Look what we do to them—what we *make* them do."

He wrinkled his nose and stared out over the churning audience. They spread over the grass like a stain, and the deputies stationed around the field were soundlessly overwhelmed and engulfed, attacked by a sudden mob.

"G-God—"

"*Look!*"

He followed her finger to several couples in the shadows of the stage—a young man moving obscenely against the half-naked girl beneath him as though he were doing lazy push-ups, two young men pressed together in a kiss . . . and then she showed him the mob's outskirts under the near goalpost, where a girl made miniature by the distance stretched her eyes and mouth grotesquely as a boy wrenched her back and forth with one hand, his other raising her short denim skirt above her waist. He fondled her roughly and struggled with her white panties until they were gone, then pushed her down flat in front of the scoreboard, where a poster rippled in the evening wind.

Aliester let his eyes rest on the graphic poster of himself streaked in makeup and hanging by his neck in front of a dozen struggling, hanging babies dressed in black robes, his photograph hands clamped around a scythelike guitar. ALIESTER C.! read block letters under the cartoon blood dripping from the enlarged blade. TONIGHT! LIVE—AND DEAD! TOGETHER!

He turned back to the blood-flecked woman who'd stolen his show from him and shuddered in the air that screamed between the old rusty goalposts on either side of the football field. The teenagers twisted with the raw metal sound of the explosive synthesizer as it roared on, jerking their arms back and forth frantically, their hands fists with the little and forefinger upraised. "God damn," he gasped, feeling the wind whipping harder and colder.

"She's gonna kill herself again!"

The mysterious groupie beside him pulled the sharp fingernails across her throat, splattering his face. The distant teenaged man gyrated berserkly on top of the motionless young woman now, shoving himself back and forth between her pale, outstretched legs. She stared blankly at the poster as he held her arms to the ground and raped her.

The deputies had disappeared.

"Death!" blared the groupie's cruel voice beside him, somehow booming from the massive speakers into the open air. *"Death! Kill and dominate—POWER!"*

"Death!" rejoiced a thousand hoarse voices, hurting his ears as he stood disbelievingly.

"Death is ended! Kill and live again! Kill your love—kill yourself—kill, kill, KILL!"

The mesmerizing edge in his new partner's chanting voice made him hold his ears, and he felt the handle of his rusted, evil machete pressed into his hand. "Fuck *me!"* she whispered.

The force of her voice unshackled him, shooting red, flaming power into his arm. He found himself waving the weapon, prancing around her as the dribbling guts fell from her body. She lay down on the plywood flooring, spreading her legs wide—

Swept with insanity, Aliester suddenly dropped to his knees before her and brought the long knife forward, thrusting it between her thighs, impaling her single-mindedly as she threw her arms back over her head against the drums— But she jeered him, cackling with hysteria when the ghastly dildo rammed inside her and splattered more of her thick red blood in his face. It impelled him with new strength and desire.

Hollering with that violent need, he jerked

the dripping machete back out and brought it down on her head hard, biting into her skull to spray more stinking blood and pieces of her crushed bone all around him. *"DEATH!"* he screamed.

The audience screamed with him, even as he insanely ran toward them on the slippery floorboards, leapt among their ghastly excitement, and grabbed a pimple-faced boy's long blond hair in groping fingers. Spitting bitter foam, Aliester raised the slippery blade and hacked deep into the screaming boy's neck, tearing his oblong head loose from the shreds of skin, and making the others around him grow hushed and still as he held it high, lunging at them with its gory truth. The dying eyes blinked as the severed head's mouth gaped open, then froze. Pieces of the torn flesh dropped at Aliester's feet and he vaulted back onto the stage to wave it ecstatically before his suddenly quiet admirers. The echoes of their voices faded into the silence . . . of . . . *death.*

"Death is reborn into life!" He held the head in his hands and laughed, strutting like a quarterback: "Hut one . . . hut two!" He grabbed the head and drop-kicked it out toward the goal into a hundred clutching hands. *"To know life— you must fuck DEATH!"*

"DEATH!"

Spitting blood, the young groupie who'd begun it staggered to her feet, limping to him and licking the wet machete lovingly. Then she took him in her arms and her lips pressed his, and he tasted the cold, tangy flavor of the freezing lust that emanated from her—through *him*.

But he pulled away breathlessly, his straining eyes darting across the field once more to the two teenagers still beside the poster as the boy's hands tore at the girl to the crowd's rhythm:

"DEATH!" the voices all around cried as the stadium's lights blinked on and off. *"DEATH! DEATH!"*

The straining boy fell onto the girl, his face covered in saliva and running sweat.

"Death," she mouthed in the blaring cacophony, and her white teeth bit his cheek, her possessed face warping as she clamped down, and the purple blood spilled from her mouth and over her lips to her chin.

"Death. Death. Death to life. Life to death."

The hysterical chant drowned out the boy's scream while violence erupted everywhere as the teenagers turned on one another.

And Aliester, feeling strong in their life that surged into him, laughed harder.

4

"I am Garcia Efstathiou."

The lusterless eyes stared back at him from between the smudges of greasepaint in the mirror, and he tried to force humanity into them but knew he could not.

"I am Aliester C.," he whispered to the stale face—his face—looking at him. He saw the words slip through his cracked lips without effort, and longed to be able to cry out in the despair of what he'd been part of minutes before. But despair was beyond him.

Almost. Only memory allowed the barest trace of that emotion. All else was lost and only a longing now.

He touched the bottle of whiskey on the dressing table. He was beyond sickness, but sick to *death*.

Carelessly, he picked up a tiny blue cardboard box of razor blades on the dressing table. In the mirror, smoke rose from the lips of the mysterious girl behind him. She smiled and stood on a bench, inhaling from the joint again and displaying herself like a strip dancer in front of the bleak, open lockers.

Aliester shivered and dared look at the body he saw ruined and torn, the body that had magically and miraculously re-formed before his eyes.

Knocking hammered the door, dragging his eyes away from her. "Garcia!"

He frowned. It was Richard Waterman, and the bitter tone made Aliester look at the door with rising hatred, made him shudder at the horrors he'd witnessed and taken part in—*instigated*—

"*Garcia!*"

He put the razor box on the table and walked to the thick door, trying not to crave what he'd been part of. He pulled the door's handle, and it creaked open to Waterman's pale countenance.

Silence. Their eyes locked.

"*Do you know what you've done?*"

"I—" The hysteria crawled back to him. "I—"

Cold fingers touched his arm from behind. "We gave 'em the best damn show of all time," sneered the girl. "*We gave 'em what they wanted.*"

"The police will be coming, Garcia. You ought to see it out there. People were *killed* tonight!"

A razor blade fell onto the floor behind him. He stared at it quietly, then bent to touch it.

"Kill him too," he heard in his ear.

"Garcia—"

"Kill him."

He took the blade between his thumb and fingers, facing the manager.

"Kill him." She shoved his hand forward. "Death to life and life to death."

"They're going to put you away, Garcia." Waterman's red eyes grew large as he backed into the archway under the bleachers. *"Get the hell away from me!"*

"Kill him!"

He snagged the hated manager's collar with a suddenly vibrating hand and sliced the blade into his nose, opening it like a zipper—

"No! Goddamn—*no!*"

Garcia ripped it through his throat.

The scream became a gurgle as blood flowed out of Waterman's mouth and stopped as the twitching body wobbled and collapsed onto the floor, spilling its life around Aliester's feet. Aliester dropped the razor and felt his heart beating and beaten. *"My God."*

"You're ready, Aliester," the groupie whispered, and tugged at his arm, pulling him back from the still form and the sounds of pain that trickled from the bleachers. "You're ready, now."

Moving with her in limp futility he refused thought. She shoved him back into the lockers and slammed the old door against the night, where the wind was rushing harder and harder. Those sounds combined with sirens in the distance, but he refused to care. Though confused and aimless, he was strong with life. Strong with life that was his because he'd taken it. He *ruled* life. Like death, he commanded life. It was his to take.

He heard the hopeless moans and screams.

"Come on, asshole. We don't need long."

He grumbled and stretched unwillingly. "Don't call me asshole," he grumbled, wiping the drops of perspiration from his hair. "I'm Aliester C. I—I commanded *death.*"

"Or the other way around. And now it's time to meet him, A.C." She laughed deeply, joining a sudden boom of muffled thunder. "But fun and games first. We'll have our time. You broke the lock. The door is weak, now. Someone will open it soon."

Her words were beyond him, but he didn't care. He felt good, and strong, though strangely distant, like he was beginning to become empty again. "What—what do you want?"

"I always *want. Just like you.*"

"I don't know what the hell you mean," he shot back, annoyed, and reached for the box of razor blades. One cut into his thumb as he fumbled with the lid and he grunted, raising that finger to his mouth. "They—they'll put us away."

She reached into the box for him and took out the darkened sliver that had cut him. "They won't get a chance to."

"I don't care."

She nodded. "That's why you're ready. It's been a long time since you have." She reached down to his belt and unfastened it, getting him out of the clothes quickly. "You can't care when you're dead."

"You're . . . *crazy.*"

"And you're a dead man. But I don't want to care." She gave him the razor with a smirk. "I just want to feel how much I can make pain and hurt. I want to feel. *I want.*"

He held the blade before her eyes while she tugged off his shirt. He smiled coldly. "Do you want to die again?"

Her dilated eyes blinked. "I don't care. It wouldn't do any good. I just . . . *want.*"

Who cares? He was dead now—they would put him away forever or gas him. Why should he care?

He put the blade to her throat.

"Go ahead." She leaned into it until the point pressed so hard into her slender neck that the slightest nudge would penetrate her skin. "It won't be the first time, you know."

He did not know, and could care even less, but an anticipation began to fill him, and he dared to smile. With a quick twist he swept the thin metal sliver across smooth flesh, forcing it deep, and felt her thick blood drench his hands. A charge of excitement twisted him and he shuddered, knowing this penetration and the warm, sticky juices dripping over him united him to her more strongly and more pleasurably than any union he'd experienced before.

She flinched but didn't fall. The blood spilled, and she moved a finger into it with purpose, dragging it into a moist scrawl on his naked skin. "Yes. It feels so good the first time, doesn't it?" Her eyelids dropped until they were nearly closed. "You have *accepted* me, Aliester." Her words gurgled. "In life you accepted me into yourself and made me part of yourself. You *wanted* me. *You fucked me.* Now I have accepted you. I came to you and you possessed me as you let me possess you. It makes us one whether either of us wants it or not. Death has been accepted and offered life through your own sacrifice—*a more than willing sacrifice.*" She cupped her hand under her spilling life and shook it, tossing the drops at him playfully. "Hey —wanna have a water fight . . . *with blood?*"

He gasped weakly, dazed. He *had* cut her. The razor blades were real. She should be dying, screaming, *flailing her arms as the blood spurted from her like it had from Richard Waterman.*

"Life and death have become one." Her spilling discharge became a trickle, stopped, and her flesh repaired itself again before his eyes. "There will be nothing to end it soon. *Nothing.* Death will live inside life, nurtured by life. We only wait for our complete freedom, *for the birth of death from life."*

Breathlessly, he slit her throat again. *He was insane.*

"It'll get boring after a while." Her words bubbled, and he felt the thick spit from her mouth on his cheek. She cupped her hands again and let them fill with the thick red liquid, then threw it in his face with a snicker. "Try it on yourself."

Hopelessness pounded him and he croaked, wiping the slime from his chin. He didn't care. The madness drove into him and he forced the wet blade against his wrist, ripping it savagely. The deep gash exposed purple flesh and white bone. A dark splatter— A startling, dizzy pain surged into a gasp. *"Damn!"*

She touched her coppery tongue to his lips, then bent and lapped at his leaking redness like a noisy dog. "But even pain gets boring."

She spat it at him.

"You *can't*—" He felt the sharp throbbing stings and stared at the flow in mystification, trying to get out of the fog claiming him. "I—*I'm dying.*"

Getting down on her knees, she touched his hips. "You've been dead for a long time."

His teeth chattered at her low tone. "Don't." He shuddered, feeling her fingers at his jeans.

"Yes." She giggled, opening the pants and licking the bare skin of his stomach. "It's all I ever lived for. *I can even bite it off!*"

Something—to live for. Aliester grit his teeth and watched his own destruction with distant panic. His body numbed, and he craved the screams of the audience he destroyed.

He had given them a show. He had outdone Alice Cooper.

She slipped the jeans down his legs and closed her teeth over him.

"Ouch." He moaned, wriggling when the incisors pressed harder into his flesh. *"Ouch!"* he yelled, trying to pull away.

She clamped down hard, tearing—

"No!" He fell to the floor, panting, his eyes wide with agony, and vomited into the spraying blood—

But she only laughed wildly, chewing and ripping him until the charges of pain made his scream unfathomable. She pulled away slowly, blinding him with a horrid blast of agony, and gnawed his torn penis in her crooked mouth.

"N-no!" he moaned horribly, nearly blacking out from the white pain.

"Want a bite?" She spat out the ruined brown flesh. "Oh, my, lookie—*a shower!*" She bent into his squirting blood, catching it in her mouth and spewing it back at him. "Just like a garden hose!" She trembled in laughter. "A *fucking* garden hose!

"M-m-my—"

Their eyes met and her laughter died to a low condescending ripple. "Does big bad Aliester C. want his poor dead dick back?"

"I—I . . . *please* . . ."

She made a face, scooted through the puddle on the floor, and picked up the torn penis. "It doesn't retain its flavor, you know." She stood on her knees and tossed it gleefully. "But it's always good to know how you taste to someone else, right? *Eat yourself, Aliester!*"

He screamed, clutching at the organ—his *penis*—shivering as paralysis spread through his body.

"See. It comes right off." She shrugged. "If I'd had the guts to do that when I was alive, it *really* would have been fun." She made a lopsided smile. *"The look on your face."*

Aliester shook spasmodically and more vomit rushed into his mouth.

"Now I baptize thee in your own stinking

blood, Aliester." She cackled. "I baptize thee into the life of death."

"God . . . damn. I—*I d-didn't* . . ."

His life and reality slipped slowly away into the dark puddle he lay in.

"I baptize thee in blood, Aliester C. The blood of the life you *had*. You have called death to life, and I baptize you in your own blood."

5

Samuel slept obliviously. His puffy hot-pink cheek was flat against the orange and green stripes of the sheet, his eyes shut beneath sparse blond hair, and his mouth puckered in an exhausted pout. His breaths were light and contented, and small pleasant noises cooed from his lips.

He lay in his baby bed in the room's center, like a showcase display. The room's pastel colors were still unsmudged, and a close inspection revealed the scent of new paint.

The baby slept. In slumber he grinned toothlessly, and his tiny curled fingers bunched together over the embroidered yellow blanket. The house slept on as the air began to crackle, and a shadow crept in through Samuel's open door, its shape becoming pronounced with reality.

"Life," whispered a toneless voice.

The shadow spilled over tiny Samuel Laster, and he withered into cracked bones and tough, leathery flesh—

Voices drifted as Vickie awoke.

". . . abnormal fetus. Performing necessary C-section—"

"God, look at this, Doctor."

"Holy God. Umbilical cord detached and extreme uteral and overical deterioration."

Samuel.

"I think a radical hysterectomy is in order, Doctor."

"Confirmed. Nurse Spencer—"

"No!"

The scream tore through Vickie's raw throat, her terror overpowering everything, even the drunken pain of her abdomen and thighs. The pungent whiff of alcohol tormented her nose and she forced her leaden eyes open to stare blindly into the white haze of the room, trying desperately to sit up. *Samuel—*

"I baptize you in the name of the Father, the Son, and the Holy Ghost. . . ."

Vickie screamed again, boiling in the fetid water of the shadows, remembering but not remembering, feeling the electricity—

Shadows—and voices crept through them.

"Doctor, she's opened her eyes."

"She's supposed to be *under!*"

"IV is hooked up and flowing. Doctor—"

"M-my baby!" Vickie forced the heavy eyelids to stay open and tried to move an arm, anything, and screamed again as she couldn't.

"Standard pentobarbital."

"Yes, Doctor," echoed a woman's loud, unfamiliar voice.

"Watch respiration."

Panting and afraid, Vickie turned to the big white-masked man bent over her. A deep, horrible prickling raked her. A woman—nurse—swabbed something she could barely feel over her lower abdomen.

She was awake.

Cold sweat streaked her forehead and she struggled to rise. But the deadness of her limbs pierced her, stabbing through the foggy incomprehension of her brain.

"Respiration abnormal," warned the woman's voice as she mopped Vickie's forehead.

Another voice: "Her heart is fluctuating."

The big sinister-browed man nodded and held up a scalpel in his blood-drenched hand, then moved it behind the sheet barring her vision. "Now, Nurse! Damn it—*now!*"

"We're losing her."

Vickie felt the sharp prick in her arm and moaned, then screamed as a numbing twitch flooded through her abdomen. *Samuel—*

"Scissors—now!"

Through the new wooziness that suddenly swept her, she saw the big man hold out dripping red fingers and exchange the scalpel for the scissors.

"No—" she screamed, fighting the darkness that drove into her. Her baby. *"NO—"*

The man lifted up a gory, bony mass of shriveled skin. "Clamps," he muttered, and panted as another woman dabbed at his shining, sinister brow with a sponge. "Goddamn thing starved inside her when the umbilical cord . . ."

Vickie sank deeper in gray fuzziness, still trying to impel muscles that would no longer obey. Sick dread pummeled her as she watched the other man remove the scrawny, dripping figure of a baby—*her baby.*

"Move. Don't stand there staring. *We're going to have to remove it all.*"

She couldn't keep her eyes open and felt weakness, the heat of the bright lights above her, and sobbed, drifting back into the dream that had awakened her, seeing her beloved baby Samuel's frail body in the horrid nightmare become the mess the man had taken from her, just as in her dream of his life. *"No!"* Vickie gasped with terror, trying to grab it with her weak arms. *"Nooo!"* she whispered, her eyes bulging in the darkness that saturated her. She didn't want to enter it again. She struggled to remain conscious, to hide from the memories and nightmares that she could never escape. A pang filled her soul. *"S-S-Sam . . . uel."*

Filmy blackness slipped in and out, dragging her into the fearsome clutches of sleep, and nightmare.

Vickie fell through the years with panic and opened her eyes unwillingly to the off-key groan of an old organ, knowing it was 1974 and she was a child again. The small, whitewashed church was filled with people, and the awareness that this nightmare was real made Vickie's skin crawl. But under the drugs she could not refuse it and it overtook her quickly, dragging her back until she was aware only of her fear and awe of death, and could not think of anything else. "Please . . . no," her shrill voice was crying those years ago. "Please!"

"It's for your own good, Vickie," Mother was whispering. "You *do* want to go to Heaven, don't you?"

Vickie drew back inside her little girl's body, feeling the staring eyes of the congregation on her and knowing she could not get away this time. She didn't want to look at the waiting minister or at Mother—could only close her eyes bitterly.

"Come on," whispered Mother, hurting her

arm. "We go to Heaven or Hell, and you don't want to go to Hell, do you?"

The small congregation was still staring at her from their seats. She swallowed at the preacher's stern features.

"Do you?" Mother insisted.

"I—I don't want anyone to die anymore," she finally choked.

"Death in this life is a small price to pay for eternal life," the minister cut in, taking her hand firmly. "You must not challenge God's laws, Vickie. The protection of innocence is stripped from us by age. Baptism in water must be your redemption now."

"I don't—"

Mother pushed her toward the minister. "Come on, Vickie. You'll feel so much better afterward. It's just like accepting Jesus as your Savior."

Vickie closed her mouth and let the minister tug her to a door. *She didn't want Jesus. Jesus only saved souls, not bodies. She wanted everyone to live forever!*

"Come on, Vickie," the preacher's gruff voice said, leading her to a stairway and up to the baptistry. "Take a deep breath before you go under the water. It will just be for a second, and then you'll be completely reborn in the spirit."

Reborn. The minister stopped with her and began to slip into the wading pants he fished in.

She looked down at her own clothes and re-membered the plain pink dress Mother had brought for her to change into.

Reborn. She did not want to be reborn because she did not want to die, but Mommy said death ruled over everyone's body.

"Come on, Vickie." The minister's meaty hand took hers once more and brought her to the small box-shaped pool above and behind his pulpit that looked out over the sanctuary. He chuckled, trying to be gentle now, and moved with her into the cool water that nearly reached his waist.

"It's *cold,*" she complained, looking out at the hushed people.

"Vickie is here to be baptized in the name of Jesus," the minister said loudly, addressing them. "In the name of Jesus so that she will be with Him when she dies."

She shivered, afraid of his words. She didn't want to *die—she wanted death to be alive!* She knew who was stronger. "In the name of death," she whispered.

"Praise the Lord," called someone far back in the church.

The preacher hadn't heard Vickie, and he smiled. "Just go limp, Vickie." He placed one hand behind her head and she did as she was told, her feet leaving the reassuring solid bottom as she floated and he held her face above the water.

"Hold your breath," he commanded.

She did.

"In the name of the Father, the Son, and the Holy Ghost . . ."

Death, thought Vickie anxiously, and felt his other hand press her under the water, felt its wetness slide over her face and saw him through it, heard the rumble of his words through—

Suddenly, a shocking tingle exploded around her and she felt powerful hands of violence shoot into her. She couldn't breathe, could hardly feel the tingling fire, could only see her body twisting as her trembling mouth filled with the luminescent water.

The minister was shaking too. Her open eyes stared through the ripples as saliva dripped from his open mouth. And then the bulging vein in his neck popped open and blood spurted out, splashing over her as she came to the surface, and it made the water warm as its red thickness filled her eyes.

Death was stronger.

Somewhere inside, she knew it wasn't real anymore, but only a long time ago.

But she couldn't wake up.

6

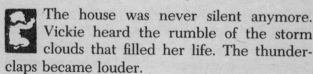 The house was never silent anymore. Vickie heard the rumble of the storm clouds that filled her life. The thunderclaps became louder.

Samuel was *dead*. She sat in a living room that was foreign to her. Her gaze wandered to the gilt-edged mirror on the opposite wall that showed a heart face. Her head was crowned with the limp strands of straw. Deep circles underlined her dull, brown eyes, and faint lines exaggerated her slender lips. Her pear-shaped body slumped in exhaustion.

Beside her sat the stranger she had married and lived with for what seemed an eternity, though she barely remembered any of that long life now at all. She watched his moving lips, trying to make the endless words separate from the violent stream fury made them become. John went on and on, his chiseled features growing harsher with each second.

"It was seven damn months ago and you still want to blame it on me, don't you?" He touched his bare, hairless chest with a thumb. "It was in your damn womb." John jerked the thumb at her. *"You!"*

Vickie closed her eyes. The vivid bleakness was always there. Even the eternity of time already passed wouldn't blur it. Instead, the pain grew daily, and sometimes hourly, until now it was as much a part of her as breathing, and it hurt so bad, she no longer wanted to wake up in the morning.

John shook his head, spitting his booze-ridden breath. "You can't get pregnant now, can't even give me a goddamn son. And you don't even want to."

"I—I need time, John."

"Yeah, you keep saying you want to start all over, you want to begin again. *How?*" His teeth clamped together and his bitter words hissed: "There's nothing left to try with! You—*you're not even a woman!*"

It hurt more than anything else he ever said, making new tears spill. Because he was right, and she wasn't a woman now. She wouldn't ever have children, no longer any more suited for it than John was. The doctors had removed everything—the ovaries, tubes, the uterus—*every-*

thing. And whatever had gone wrong inside her killed Samuel too, and his death brought back the nightmares.

But that wasn't the worst of it. The dreams were bad, like they were a long time ago, but not as awful as going through the pained expectations of motherhood only to lose her precious unborn son and then be mutilated by the scalpels of doctors. She woke up: *Surprise!* No more hope of a second chance at that joy—or any chance of being a real mother or even a real woman. "I—I need *help,* John." She wiped her cheeks and scooted on the fraying cotton of the red couch, trying to get away from the smell of his liquor. She wanted so badly to forget, had tried for these endless months to forget, not to care.

"You need help?" He curled his lip as he spat out the words. "You need to grow up. You think a lot of damn money spent on a psychiatrist or some doctor will *help?* You said you went through that when you were little and that you were fine now." His square face was hot and twisted with bitter anger. "Fine, my ass. Your head was all screwed up then, and now, look at you; you don't even have a real woman's body."

The TV, tuned to one of the two channels they received, showed a barely discernible human image. John had turned down the sound when he'd started in on her, and now his breathing overpowered hers in the silent room.

"You don't care. *You don't even appreciate what I do for you!* I wanted a son, and you killed him." He ground his teeth loudly. "You *killed* him."

"John . . ." She was so tired of this. Nearly every night they replayed this scene, leaving her in the tears that were already spreading down her cheeks, but he wouldn't leave it alone. She *knew* it was her fault. How could she help but know that? Her baby was dead and she would never have another chance to have one. He was dead because of that accident in the church that haunted her. She had even begged death to let her unborn child live, but her words were useless.

Her soul felt dead now too, and her womb was dead and she could never bear life like other women.

She only brought forth death.

Vickie opened her mouth, trying to find words. "John, please—for God's sake, just leave me alone! You've—*you've done enough.*"

His brown eyes gleamed with hate. "I've done enough?" he wheezed. *"I've done enough? You don't even care. You killed him because you don't really have a woman's body—and now all you do is lie around the house like a damn queen!"* He belched and picked up the open

Coors can on the coffee table. "You're just like a faggot with a sex change. You even have to take those frigging hormones."

The words made her flinch. *She still felt dead inside,* and though that death had been physically taken out of her, it only left her empty and mangled, a murderer of the innocent life she helped create. He, Samuel, starved to death inside of her. The tiny kicks she rejoiced in had been his death throes. He died and shriveled, never to see her or know her love.

"Your tits have shrunk so small, you don't need a damn bra! Without those hormones they'd just dry up and fall off!" John shook with intensity, taking another gulp of the beer and squashing the aluminum container between his fingers. "You're not a damn woman. You're not even a man. You're nothing—*fucking nothing!*"

The blood drained from her face. She hated him more than she ever hated anyone. "You b-bastard," she stammered thinly.

His nostrils flared. "What?" He raised his hand and looked at the crushed can, as though weighing a gun, then guffawed. "You don't have a right—"

She stared at him, cringing. "Y-you *bastard,*" she murmured again, her voice quivering.

His laughter became a snarl. "You *bitch!*" He hit her hard in the face with the bent metal, making her ears ring. *"You don't talk to me like that!"* He raised the can again.

White-hot agony stung her forehead. "No!" She covered her head and the pulsating memory burned in her. *"No!"*

"You're the damn baby killer!"

Screaming, she kicked hard, her toes rising into the giving flesh of his groin.

His face went pale, and he bent over in a howl. "I—I'll kill you for that!"

She screamed again, clawing the air to get to her feet, and charging to the front closet. She had to get out! Out! Throwing open the closet door and pulling on the hangers, she grabbed her coat, frightened by the roaring curses that followed, and forced her heavy feet to the front door. She opened it frantically, and stumbled into the frigid night wind. She was nothing. She had *nothing*.

The futile scream boiling in her lungs exploded, and she ran on toward the tangled woods that surrounded the tiny frame house, no longer caring what became of her. Her baby and her insides were dead—dead and buried.

She was dead.

Dead.

Like Samuel, like the shadows.

"God," she wailed, dropping to her knees in the crackling grass. "God!" Hot tears ran down her cheeks and she pounded the ground. *"I want my baby back! I want a baby. More than anything . . .*"Her voice fell. "God . . . damn *life!*"

The house door creaked behind her and she froze, cringing and waiting.

Silence.

Vickie cowered and held her head, waiting.

"Get . . . out of here," John's pained voice wheezed from far away, and she heard the door slam shut.

7

Vickie shivered in the chilling breeze, surrounded by a quiet broken only by her short breaths and the rustle of the October leaves stubbornly clinging to the trees.

"Son-of-a-bitch." She touched her stinging face where he hit her.

The leaves rustled in agreement.

"And so now what do I do?"

Another rustle, and the wind cut through her. Her teeth chattered.

But what could she do? She was far from anywhere but the home she'd walked out of. Mother lived miles away. And it was dark and cold.

Vickie stopped at the roadside indecisively, wrapping her arms around herself and staring back the way she came. Was her self-respect worth freezing to death out here? Then again, *did she care?*

The memory of John's hate, and the way it permeated that house, made her squeeze her eyes tight. He wouldn't let her care, wouldn't even let her have a life, and now she couldn't have a child, *couldn't be a woman.* She *was* nothing.

Just like he said.

Vickie released a deep groan for the demise of her ambition and desires. The fun and challenge of college had disappeared when she met and loved John. He enthralled her with his leisurely way and the private backwoods heaven he promised her, far away from the city lights she grew up in and the nightmares that made her so alone and urged her into his bed. She wanted children desperately even then, and he promised those too.

Then all those things she'd wanted dissolved during her first months with him. The material objects never appeared as he used his meager paycheck on cockfights and liquor. The happy, loving relationship with a man who cared for her frittered away like dandelion fuzz in the wind. She tried hard to make it work, but each happiness she and her high school friends had planned for and wanted disintegrated. She was lost in her imprisonment of housecleaning, mending his clothes, cooking his dinners, and tending the land he wanted to make into a farm one day, and all her desires had slipped away, leaving only the old nightmares that made her wake up screaming until he slapped her. She'd wanted to divorce him—

He got her pregnant.

Her first wild horror dulled overnight as she'd focused on the remaining hope of motherhood she so craved.

Now that promise was gone too.

She needed time, and help—and he wouldn't give her either. John wouldn't give her a damn thing because she was only a woman and now she couldn't give him a son to further his family name! "Dead," she murmured, fumbling inside the coat pocket until her fingers closed around a stick of gum. She unwrapped it mechanically and put the hardened refreshment into her mouth. But it was old and almost tasteless. *Like life.*

She shivered again. Even death had turned on her now.

"I don't care. It would be better to freeze," she whispered. She turned back to the road.

And stopped, her brown eyes wide.

A sleek van waited beside her, its long-haired driver so close, she knew she could stretch out her arm and touch him. His irises were deep blue and so dark, they were indistinguishable from his pupils. His crooked mouth grinned at her. Vickie broke off a cry and jerked back.

"Sorry," his deep words rumbled, and he

scratched the brown skin of his stubbled chin. "I didn't mean to startle you. Need a lift?"

Vickie couldn't make herself smile back.

"Hey—you all right?" He poked his head out the window.

She flushed. "You scared me. I—I'm sorry, I didn't hear . . . you . . . drive up." She shook her head in shame. "I didn't see your headlights."

His smile remained. "This baby's got a quiet engine." He patted the side of the orange, green, yellow, and pink vehicle. It had been painted with a bird's-foot peace sign and a dozen horned centaurs with a baby in their circle. The man followed her gaze with a chuckle and drew back into the cab. "Need a ride, babe? It's awful cold to be out tonight, real cold for this time of year. It's at least five more miles to the nearest farm."

She watched him silently, uneasy with his manner and unwarned appearance. "I—" she shrugged—"I kind of need the walk."

"Did your car break down?" He glanced behind on the silent road. "Maybe I can fix it for you."

"I—I don't have a car," she said quietly.

"Don't tell me you're out here jogging?" He chuckled.

She choked back a sob. "No," she managed, feeling very, very alone. Three years had disappeared down the drain—three years of a life that had been finished from the moment she awakened and saw Samuel's dead body in the drugged horror of the emergency operation. It destroyed all the goals she wanted to renew with John. Samuel had been taken from her like everything else. She could never have another. And now she had closed the door on her marriage and there was nothing left.

Bitch, John said. *You useless bitch. Who wants a horse with a broken leg?*

She had nothing. She wanted to die.

The hard knowledge made her wince and she chewed bitterly. It was only herself now—only herself—and no one cared, not even herself. Agony passed between her dry lips in a whine. She was alone, on an untraveled rural road in the dead of a cold, damp night.

Alone . . . and *dead*.

She closed her eyes as the wind made her tears like ice. Then the car's door clicked, and she listened to the crunch of heavy feet on the gravel and felt the stranger's gentle hand on her shoulder. "Hey. Are you okay?"

She tried but couldn't answer him. Exhaustion poured through her. She wanted—needed —to rest.

"Come on. You're freezing. You'll catch pneumonia out here." He clutched her arm in his own cool hands and guided her to the passenger door, opened it, and boosted her inside onto the leather bucket seat. "Just sit tight." He shut the door and went back around to the other side.

Vickie closed her eyes, not wanting to be there.

Not wanting to be anywhere.

She wanted her child.

"My name's Garcia," his voice intruded softly as he clambered into the driver's chair. "I was on my way into town for something to eat. Are you hungry?"

No more babies, no more pukes, no more doctor's dirty looks. "N-no."

He stared at her placidly, soothing her with his silence for long moments, then: "Where you headed?"

"I—" she closed her mouth tightly, then had to relax in the soothing warmth, shedding the iciness her walk had driven into her—"I'm Vickie," she told him.

"Where are you headed for, Vickie?"

Where indeed? Where am I now? "Where have I ever been?" she breathed to herself.

He smiled and raised an eyebrow.

"I'm sorry." She sighed as the warm air from the vent blew over her. "I don't even know you . . . uh . . ."

"Garcia." He smiled, and his eyes gleamed.

The smile touched her again and she returned it as well as she could, wanting the simple conversation to cover up her horrid experience. It was so cold. If she stayed out there, she would die of exposure soon. She would be as dead as she felt.

Dead. Don't I want to be dead?

"I"— her jaw worked back and forth—"I can't bother you with . . ."

"Hell's bells. You won't bother me, Vickie. What's wrong?"

His concern was perceptive and easy, unlike the brusque manner he expressed it with. It almost made her smile. Despite a stiffness in speech he cared. Not like John. Not like John at all. He made her blush, and it made her like him.

He touched her hand and squeezed it before starting forward. He didn't say anything.

Long, silent moments passed.

Garcia chuckled. "You're too old to be running away from home, aren't you?"

Her hands tensed on her knees, and she suddenly laughed with him stupidly. "I—but I *am* running away from home."

A twinkle was in his eye as he glanced at her. "Parents?"

"No." She sank back in the soft seat. "I'm leaving my *husband.*"

"On a night like this . . . on foot? Couldn't you have picked a better night?"

A giggle captured her until she was in the

midst of a panicked release, and she gave in completely, trying to purge herself of all she'd gone through.

After a few minutes, she nearly choked on the bland gum in her mouth, and went silent. But she didn't flinch when he reached to touch her hand again—was even able to return the slight pressure. "I had to leave . . . *I had to.*" She looked at her chewed nails, not telling him why. She wasn't a woman. Not anymore.

"Do you have any family nearby?" he asked.

She shook her head. "My mother's in Tulsa."

He cocked an eyebrow. "That's not so far."

She sniffed. "I don't dare tell my mother."

"Oh? So what are you going to do now?"

Vickie huddled in the seat. "I don't know. I don't even have my purse." She gulped and balled a fist with frustration. "I don't have anything."

"Where you going to stay the night?"

"I don't know." She made a face and took the gum from her mouth between a thumb and forefinger. "I am tired."

He shook his head. "I have the same problem. I've been staying in an old football locker room." After a pause he winked at her smoothly. "You're welcome to stay there with me for the night, Vickie. It's not real comfy, but it's quiet, and as good a place as any to rest your bones."

Suspicion crept into her. "Why?"

"Because you need someplace to stay." He grinned his easy smile at her.

"I—" But she couldn't finish. She was warm now, but shivered with the inner chill of loneliness. What else could she do? Where else could she stay? If she didn't accept his offer, the only alternatives were to get out and wander until she really did freeze, or go back home to John.

Mother.

But calling her wouldn't make things any better. Mother had lived her life around Vickie, taking her to psychiatrist after psychiatrist. She'd just want to take control of her again. Being with Mother was just like being alone, sometimes even worse. Besides, she never wanted Vickie to marry John, and Vickie shuddered with the dread of how she would smile sorrowfully and say, *"I told you so."*

And with her mother came the nightmares. She would be more than alone.

Alone with the memory of Samuel.

"So what's it gonna be, babe?"

There was nothing she could imagine to say. "Take me with you," she whispered.

He laughed mildly. The sound of drizzle on summer leaves.

The next mile passed in silence. They entered the outskirts of town, passing the scattered warehouse buildings and frame houses in the blink of an eye, and he turned off the two-lane highway onto an overgrown dirt road. Two farmhouses went by, their fields brown and empty, and then a two-pump gas station with blinking self-serve lights and an old neon sign that sputtered shimmering red. She looked at the small house-building and adjoining garage that served as a prop to several tall stacks of tires, then turned back as the van pulled up several yards farther on. Garcia hummed to himself. A dilapidated chicken-wire fence ran along beside them, its warped wood posts covered by peeling green paint.

"Your palace awaits, princess," laughed Garcia, pointing beyond the fence.

Vickie squinted through the shadows. The gutted football stadium behind the tangled bushes did appear a little like some old European castle, but it was nothing to make her feel better. It was dark and creaked in the breeze like it would collapse any minute.

Garcia shut off the vehicle's engine and got out, then walked around and opened her door. He wore a black, sleeveless shirt. "Aren't you cold?" She dropped her gum on the dirt.

"I'm tough." He rubbed his rough hands briskly. "I'll take you inside and find some blankets, babe, and you'll be okay. You can get some sleep and try to figure things out."

Nodding, she let him walk her inside the gate. The silent bleachers ran down over a tiny shack whose shingles were black and curled with age. The whole structure creaked in the breeze as if it would collapse at any minute. Garcia pointed at the stands, their weather-beaten wood like a sunken ship's hull. "This is my home away from home."

Vickie shivered in the wind, and looked up at him, really examining him for the first time. She liked the softness of his Latin features, crowned with that wild, stunning black hair. Despite his scroungy dress and manners he made her feel better.

She caught a breath. "C-could you just talk to me?" She blushed again. "I—I'm sorry. I just . . ."

His easy voice was already familiar to her. "Feel lonely?" He smirked, curling his wide upper lip. "I know just how that is. I'd like to talk to you, Vickie. I'd really like to."

"I don't want to be by myself. I . . ."

He touched her slowly, then wrapped one arm around her as he guided her through the carpet of crackling, dead leaves. They stopped at the dark doorway of the shack under the bleachers. "I know how you feel. But you're not alone anymore, okay? I'll be right here with you tonight."

Standing beside him made her hope, and she tried to forget the way she was driven from her own home. She leaned against him, but flinched at the temperature of his skin. "You're cold . . . Garcia. You should be wearing a coat."

"How do you think I stay 'cool'?" He laughed. "Here we go." He grunted, pushing hard to open the discolored door.

"I . . ." She gulped, and let him escort her inside the darkness. "I . . ."

He lit a match and touched it to a candle on a rickety table. Their eyes locked together a moment, and he looked her up and down, lighting another candle. "Your husband's a stupid man. You're a very pretty woman, Vickie."

She swallowed, and felt a tingle. Not a woman —*dead.* She pushed past him with the taunts raging through her, remembering the hard curses and hatred—the failure—that drove her out of her house. She had to take hormones—

"—like a faggot."

In the dim light the empty metal lockers stood open like thousands of gaping, hungry mouths. A pile of mildewed blankets lay in the room's center. She knelt on them, causing a tiny cloud of dust. Again, she found herself fighting back sobs.

"Hey—"

Burying her face in the damp, stinking fabric, she shook with emotion. She was incomplete, not a woman or man.

She was dead. Her baby was dead.

"There." Garcia's voice was awkward and

stilted. She felt his fingers on her shoulder and tried to shake them off. "Hey . . ."

"No!" She clawed the blanket wildly, lost in self-hatred, angered by his pity. She didn't care —she didn't *want* to care! *"No!"*

"Darlin' . . ."

His voice was uncannily soothing to her pounding head, but as he touched her she jerked away. "No!" she screamed hysterically. "You don't know. *You don't know."* She broke off in a pathetic wail and huddled on the floor, her arms thrust out defensively. *"I'm not even a woman. I'm dead. Dead. Something was wrong inside of me. They cut my body. They took away part of me."*

"Vickie, baby . . ."

She bolted up and stared at him glassily. "I— I'm not a woman anymore—and—and I don't *care!"*

His hands stroked her, sliding over her coat.

"Garcia—" She felt the hot tears run down her face and tasted their salty moisture.

"You're *alive,* Vickie," he said gruffly, slipping the coat off her shoulders and letting it fall behind her.

"I . . ."

"You're a woman." He touched the top button of her shirt, then unfastened it slickly.

Vickie tensed, feeling her thoughts cloud,

grow incredibly dark. She squeezed her eyes tight. "But I . . ."

The fingers continued, opening her shirt, and she felt those cool, careful hands. "I—I'm dead, Garcia." She panted for breath. "I'm dead *inside.*"

His face moved near. She felt his lips cover her mouth and let her bizarre longing open it to him.

The kiss was nearly timeless. It seemed that days passed . . . and she slipped into that unending excitement.

"Vickie?"

"Wha—" She opened her eyes dizzily to the flicker of candlelight.

The muscular, rough-looking man lay next to her on the scatter of blankets, naked, cradling her head on his shoulder and resting his fingers on her side. She stared without understanding at the pale scars on her own naked body; felt goose bumps . . . and weak.

"What?" Vickie stared at him, confused, afraid, and cold. She couldn't control her tremble.

"It's okay."

"N-no." She gurgled.

"You *are* a woman, Vickie."

She shook her head, trying to remember. "You took off my clothes."

Garcia nodded and touched her hand. "You're a woman, Vickie. A stunning, beautiful woman. You're *alive.*"

"No." She shut her eyes again and shook her head desperately. *"No. John says—"*

He raised an eyebrow.

"They took away my u-uterus . . ." She blinked as his icy fingers touched her shivering breast. "I—I can't have children. *They took away my—everything . . ."*

But the fingers were smooth. "You're alive and you're a woman, Vickie. You *are* a woman. You are *alive.*"

"I can't have a child."

His hand moved down her stomach slowly, growing warmer . . . making her moan and writhe. She moved into his strokes hungrily, disoriented from the unexpected pleasure. "A child?" he asked.

"I . . . can't get pregnant." She gasped, shaking. "But, God . . . I—I want . . . one . . . I want one . . . more than anything. I . . . *want—"*

He licked her navel, and slid lower . . . teasing, making her shudder. . . .

It was insane. She could not be doing this. No one wanted her. John said— Who was this man? Why was she *here?*

Why was *he* here?

"Do you want my baby in you?"

Why? Was any of this really happening, after all? Hadn't she been walking and walking and walking . . . until she stumbled and froze to death in this horrid final delirium?

"Vickie?"

Baby.

"God. If you could. If only you could."

He moved up between her legs, and she sighed at the hardness that suddenly teased her, losing the fears in an insanity of desire. She wanted—

"Do you want me?"

"God . . . yes. Yes, Garcia. Yes. *Please.*"

"I need you, Vickie."

". . . I want you." She winced while he grinned, forcing roughly into her dry body. *"Please . . ."* She bucked against him fast and hard, rubbing raw, then feeling blood's lubrication.

He pushed in and nearly out, then deeper, and back again. "I need you, Vickie. I *want* you."

She closed her eyes, swallowing every move, craving the meaning he was bringing her. "I—I *need.* I need *you,* Garcia."

"We fulfill . . . one another . . ." he breathed, "we *exchange*—"

"Oh . . . oh . . . Garcia—" Her thighs trembled, driving out the nightmares, the memories that welled inside. Sweating, she pulled on his bare hips, dragging him in deep, fastening on the pleasure she found. She wanted so much.

"Oh—yes! Yes—yes!" Her frustration crumbled as the power mushroomed and shook every nerve in her body, burning her in violent, crushing orgasm. She screamed, feeling the painful pleasure suck out her very soul, and fell back gasping, weak in satiated emptiness.

Then, as her last waves slipped away, he began to shudder, and Vickie held his tense body thankfully as his own explosion drove him so far in that the force almost tore apart her throbbing flesh.

Cold sticky wetness shot into her.

"No." She screamed at its frigid intensity.

His icy lips rubbed hers.

"Noooo . . ." She gasped.

His smile was dark now, and he pulled out with a ghastly, ripping effort.

Blood sprayed out from the torn hole between his legs. The cold, rigid flesh of his penis remained lodged in her still.

"NO!" she screeched.

"Yeah," giggled a high falsetto.

The young red-haired woman appeared beside him in the candle's wobbling shadows and laughed gleefully. She cupped his blood in her hands, then splashed it over the shack's walls and over Vickie. She threw handfuls into the air. She spilled them into Garcia's mouth. A razor blade danced in her fingers, and she slashed it across his throat.

Vickie screamed hysterically. With shaking hands she pulled out the penis still pulsing inside her.

"Something to remember me by," he gurgled, spitting his blood.

Vickie screamed, finding herself on trembling legs and lunging drunkenly for the door. Adrenaline pumped through her system as her hands closed on the doorknob and she pulled—got open the door—and ran outside into the frigid air. A sharp rock dug into her foot and she stumbled, fell.

The ground was freezing and she choked on dust. Tears streamed from her eyes. *No . . . no . . . no . . . no.*

She pushed herself up from the frigid earth and staggered through the black night for the rural gas station down the road. Her numb feet crushed the dead, tumbling leaves. At some distance she heard her teeth chattering, joining her pounding heart. Hours and years passed in the wind that caught her hair . . . decades . . . and then she was through the gate and hurtling frantically down the road. As the gas station approached, she stumbled over a discarded muffler, then finally slammed into the office door and fell inside screaming.

"Please help me!" She was sinking into a dark, dark hole. Sinking. *"Help me!"* she screeched, and barely felt the hardwood floor as she crumpled upon it.

8

" . . . came in hollering like she was killed."

From deep inside an echoing cave the words filtered into Vickie's thoughts. She made a halfhearted effort to open her eyelids, mystified by her exhaustion.

"Did you see anything?" asked a deep voice.

"Nawp."

"What's her name?"

The other voice grunted. "Don't know. I think I seen her before, though."

Vickie opened her eyes, suddenly remembering the violent, inconceivable nightmare she witnessed. Her heart lurched, and an emptiness like when she saw Samuel's limp, ruined body filled her. *Garcia. That woman* . . .

" . . . who she is?"

Shivering, she looked down at the coarse gray blanket covering her, then at the policeman

who was speaking before a tall counter. His gray
hair was thick under a felt cowboy hat, and his
rocky face was like someone had taken a ham-
mer to it when he was born. His thin lips were
pursed quizzically under a flat, blushing nose.
An unshaven, oil-smeared garageman leaned on
the other side of the counter against the cash
register and his mouth moved soundlessly,
chewing tobacco. Behind him waited a younger
man in a plaid jacket, his eyes huge and white.

"Don't know her," that young man said carefully, "but I think I've seen her before. I just
moved here last year to go to school. Classes are
full of shit, but the fishing's real good."

The sheriff nodded and wrote on the pocket
pad he was holding. "Did you see anyone
around here tonight you haven't seen before?"

"Hmmph." The older man rubbed at a grease
spot on his hand and shrugged.

"He—" Vickie stopped. Her throat was sore
and parched. "He . . . this man who was with
me—"

The sheriff looked her up and down, then
glanced at the men and rubbed his chin
thoughtfully. "You boys didn't do anything to
her, did you? Nothing illegal?"

Jerry shook his head in boredom, and the
younger man blushed. "Hell, no. She ran in here
naked like that. Honest, Sheriff."

He walked closer, creaking the boards with

his steps, then bent beside her. "Steady down now, miss. No one can get you in here." He patted the golden five-pointed badge under his open coat. "Not now."

Pulling the blanket up to her chin, Vickie swallowed nervously. "They—they're *dead,*" she burst out.

The sheriff frowned, narrowing his eyes. "Who?"

"I don't *know.* A man . . . a woman . . ." She saw her destroyed son held in the doctor's bloody arms. "In—*in the stadium!*"

The sheriff looked back at the desk, then lowered his palm to a holster and unfastened the leather strap over his pistol.

Vickie shook her head. "There was blood all over the place! It was awful—there was blood *everywhere!*"

The sheriff looked at the men.

"We haven't had a customer all night except for Barney down the road," Jerry grumbled, smacking his tobacco loudly. "These damn kids go in that place when they ain't wrecking their cars and they're always seeing some kind of shit."

The uniformed man frowned harder, then shook his head at Vickie. "I'll need to ask some questions if you want me to file a report, miss." He reached down and pulled the slipping end of the blanket over her foot. "Are you feeling good enough to answer some questions?"

A haze of unreality foamed around her. The gentleness of Garcia's voice flowed over her. "Y-yes."

"What's your name, miss?" he asked, touching his pen to the notepad.

She took a long, deep breath.

"Miss?" he asked softly.

"Vickie. Vickie Laster."

Recognition crossed his face and he smiled honestly. "Yes . . . I've met your husband. My name's Kelsor, but everybody just calls me Sheriff." He scratched his head, then spoke more softly: "I'm sorry about . . . what happened with the baby."

She closed her eyes, refusing his consolation. Overpowering sorrow throbbed in her veins. "God . . ."

"You sure you haven't seen or heard anything unusual tonight?" Sheriff Kelsor asked Jerry.

Jerry spat on the floor. "Nawp. Not till she came running in, I didn't. Been damn quiet. Kids are usually tearing up and down this road drinking and smoking their shit till daybreak, but it's too fucking *cold* tonight. Still, that's where your money is. She was probably getting stoned with some damn student from the college and just freaked out. Used to be a lot of that back when the hippies hung around."

Kelsor bit his lip. "Who's that pickup out front belong to?"

"Barney," Jerry answered. "He got pretty drunk while we were playing cards and started walking for home a few minutes before she showed up." Jerry shifted his tobacco to the other cheek.

She shook her head. "I—I *saw* them *die.*"

Shrill sirens broke through the night, and Kelsor glanced at the door. "Ambulance will take you to the hospital in Stillwater, Mrs. Laster. I'll do some checking around that stadium and see if I can find anything." She flinched as he touched her hand with cold skin that reminded her of Garcia. "Shh—don't worry, now, miss. I'll check around." The sirens grew loud, and flashing red and blue lights showed above the stacks of multicolored oil cans in the big front window. "I'll tell your husband where you are."

New fear surged into her, overcoming her panic. Her mouth went dry. "No . . . don't . . ." But she was the type of person people often didn't hear, and he had already stood and was walking to the door. A blast of cold air struck her as it opened and two men in white entered with a stretcher. They laid it beside her and moved her onto it, scraping her bare ass over the frigid canvas.

"Jerry," said the sheriff, "have your boy come with me."

"Hey," the young man cut in, "I got class tomorrow. I don't want—"

Vickie held herself in her arms as she was taken outside. The flashing brightness of the ambulance cut brightly through the ebony night, illuminating the bare-limbed trees. Then she was lifted inside. A flabby-cheeked man took her pulse and checked her eyes with a tiny bright light.

"Sheriff Kelsor!" called another paramedic at the ambulance door.

She heard whispers and closed her eyes again, slipping back into the exhaustion that still held her. The scene of Garcia and that woman bolted across her thoughts, filling her with the memory of the cherished orgasm that became a nightmare. Over and over. It seemed that long hours passed.

"Hey!" cried out a squeaky voice, far away but growing nearer. "Hey, Sheriff—"

The sheriff's answer was muffled.

"Over here on the road!" came the young man's high, breathless tremor. "Barney—he—he's dead. It's like . . . *God damn. It's awful— never seen anything— His body's all crushed and like it's—like it's fucking melted!*"

The sheriff mumbled something again, then stepped back into the ambulance's doorway and looked in at Vickie. "I'll come by and talk with you tomorrow if you're up to it," he said, his face briskly gentle, then turned away again. "Send another ambulance, Bill."

The second paramedic got in beside Vickie. "Will do," he replied, then shut the door.

The engine started up, sending its vibrations through Vickie, and the siren accompanied it.

9

You're alive, Vickie.

The voice was hollow, but right at Vickie's ear. She started to open her eyes as she awoke, but then squeezed them tightly shut. "No," she whispered through clenched teeth. Garcia and that woman weren't real. They *couldn't* be real.

She brought her fingers to her ears.

Do you want my baby in you?

Confused, Vickie opened her eyes. An empty plastic chair sat beside her bed. The white wall behind it emphasized its emptiness, and she sighed. Like the horrid nightmare images that consumed her sleep, the words were only memories. *Dream words.*

A yellow plastic curtain hung on her left and a counter across from her was covered with a box of gauze and bottles of lotion. A hospital room. Hospitals were the gateways to death.

"No," she murmured, seeing her child being torn out of her again, feeling the horror of his tragic, incomprehensible end.

It was all real. The past months flashed back terribly, and she knew they were true. And then that ragged man came, giving her meaning and strength, taking it all away in a ghastly nightmare that was *real*.

The knowledge made her cold. "Oh, God," she murmured, and closed her eyes again, though too terrified to sleep. After a while she heard footsteps near and then felt a damp hand, and something cold on her breast. She made her mind blank—and after what seemed hours of consciously holding out the terrible visions, she opened her eyes once more.

"Good afternoon, Mrs. Laster."

Turning her head, she saw the big sheriff from the night before sitting in the stark chair beside the bed. His leathery face was worn, and he wiped a ragged fingernail along his bristly right cheek, then bent forward. "How are you feeling?"

"Tired," she managed.

He nodded. "You had quite a night."

She didn't answer.

"Are you better now? They had to put you under sedation."

She kept her dry lips together.

"Do you feel up to talking a little?" He rubbed

his rough hands together. "I'm sorry to disturb you. I can come back later if you'd rather. Might be tomorrow, though." He smiled briefly. "All sorts of crap going on in this county the last couple of days."

"Did"—she licked her dry lips—"did you find *him* . . . or the woman?"

Kelsor stared at her carefully, then shook his head.

The fuzzy wonder of her dreams returned. "Th-there was blood *everywhere.*"

"We didn't find any blood, Mrs. Laster."

Vickie stared at him with disbelief. "I saw it!"

"Easy, now." Kelsor leaned toward her slowly. "That's why I'm here talking to you. You're the only witness, and I can't seem to discover any evidence." He regarded her steadily. "We're not even sure of what you saw."

Vickie's throat was tight. "I didn't make it up."

He nodded. "They did a thorough examination of you last night, Mrs. Laster. Routine for an emergency patient. No evidence of drug use or drinking." He rubbed his broad nose. "A man did die last night—they don't know what happened to him either. He was . . . Did you say that this man you saw killed picked you up on the road?"

"Yes."

"Awful cold to be out."

"Yes," she agreed. "I—I was leaving my husband. I—he—I didn't have any money and that man didn't either. He said he was sleeping in that locker room. He took me *there*."

Kelsor frowned thoughtfully, causing his thin eyebrows to struggle across the chasm above his nose. "Were—were you spending the night with him, then?"

"Y—" She stopped, understanding what he was asking, and felt herself blush.

Kelsor seemed uncomfortable too. He cleared his throat, not looking at her. "Did—did the two of you . . . have relations?"

Her face felt hot and her mouth was bone dry. It was so distant now. But no less vivid. "I . . . no. Yes. H-he—"

He stared at her silently, took a large manila envelope from an inner pocket of his coat, and unfolded it. "Mrs. Laster, the examination you were given here showed no evidence of your having had, uh, relations with anyone last night." His voice was slow and careful.

An icy hole opened in her stomach.

Kelsor opened the envelope with the crackling fire-noise of paper being torn and took out a newspaper clipping, then held it up before her.

"Wh-what's that?" Vickie scooted back on the bed and sat up against the headboard; touched the yellowed paper. "He—"

"Is that him, Mrs. Laster?"

Garcia stared at her from the newspaper photograph. His soft eyes and easy smile just as they were last night, before— "Who—how—"

Taking the paper back, Kelsor looked at it himself. "Was that man's name Garcia Efstathiou?"

Pressure thudded in her brain.

"Mrs. Laster?"

"Yes . . . *Garcia.*" She sighed.

The sheriff shook his head. "Then I don't know what to tell you, Mrs. Laster."

She reached back for the paper. "I . . . Wh-who is that in the picture?"

"Garcia Efstathiou—alias Aliester C." He stared at his rough hands. "He died several years ago in that shack you said you stayed in."

She put a finger into her mouth, biting it. *"God—"*

The sheriff paused and swallowed. "It . . . was before my time here. It, uh, seems he's become something of a local spook, though. From time to time we get reports of 'him' driving the country roads around Stillwater, clear up to Lake Murray and sometimes as far south as the Cimarron River. He cruises in a painted hippie van—just like the one he came here in before the Eagle Stadium rock massacre."

Vickie felt her heart beat faster.

"No one knows exactly what happened to him. When the police found him an hour later he was dead—mutilated. They don't know who did it, and no one really cared about finding out after what happened. Did you ever hear that story before?"

Vickie shook her head stiffly. "Just vaguely. Sometimes people say things about—"

"Yeah." The sheriff frowned again. "Seems to me that if you heard that story, and being out in the cold after a fight with your husband—"

"B-but I didn't walk all that way!" Vickie felt a hole blossom inside her, sucking her into its fear and confusion.

"I don't know what else to tell you." The lawman shook his head and turned his lips down apologetically. "How could it be, right?" Kelsor put the clipping back into the envelope and shook his head. "It's okay. A dozen other people see him every year. . . ."

Vickie coughed.

"Do you want me to get the nurse to give you another shot, maybe? After some more sleep and rest you'll feel a lot better."

From deep inside her a high-pitched howl began, tearing her lungs, and she drifted with it out of her body into dry stagnant air until she was falling through a dark nothingness . . . into that formless pit that knew no end.

10

Vickie sat restlessly in the soft-contoured chair, keeping her eyes averted from the two doctors and taking in the surrounding room instead. It was clean and businesslike to the point of being uncomfortable. Fat hardcover books were stacked uniformly on the shelves covering the far wall, and the big desk in front of her was arranged flawlessly, pens in a silver cup on one end and the clean white phone beside two looseleaf notebooks at the other.

Time passed, but it had no meaning. A lot of time had passed—months—but the fear begun so long ago was still as near.

"What do you dream, Vickie?"

She shrugged, edgy in the presence of this newest doctor—Sarah whatever-her-name-was. The blond-headed woman was about thirty-five, Vickie guessed, and even though her blue eyes were mild and her words soft spoken, the questions were endless—and they were always the same. She'd repeated what happened so many times it almost wasn't real . . . and at times, like right now, she could almost pretend it *hadn't* been real, or at least that it happened to someone else. "I just dream. Everybody dreams."

"Yes. Everyone dreams," Dr. Sarah agreed. "Do you dream much now?"

She shrugged again and took a half-empty package of Wrigley's gum from her leather shoulder purse.

"I'll be more specific." Sarah glanced over at Dr. Drake standing on the other side of the office beside a four-drawer file cabinet. Bulges overpowered Dr. Drake's middle and caused his yellow shirt to spout over his belt like a geyser. Sarah looked back at Vickie. "Do you seem to dream more now than before that night?"

"I have more nightmares."

"That's natural." Sarah smoothed her brown plaid skirt and picked off a white thread. "Are they vivid?"

Vickie frowned. "I don't remember much about them when I wake up. I've told Dr. Drake that before. But what happened wasn't like that at all. It was nothing like a dream. It—it wasn't a dream." She looked down at her swelling belly, which was beginning its short-lived challenge to Drake's. Her first feeling of joy had given way to anxiety now. She knew it was *his*—that man who'd picked her up. He made her pregnant. *But she could not be pregnant.*

Impossible. "It really happened. *It really happened!*"

"I don't necessarily disbelieve you," answered Sarah quickly. "Easy now . . . okay?" She held one of Vickie's hands.

"I'm . . . okay."

Sarah stayed close. "What do you think you saw, Vickie? Was it real—are you *sure* it was real?"

"I didn't walk all the way by myself in that cold," she whispered. "I—I was half frozen when . . . *he* . . . drove up." She rubbed her bulging tummy, her voice brave with the repeated telling of these past months. "I didn't do *this* by myself either."

Looking down at her, Sarah raised a dark eyebrow. "Did you see him drive up?"

"Not exactly." She sighed. "I just looked up and there he was. He called to me and asked me if I needed a ride." Vickie's brown eyes went from Sarah's thin angular face to Dr. Drake's chubby one, then back. She grew serious with the remembered need and chewed hard. "I—it was cold. . . . I was freezing."

Sarah squeezed Vickie's hand. "Then what happened?" she asked.

"He acted like he really cared. I don't . . .

remember everything now. I—I guess I should, as many times as I've been asked. But he asked if he could *help* me."

"And you told him what was wrong?" Sarah asked.

Vickie blushed. "He . . . took me to that place. I felt so empty and alone. I wanted to talk to him—I wanted to talk to *anyone.*"

"You liked him?"

"No . . . yes. Yes. I needed to be with someone." She took a deep breath, looking nervously around the room.

"And you made love with him?"

The words hung too close for long seconds. Vickie bit her gum in half. "Y-yes. God, but then—" She stopped, knowing she couldn't talk about that even once more. The horrible things that had followed brought it too close. She shook her head slowly. "He—he must have gotten me pregnant." She bit her lip now, feeling its pang. *"But that can't happen. They told me it could never happen again!* They—I didn't believe it for months. I thought—the books I read said it was psychosomatic. I couldn't be pregnant. I didn't believe it . . . but"—she chewed the gum furiously—"Mother made me go to an obstetrician. He said I'm at least six months pregnant. He wants me to have an abortion!" She screwed up her eyes. "I won't. I want the baby. *I want it! I want . . . a baby!"*

Sarah touched Vickie's shoulder lightly.

"Was he real?" Vickie stared up. "God, how could he not have been. How could I just imagine something like that? *How could I imagine anything like what happened to him?*" She gripped the arms of the chair tightly, remembering the experience so vividly now, she almost swallowed her gum. "How—*how could I get pregnant?*"

Dr. Drake cleared his throat and raised a stubby finger.

Directing a frown at him, Sarah stroked Vickie's hand with a soothing touch, running her dry fingers up to Vickie's wrist. "Could you give me a moment, Doctor?" she asked coolly. "Could you go get me a cup of coffee and give me just five minutes?"

Dr. Drake didn't answer. He turned back to Vickie and twisted his thick gray eyebrows between a finger and thumb. "You just can't be positive that the baby *isn't* your husband's, Vickie. You've got to accept reality—that you created this incident to make the baby solely yours, because of how you feel toward John Laster. You've talked to other psychiatrists. You must be aware of how dangerous the situation is to you. The tests made have shown that the baby is abnormal, and its birth will almost certainly prove fatal to you. If you'll just admit to yourself that John Laster is the father, it will be a lot easier for you to give it up."

Vickie looked away angrily, wishing he were right. At least then she would know those horrible memories weren't real. But the baby inside her had been growing for only a little over six months, its inception pinpointed almost to the night she left John. And she hadn't slept with *him* since Samuel's death months before that.

"You just—" Drake shook his head, at last facing the tall woman he'd asked in. "I won't have you encouraging this difficulty she's having, Sarah."

"I won't encourage anything," Sarah said honestly. "You asked me to come here. You thought that my special studies might help."

His mouth worked silently, making his jowly face look like a pig imitating a cow. Then he looked at his watch. "Five minutes, then." He sighed, stood still another moment, then picked up one of the notebooks on the desk and went through the door, leaving it slightly ajar.

"Is that better?"

Vickie took a tissue out of her purse and wrapped the gum in it. "Yes . . . yes. He makes me feel—threatened. Does that make sense?"

"More than you know. Did this Garcia make you feel threatened, Vickie?"

She didn't answer.

Sarah reached for her oversized black purse

and got out a pack of cigarettes and a small note-book. With a glance at Vickie she dropped the cigarettes back into her purse. "You said he was nice, though, didn't you? A kind and caring man always catches a woman off guard." She stared directly into Vickie.

"He"—Vickie rested her eyes in the gentle plaid designs on Sarah's outfit and fought her thick tongue—"made me feel like a person again . . . like a *woman*. But—but then—" She clenched her fist.

"How did it feel when Garcia touched you and when you touched him?"

Vickie blushed. She fingered a button on her blouse and pulled at it. He had unfastened her shirt so carefully. . . .

"I'm sorry. I didn't mean— How did his skin feel? Was it warm, cold? Rough?"

"It—it was cool." She scooted back in the chair as far as she could. "Almost cold, I think. I told him—I told him he needed me to warm him up. But what he did to me—I've never felt that good before. It—it . . . and then . . ." Vickie blinked with the wetness in her eyes. *"God, it's horrible."*

"But are you sure it happened, Vickie? Are you sure *he* was *there?* Couldn't someone else have taken you to the stadium and left?" She took a Kleenex from Drake's desk and gave it to Vickie.

"No." She took the tissue thankfully and dabbed at her eyes. "He *was* there."

"Vickie, if what you described was real, it should have nearly killed you." Sarah picked up a pen and touched it to her lip thoughtfully.

Vickie breathed slowly.

"But you're all right, aren't you?"

"Y-yes." She squeezed her eyes shut.

"Had you ever been out to that stadium before, Vickie?" Sarah asked, leaning forward. "Did you know that other man they found out there later that night?"

"You mean the one who died?" She interlocked her fingers and squeezed them tight, listening to the rapid beat of her heart. "I don't know who he was. His name was Barney something, wasn't it?"

The older woman wrote something down. "Had you ever been there before?" she asked again.

Vickie shook her head vigorously. "Never. I had heard about it being there, but that's *all*. I didn't even care about where I was that night. I was just tired and upset. It seemed like no one cared about me, just like when I was little and Mother sent me to the doctors. When Garcia came, he acted like he wanted to help." That betrayal on top of all the others made her wince, and she narrowed her eyes. "But no one really *cares.*"

"That's not true. I want to help you, Vickie."
Sarah smiled at her with warmth. "I know you
want to understand. I want to help you understand. I want you to *know.*"

Vickie grit her teeth. "I . . ." Behind them
the door squeaked and Sarah looked at her
watch with a sigh. Exactly five minutes had
passed.

Drake peered in. "I have more questions I
need to ask."

"Doctor—"

His brow furrowed. "I should be in here. She's
my patient, Sarah."

Sarah took out an embossed card and slipped
it into Vickie's hand. "Call me later and we'll
talk some more," she whispered, then put a cigarette in her mouth and went to the door.
"That's all I can do then, Doctor. Ask her your
questions and I'll meet with her another day. In
my work I prefer to deal directly with the subject . . . without having someone over my
shoulder." She didn't smile as she stepped past
him. "I've got another appointment, so I'll have
to leave. Call me later at the office." She faced
Vickie and smiled again. "Nice to have met you,
Vickie."

Vickie nodded and looked at the card in her
hand. *Sarah Finley,* it said, *Psychiatrist.* She
watched the blond woman's back as she went
out the door, then turned to Dr. Drake as he

opened his notebook and sat down. She unwrapped another slice of gum, wishing she were
going to be talking more with Sarah instead, and
waited for Dr. Drake's questions, and his lec-
tures of what *must* have happened rather than
what *had*.

11

 "Vickie . . ."

She sighed, stretching out on the bed, wanting. She wanted . . .

"Vickie . . . darlin' . . ."

"Yes. Yes, please."

"You feel so good. . . ."

His fingers moved below her stomach carefully, touching the right places—caressing them, taking away her bad, lost feelings.

"Yes." She gasped. "Garcia . . ."

He was a ghost. Garcia had never been there. He was dead—killed years ago. He was dead like her baby.

Like Samuel.

The name touched the shadows in her.

Samuel was dead.

"Like me."

Vickie heard her own sleepy words and opened her eyes to the dark bedroom. Then the desire that was mounting in her dissolved in self-disgust; it was her own hands that were rubbing through her pubic hair! She clamped her mouth shut and pulled them away, a cry in her throat. *Garcia did not exist.*

She stared at the bulge low on her pale stomach and sat up in bed, her breaths ragged as she closed her nightgown. She wiped her hands on it sickly, knowing she was tormenting herself in her dreams with something that was no more than a dream itself—the dream of a dead man. She wanted and lusted for a dead man.

"God," she whined, wanting to be rid of it all. Yet . . . and yet, she knew it was not a dream, could not be, any more than was the baby she carried. Garcia had to be real, because he gave it to her. He gave so much to her, and then took it away.

But the baby proved he was real.

The warning of its abnormality frightened her, and yet . . .

It was another chance. Despite the horrors she witnessed, it was the second chance she so needed.

She remembered Garcia's spurting blood and was dragged back past it to the horrid nightmare memories of the minister all those years ago.

"No," she murmured, pushing herself to the edge of the bed and then lowering her feet to the carpet. "Oh, God. What have I done to myself?" Wetness crept into her eyes and she staggered to the light switch, blinking at the pale yellow room in its glare. She stared at the curious familiarity of the surroundings she grew up in, seeing her past lurking behind the new paint that sought to cover it, in the dolls and fuzzy teddy bears she had left behind. They stared at her from the dresser top where she abandoned them for marriage to John Laster. They each had names, though those identifying handles were nearly forgotten now, and she looked away from their mournful glass eyes to the dresser mirror that reflected the undeniable enlargement of her abdomen, and her pale face . . . the dark, deep circles under her damp eyes. "What have I done to myself?" she whispered pathetically.

What indeed? She escaped the life of hell alone with her nightmares to marry that bastard and live in the sticks as the subconscious horrors continued to overtake her. Now her own private hell wrenched her sleep and her waking hours as well. All the attempts by the obstetricians at a logical explanation were hollow: her memory of Garcia and that terrible night was more real than life itself. After they had made love, she'd stood face-to-face with the violent impossibility of a nightmare—a nightmare that everyone said couldn't be real.

"Please!" she screamed, grimacing. But she held in another wail as she remembered her mother. "I . . . need . . . *help*," she told herself, and thought of the psychiatrist, Sarah Finley. She'd given Vickie her card. At least she did not dismiss all this with a wheedling argument. Her words and voice were soft and caring.

Vickie went to her handbag on the other side of the room and opened it, digging through keys and makeup until she found the already bent card. She glanced at the clock and walked slowly to the phone. It was late, almost one A.M., but if Dr. Finley were the kind of doctor Vickie needed, she wouldn't mind a call from a—a *patient,* no matter what the hour.

Hot desperation stung her as she sat down at the phone and picked up the receiver, then pushed in the numbers to the residence listing on the card. The phone rang . . . and rang. . . .

12

Sarah jerked up with a start at the shrill sound in her ear. Her skin was slick on the sheets as she reached up the bed's smooth frame for the alarm clock, trying to shut it off. It was still city black beyond the open curtain across the room, and she blinked, at last knowing the sound was from the phone.

"You going to get that?"

His voice almost made her jump, and she saw Mitch sit up on the other side of the double bed.

"It's the phone, Sarah; want me to answer?"

Sobering, she pushed the sheets down past her legs, sat up, and stood. "Jesus . . . what time is it?" she groaned, then yawned, her rubbery legs taking her gracelessly to the dressing table at the side of the room. She ran her hand blindly across the books she'd left there and lifted the receiver. "Hello?"

"Dr. Finley?" a thin voice at the other end of the line asked.

"Yes?"

"I—I saw you this afternoon in Dr. Drake's office, remember? My name is Vickie Laster. I—I'm sorry to be calling so late, but I needed to talk to someone. I thought maybe that you—"

"Uh . . . it's all right," Sarah replied, yawning again. She rubbed her eyes, finding and sitting on the half-backed chair before the makeup table. "I don't mind."

"Who is it?" asked Mitch's deep voice from the bed.

"I keep dreaming, Doctor." Vickie's voice was nervous and flat. "I . . . I don't know. It's hard to explain."

"Who is it?"

Sarah glared at Mitch's shadowed countenance and covered the receiver with her hand. "Shh," she hissed loudly, then spoke quietly into the phone. "Would it be easier to talk to me in person?"

"It's so late," Vickie said, her tone taut. "I shouldn't have called you. It's just that you seem— I'm sorry. I'll call you back in the morning."

"Would you like me to come over and see you now?" Out of the corner of her eye she watched her guest's small but trim physique as he got out of bed and passed the open window to the bathroom.

"That's too much to ask, Doctor. I really shouldn't have called. I don't know why I did. I just . . ." There was a long, muffled silence. "I —I'm sorry I bothered you."

Sarah blinked as the bathroom light came on. She heard the splash of Mitch urinating a second later and wished he'd shut the door. "You're not bothering me, Vickie. I want to help you." She hesitated. "I could meet you somewhere."

"Would you? Do you mind?" She seemed eager.

"An all-night restaurant, maybe?"

"There's one a couple of blocks away."

Sarah took a pad and pencil from the table to rest on her legs. "What's the address?" She breathed in to control another yawn.

"It's at the corner of twenty-first and Sheridan. Are you sure you don't mind, Doctor?"

"Not a bit," she said sincerely, coming fully awake with the questions that were reviving in her. "Say in a half hour?"

Vickie's reedy voice sounded relieved. "Thank you. Thank you. I'll see you then."

Sarah listened to the line click dead, then hung up. The toilet flushed. She wanted to tell Mitch more about Vickie, but needed to hold back. Mitch had come far since Dr. Drake first introduced her to him. Drake told her about his nightmares and their causes, all the way back to his mind-fuck as a child when he was playing with his sister and accidentally locked her in an old dumped-off freezer. It had taken years to bring him around to dealing with that guilt, and he'd been fine until he married. Then his wife became pregnant with a child he couldn't cope with because of his past and he'd left her. She aborted the baby a few days later . . . and then she had committed suicide. The pressure of guilt had exploded in Mitch, combining with the things that happened to him before: both he and this girl, Vickie, had undergone ghastly traumas in childhood that had been seemingly put to rest but had been reactivated by disaster years later.

"Boy, did I have to piss," he grumbled, yawning.

"Yeah," she said, jarred from her thoughts. Her eyes roamed over him in the bathroom's glare—tall and normally well groomed, his broad cheeks were darker than the rest of his brown body with the evening's stubble.

"Life is hard when you can't find an answer," he'd told Sarah one time.

He said that a long time ago, and Sarah had looked at him uncertainly. *"To what kind of a question?"* she'd asked.

"Why?"

Not why does this happen, or that. Just "why?" She had no idea of the answer, but that simple word of complexity was behind it all. That question had destroyed his innocence as a child, and then his rationality as an adult. It made her try to keep her words to him cautious, even though he usually seemed more than able to listen to the problems *others* had . . . sometimes with blinding insight.

Why?

"Who was on the phone?"

"Why—what?" Sarah swallowed. "A patient. The one I met at Dr. Drake's today." She shrugged at him apologetically. "I have to go meet her." She passed him and flipped on the overhead fixture, revealing their wrinkled clothes on the floor, the books she'd left open on her desk, the wedding picture of her and her deceased husband, Lesley, beside the window.

Mitch raised his small, childlike hand to protect his vision, then walked to the bed and rapped that hand on the mattress. "Is that my cue to leave, or do you want me to stay?"

"It . . . would probably be better if you left, Mitch."

"Do you really think she's another possibility for the institute?" He frowned, picking up his wrinkled slacks from the yellow carpet. "I thought you professional types didn't have time for anything but that Jim Whitten guy these days." He flapped the slacks in the air to straighten them, then hesitated.

"I'm not that involved with Whitten."

"Not unless you want me to be jealous." Mitch smirked and rubbed his cheek. "Well, how about spilling the reasons why this girl is so fascinating, then?"

She bent down to his green shirt and handed it to him. "You do have your own problems, Mitch. More than enough without trying to handle another."

He put fingers in his ears and wiggled them. "Come on. I don't think I'm Napoleon anymore . . . or even Jesus Christ. Besides, it isn't *my* problem. You and Drake both said it helps everyone to hear the things that go wrong with other people so that they know they haven't got things so bad as they think they do."

It made her laugh weakly. "That's true to a point, but you're just barely out of the woods." She let her hand rest in his; Mitch was careful in what he said these days, even careful with how he moved. It was so easy to forget how he was: his sessions with Dr. Drake had been growing less and less frequent and he guarded himself well, even better with her help. "I don't think you've ever *really* gone over," Sarah finally continued, "but sometimes I can't be sure if you act so crazy because you really are, or if it's your defense against really *going* crazy."

"I'll never tell. But seriously, with all the things we've told each other, I can't believe the way you keep your work some kind of hush-hush secret."

"You know it's not that, Mitch," Sarah said quickly. "It's just—like I told you, she's been having nightmares. When I read her file there were . . . some things about her that made me think of you."

"Come on, Sarah—like what? We're both having nightmares? Hell, you talk to people that have them every day."

She kept her voice cool and controlled. "It's just that she had psychiatric problems when she was younger, *too,* and after the baby died in her womb it brought her back to the edge. I told you that they guess the baby was dead at least a week before they took it out."

He arched his eyebrows. "You just said she had a hysterectomy and it gave her some problems with her husband."

Sarah crossed her arms, wanting to shut up. But she wanted to keep talking at the same time, because talking was how she figured things out. "But that's only part of it, Mitch. Vickie left her husband . . . walking. A man picked her up on the road and took her to a shack where he was staying. She said she watched him die. She said he began coming *apart.*" She tried to keep her voice from shivering. "She said he covered the whole place with blood."

"He . . . God, *how?*" Mitch's jaw went slack. He clenched his small fists and unclenched them slowly.

Watching his expression, Sarah slowed down. "Nothing was found. No blood . . . nothing. There was no evidence for anything she saw, but she dreams of it constantly, and she's pregnant again. Very pregnant."

Mitch frowned. "Wait a minute. I thought you said she had a hysterectomy."

"Yes," Sarah replied, not blaming him for his incredulous tone. "The coroner's report attributed the death of her first child to a deterioration of the umbilical cord. They had to do a C-section to get it out, and they tied off her tubes. The fact that she still got pregnant after that is one of the reasons this case interested me." She took his palm and squeezed. "And she's saying the man who picked her up has to be the father. She identified him with an old newspaper clipping as Garcia Efstathiou."

Mitch raised an eyebrow, but his fingers stayed calm in hers.

"Aliester C.," she went on. "The Eagle Stadium Rock Massacre. She says he took her to the locker room where the police found his body, and that he went to bed with her. It seems like a queer fantasy under the circumstances, but it *could* fit in with her trauma. Except her description of his death matches almost exactly the police report Dr. Drake passed on to me of what happened in that locker room years ago, *even to the details never released.*"

Mitch finally shook his head. "I remember enough as it is. But go on; this person makes me sound normal."

Sarah smiled briefly. "Her being pregnant is as psychologically impossible as it is physically, considering her state of mind at the time it must have happened. I don't think she would have willingly had relations with any *normal* man. She was near suicide."

Mitch's mouth twitched and he clicked his tongue loudly against the roof of his mouth.

Seeing his frown and hearing that noise, Sarah realized what she had said and squeezed her lips together quickly. Though at first Mitch had only satisfied the need for companionship Lesley's death impelled on her, she felt more for him now, and knew she had an unfair dependence on him considering his delicate state. "Mitch?" Sarah closed her eyes briefly. "Mitch, that's enough for now, okay? I've got to get dressed and go."

"I could just wait here till you get back."

"When I get back I plan to go straight to sleep."

He put the pants down on the bed and pulled the shirt's sleeves up his arms. "Fine. I *love* going home in the middle of the night, especially after a bedtime story like *that*."

"Mitch, please, don't be angry." She began to put on her own clothes silently, choosing fresh ones out of the closet rather than the boozy-smelling plaid skirt and blouse she wore earlier. When she finished, she saw that he was watching her.

His big lower lip pouted, and his cheeks were drawn under his suddenly dull brown eyes. Sarah sighed. "Look, I'm sorry, Mitch. I'll tell you more about this tomorrow, okay? It's just something I want to find out more about. It's nothing to do with you."

"Is that a promise?" he asked, crossing his heart ritualistically.

Sarah nodded slowly. "I promise," she said earnestly. "Hey, I enjoyed this evening."

He moved nearer her, resting a hand on her hip and squeezing gently. "So did I."

She picked up her big purse and went to the apartment door.

"But you're still real moody." He laughed.

"Me?" She thought to tell him that he was so moody, he was nearly a psychological study all on his own, but the words were nasty on her lips and she swallowed them fast, opening the door without another word and waiting for him to move into the wide, flower print hall. She stepped out and locked the door securely. "See you tomorrow," she breathed, and walked away, hurrying to the railed stairway, past other numbered doors.

"Right," he called after her. "And next time you come over to my apartment, okay? I don't like going home so late . . . in the cold."

She almost changed her mind and asked him to stay, but just waved her hand and started down the stairs.

13

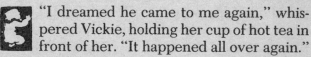"I dreamed he came to me again," whispered Vickie, holding her cup of hot tea in front of her. "It happened all over again."

Across the restaurant, a pockmarked man sat at the front counter, his wispy white hair trailing over his collar. Three booths down another craggy man in a lavender jacket was seated across from an older gentleman. Near the entrance a spaced teenager in a worn Led Zeppelin T-shirt played a whining video game and groaned and cheered himself on until he was breathless. The only visible waitress pulled a loose hair from her eyes and wiped the counter persistently, avoiding the pockmarked man's space. Her lazy jaw worked as she popped sequential bright pink bubbles.

"But you knew it was a dream this time." Sarah cleared her throat faintly. "So how can you be so sure the man who gave you a ride stayed with you, and you didn't just fall asleep and dream that too?"

Vickie pushed away her mug. "That's what Dr. Drake said. That's what everyone says."

"It's the easiest thing to believe, Vickie," Sarah replied. "Sometimes we let ourselves escape into a fantasy to avoid a reality we can't face."

Vickie pulled out a stick of gum and began to toy with it. "How could I dream up something like that? What do you really think, Sarah? Do you think it happened—or do you think I'm insane? I'm pregnant when I have nothing to be pregnant with, and—and the people at the hospital told me there was no evidence I—" She shook her head. "My husband wouldn't sleep with me after Samuel . . . died. I haven't slept with him in months. If the baby was somehow his, I'd have already had it."

Sarah twisted her lips indecisively. "I'd like to talk to Drake about this some more—about letting me have some sessions with you. He means well, but you need more than a psychiatrist. You should have been seeing someone with parapsychological training from the beginning." She frowned, pouring more sugar from the clear hexagonal container into her coffee. "Vickie, Dr. Drake asked me to see you because of my background, did you know that?"

Vickie shook her head.

"I'm a psychiatrist, but I'm a little different from the others you've met." Sarah's spoon made steady reassuring clinks inside her cup. "I work with a group that does parapsychological studies—experiments in psychic phenomena. Dr. Drake thought my input might be enough to prove to you that everything you saw and felt was only in your imagination."

The man in the lavender coat and his companion got up and passed them, chuckling at some unheard joke. "I don't want to go back to Dr. Drake," Vickie whispered urgently. She waited until the men were at the cash register to continue. "He doesn't help. No one helps, Sarah. It makes me feel so alone." She shrugged her shoulders with limp resignation. "I need someone to talk to. . . . I wanted to talk to you. I think . . . you seem like you care."

"I'm sure Dr. Drake cares, too, Vickie," the older woman replied. "And he can help you in ways I can't. I might be able to convince you that your experience wasn't real, but that's only part of it. You'll need his help too. You are pregnant, despite the unlikelihood of it. My problem is how it happened, and his is helping you deal with it. All I'm trying to do is to get you to remember how it began so we can figure out if it happened in the way you believe it did, or maybe not. Either way, your first step is to try to stop thinking about it. That's the best way to get over these nightmares." Her lips turned up. "It'll be kind of like quitting smoking. I've done that before, and believe me, it isn't easy." She tapped her fingers on the table, then sighed. "I want to help you, Vickie, and to try to help you find out what really happened, and so does Dr. Drake."

Vickie kept her voice low. "Did you say 'psychic phenomena'? You study *ghosts?*"

Sarah smiled. "Not exactly my wording, but close enough. I talk to people like you who believe they've had an experience with the supernatural to find out if they actually have, or if maybe it's a fantasy due to some other problem in their lives."

"You really believe in ghosts?" Vickie looked at her more closely, her eyes wide. "Have you ever seen one?"

Laughing mildly, Sarah lowered her voice and leaned closer. "I don't like to call them 'ghosts,' myself, Vickie. I'd rather just call them 'phenomena.' Some theories are that memories imprint themselves into the fabric of this world through a violent act." She slid a finger up to her cheek and almost closed her eyes, as if she were quoting something: "Other people believe a presence is formed by a personality so strong, it manages to break into our world for periods of time." Then she shook her head quickly, meeting Vickie's gaze once more. "But most researchers would tell you that if you saw what you thought you did, it would merely be an interpretation of physical phenomena brought on by the psychic powers inherent in either your location or your mind." Sarah tapped the table. "If you actually saw anything—"

"I *did.*"

Sarah raised a thin eyebrow and spoke carefully. "What have you done since you came back home?"

Vickie's words came faster as she recalled days spent in front of the TV or with the baby magazines in her room as she tried to forget and pretend her coming child was normal. "Nothing. I was freaked out when they let me out of that hospital. Mother came for me. She stayed at a motel until they released me. But I couldn't tell her what happened. She took off work to be with me and bring me back. I feel guilty about that, but she . . . bugs me too. There's nowhere for me to go all day long, and she's always telling me how I never should have married John anyway. I tried to call some of my old school friends. They're all married or moved away. It—it's like I died and came back . . . and no one remembers me."

"*It's a Wonderful Life.*" Sarah smiled wryly.

"It's a terrible life!" she shot back.

"No—I mean that movie with Jimmy Stewart."

The intended cheer didn't make it any better. "It's a terrible life," Vickie repeated.

Glasses clattered together in the kitchen and Vickie jumped as they crashed on the floor with an explosive shatter. "Shit!" cried out a voice.

Vickie flinched and glanced toward the noise, then at the waitress, still scrubbing the counter uselessly. The boy in the Led Zeppelin T-shirt smirked and put a hand in his pocket, taking out another coin.

"Sheriff Kelsor said other people"—Vickie went on shakily—"have seen Garcia too. I feel . . . G-Garcia made me feel so good, and then . . ." She put down the cup with her trembling arm. "Now I feel he's part of me. He—he—" She gulped audibly. "I wake up screaming when I dream about him."

"Exactly," Sarah murmured, laying her hand over Vickie's fist. "But Dr. Drake—and the other psychiatrists you've seen—are convinced that if a man picked you up, he left, and you only pretended he stayed with you, and your need made him as real as me. They say the dreams are caused by the frustrations you've described, and your refusal to accept a pregnancy by your husband."

"No." Her voice was flat. "I *know* it's not his. God, sometimes I wish it was. . . ."

The grip on Vickie's fist was firm, but not imprisoning. She pulled her hand away slowly.

Sarah didn't try to grab her again the way Mother would. Vickie opened her palm, moving it back.

"The investigation by the police and highway patrol was extensive, Vickie. No one of the description you gave was found." Sarah entwined her fingers awkwardly with Vickie's. "I read the reports over twice myself. The man who did die that night was nothing like—"

"But"—her jaw quivered and she was silent for several moments—"did—did you read about what that man was like . . . when they found him on the road?"

Sarah hesitated. "I read all the reports, Vickie. Dr. Drake gave them to me and asked me to."

"I didn't read them . . . but I heard about what happened." Vickie remembered the horror that overcame her shocked exhaustion. "I heard them. It"—she pulled away from Sarah—*"it was like my dream . . . of Samuel."* She trembled, trying uselessly to blank it from her inner eyes. "My first baby."

Sarah circled the spoon again in her coffee cup. "Vickie, no one else saw the man you said you were with that night. The sheriff went to that stadium himself and searched it. There was no sign of the van you described."

Vickie breathed. "But he—wouldn't admit to seeing it if he had."

Sarah cocked her head to the side. "Maybe.

But as you say, others *have* claimed to have seen that man and his van cruising the roads late at night. Although considering what he did and how he died, it's not surprising. It was the most terrible thing that ever happened here. He's become kind of a local spook." Sarah studied Vickie solemnly. "But they've only been vague sightings. There's no proof they're the product of anything more than active imaginations." She smiled with caution. "If you really were with Garcia Efstathiou—Aliester C.—then you were moved several miles in a van that hasn't existed for years, driven by a man who was dead. That alone would stand as a unique experience."

Vickie repressed a shudder, half listening to the whispered cursing in the back of the restaurant ending with the distinctive clatter of the swept broken glass. She watched the waitress brush her hands on her yellow apron and walk to stand in the doorway to the kitchen. The boy in the T-shirt finished his newest game and walked to the counter behind her, then put on a torn jacket with a low whistle. He turned to Vickie and she shivered at his deep eyes, turning away.

"I've known a lot of people who thought they saw something or experienced something become very disturbed," Sarah said. "A lot of people dream about things that have happened to them, or people they loved, or who touched them deeply. Sometimes, if those people are dead, they want to believe it was a ghost. Sometimes we even dream something to take the place of reality, of something we can't face. It looks like you've got a combination of both. You want to believe that a *ghost* made you pregnant."

"But I don't."

"Not consciously. But perhaps the guilt for your baby and something you remembered—"

"No." She clenched her teeth. "I *know* I was with him, Sarah. And maybe I do dream about it now, but I wasn't dreaming then."

"And the dreams started in the hospital?"

"The *dreams* did."

"Vickie, I just don't think your experience was necessarily real," warned Sarah. "You've never had anything like it happen before. It's very unusual for *anyone* to have an extended contact, especially one like yours had to have been. Even more since you've never before indicated a real psychic potential."

Vickie grit her teeth and hit her fists together. "But if it didn't happen, what does it *mean?* How—"

Sarah's tone was still cautious. "What I mean is that phenomena—ghosts for want of a better name—must draw on something from our plane for their 'physical embodiment.' If it had used *you* . . ."

Vickie's mouth drooped as her eyes grew wider.

"But we don't want to get into that. I just don't think you should be afraid of your dreams, Vickie. It's all they are. Even if you did encounter something, it couldn't come after you. Phenomena are not mobile. If it happened—*if*—then it was due to the memories in that locker room, and what happened there. You've got to remember that. Try, Vickie, and we'll do our best to figure it all out." Sarah frowned and looked at her watch. "It's way past our bedtimes," she said distantly, as though her thoughts were on something else.

"Yes." Vickie held to the reassurance Sarah tried to offer, even though she still knew her experience had been real. "Thanks. Thanks for talking to me and trying to help. Maybe I can at least go back to sleep now. Thanks for meeting me."

Sarah stood up, leaving two quarters by her cup. "I'm glad if I helped, Vickie. The things we don't understand are the hardest to deal with. If you'll call me tomorrow I'll set a meeting up. If I can help you at all, maybe you'll feel different about going to see Dr. Drake."

Vickie nodded thoughtfully and got her coat. "I just—" She shook her head. "Thanks, really."

A tired smile crossed Sarah's lips, and she followed Vickie to the cash register. The dull-eyed waitress took their money, smacking her constant gum in thanks, and the older, pockmarked man watched them with a superior look, as though proud that he was now the sole customer in the restaurant. Vickie closed her purse and went to the foggy glass doors. They walked outside, buttoning their coats.

"I used to like the cold weather," Vickie whispered. Beyond the parking lot's lights the hazy sky was filled by more distant, twinkling pinpoints. "I loved the way my breath would fog. . . ." She watched her breath disappear with the words and took a stick of gum from her purse, ripping off the wrapping and foil and discarding them on the pavement.

Sarah stood by her. "It's starting to get warmer now. Before long it will be summer. I think that will help you, Vickie. Getting out in the sun will help you to forget."

Vickie slid the gum between her lips. "Maybe. God, I hope so. I really do appreciate your meeting me, Sarah. I was desperate, and you seemed so understanding earlier. Thanks—thanks again."

"Forget it," Sarah told her, walking Vickie to her mother's white Oldsmobile Cutlass. "Just get home and get some sleep, okay? No dreams, good or bad."

"Okay." Vickie nodded, sliding the key in the door. "No dreams."

14

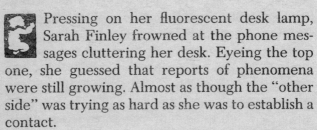 Pressing on her fluorescent desk lamp, Sarah Finley frowned at the phone messages cluttering her desk. Eyeing the top one, she guessed that reports of phenomena were still growing. Almost as though the "other side" was trying as hard as she was to establish a contact.

She snorted and dropped into her swivel chair, scanning each with halfhearted purpose. She was thinking of Vickie Laster, had been thinking of her constantly since leaving her in that parking lot hours ago, and wondered if Vickie had called. Sarah hoped that her underplaying of Vickie's experience had given her some rest.

After a second unfruitful investigation Sarah yawned, stretched, and looked at the picture of Lesley she still kept here on her desk, wishing he were here to help now. Her moist vision stud-

ied the slender, pale countenance that watched
back immobilely. Lesley's stony eyes seemed to
be studying *her* from behind the glass as she let
herself remember him:

She had liked him from the first. Even though
he was older than she, he had never really gotten involved with anyone before she came
along. He told her once that people always
thought he was kind of a freak because of the
way his mind could abruptly jump from the
present into the far past without his awareness
that he'd made that leap. There were many
times when he would start out telling her of
some minor incident that had occurred only an
hour or so before and splice it into something
unrelated that had happened to him years ago.
But that was a minor drawback compared to his
incredible talent. Sometimes he suddenly knew
things, like that time when he was holding her
close and pulled away with tears in his eyes. He
had stumbled upon a long-forgotten sorrow inside her—the anguish she'd felt when she was
only fifteen and found her cocker spaniel dead
on the street in front of her house, crushed by
some speeding car.

His extraordinary perceptions scared her but
fascinated her, too, just as Vickie's unusual experiences did now. When she'd married Lesley a
year after their first meeting, she was completely caught up in his psychic world and had

eagerly come here with him to work at the institute. Then, only months ago, she'd watched him die in an experiment to contact his own father.

Sarah sank into the bitterness it still drove into her, remembering how she had helped push him on, blinded by the driving curiosity he'd begun in her. He'd grown weaker and then had confessed their success: *the apparition of his father had come to him.*

Lesley said his father needed him. He'd told her and the others on the team that his bastard father made him feel guilty that he was alive. And that night she'd woken to an empty bed.

Sarah shivered even now, remembering how she went through that silent hallway of their apartment to the light under the bathroom's door. Inside, she'd found him lying partially submerged in the bathtub's muddy red water. His blank eyes had stared at her endlessly, just like in his picture, now. His father had called to him, and he had left her.

It was worse than betrayal. Lesley's choice of death left her alone with a new dangerous craving to understand what death really was, and how and why it had called out to him. Sometimes the compulsion frightened her. Rather than quitting the institute that had used him to death, she stayed and worked even harder to understand the mystery of the afterlife. She studied philosophy and religion, working her experiences into them as she did. Death awaited everyone and everything. To understand life she convinced herself that she must understand death.

To understand what had happened to Lesley, and maybe to Vickie Laster, too, she had to understand death.

Breaking out of her trance, Sarah went into the hall to get some coffee. Two or three strong cups would put her in a better shape to function. At least, she thought with a grin, a more lively shape!

Sarah yawned three times before she reached the coffee maker in the hall pantry. She took down her usual cup, decorated by a cartoon cat sipping from his own mug. While filling it and adding a cube of sugar, she decided against one of the pink packets of cream despite the first hints of fire in her abdomen. Her life-style and anxiety over the events months past were steadily taking their toll. But without the pressure of her work and occasional mindless activity after, she would be constantly up against the memory of Lesley.

"At least most of my body parts can be replaced," she said aloud, starting back for her office.

"Have you lost any part in particular?"

Sarah glanced sharply to her side, then made

a face at the olive-skinned man in baggy slacks and a button-down shirt as he stopped beside her.

"Good morning, Dr. Finley."

"Doctor? G'morning, Mitch."

He grinned pleasantly, showing the white teeth behind his lips, then nodded toward her door and walked her to it. "Did I miss the party after you threw me out?"

"I was working," she said quickly. "I met that girl. I stayed with her until it was late."

"Sure it was that *girl?*" Mitch made a swirling gesture with a hand. "Now that Dr. Drake's got me about straightened out, you're not trying to replace me, are you?"

"I don't think so." She touched his elbow gently.

"You know, I could almost bring myself to move in with you. Maybe even marry you."

Avoiding his eyes, she ignored the often-heard remark. "I felt—*feel*—sorry for that girl. She was upset and couldn't sleep. I guess she just wanted to talk. I was thinking that maybe you ought to meet her, Mitch. I thought it might help both of you to talk to each other."

Mitch raised an eyebrow. "Me? Are you trying to set *me* up with someone else?"

Sarah shrugged, leading him inside the cluttered office. "Mitch . . . if I didn't know how affected you were by your dreams, I might not have done anything more than her other doctors have done for Vickie. I might have just nodded my head and refused to find another reason besides theirs." Her eyebrows were knit close as she looked at him, and earnestness seeped out of her pale face. "She's already been to so many analysts, it would fill a phone book." Instead of clarifying anything, Sarah's investigation was causing the puzzle to become more and more complex. "I read all the medical stats about Vickie, Mitch. I'm starting to think that all this is wrapped up into a bizarre psychodependence on her father, who died when she was nine. It's an age when a lot of people develop and experience supernormal abilities. The trauma of her father dying would have enhanced that by itself, but then, about a month after his death, Vickie's mother decided to get her more involved in church." Sarah took Mitch's hand. "She brought Vickie to be baptized and there was a sudden storm. It appears that lightning struck the church, electrocuting a minister and nearly killing Vickie while they were in the baptistry. Vickie thinks she caused it, and there's no doubt that the new pressures *it* caused warped her further around the bend and added a religious mania to her problems." Sarah watched his expression again and hesitated.

Mitch picked up an open book from the chair in front of her desk, then sat down. He laid the

book on top of several others piled on her floor.
"This is the same girl who claimed she saw Aliester C.?" Mitch asked.

"Yes." Sarah sat behind her desk. "Is it . . .
getting to you?"

He started to shrug, then spoke instead. "No
worse than the six o'clock news. I'm fine, Sarah."

She sighed, wanting to believe him because
she needed someone to listen. She needed him,
just as she once needed Lesley. "She was in a
coma for days," Sarah went on, eyeing him
closely, "and when she awoke, her mind had
totally blacked out the memory of her father's
death. All her doctors since then have felt it's
too dangerous to force that memory back on
her. But maybe if she had to face it—" Sarah
shook her head. "It's the only thing that even
begins to tie all this together, Mitch. When her
mother remarried a year later, she just accepted
that man as her father, and used to question him
about the things she'd done with her *real* father.
But she was going to name her unborn child
Samuel, *and that was her real father's name.*"

Mitch held the fingers of one hand with the
other and waited while she dug through her
purse and dropped a package of cigarettes on
her desk. "So what does it have to do with her
delusions of seeing Aliester C.? What's the
point?"

"It's just that I told her she couldn't have had

a contact with the supernatural that was so specific, and I supported that by explaining how the talent has to be *developed*—how it was unlikely because she'd never experienced anything like it before." Sarah drew out a cigarette, flipping the lighter on and watching its flame briefly before moving it to the tobacco. "But she might have had an experience back *then*, Mitch. I didn't really think about it until I got home, and then"—she pushed aside a notebook, uncovering a ream-sized cardboard box with the name *Vickie Laster* printed boldly across it. "I opened this box and started rereading everything of her case history."

"I should have stayed over, then," he muttered. "Look, you and Drake just spent the past six months convincing me that my nightmares of Tabitha were just an extension of a guilt her death reawakened from"—he stopped and swallowed—"my little sister, Tammy. And now you want me to think that this Vickie is actually dreaming about a *ghost?*"

"Her presence in that stadium may have linked her up to an energy source that allowed her to see a psychic memory," Sarah explained. "Her hysteria may have connected somehow to the past. Time is irrelevant to psychic phenomena." She remembered how Lesley had once said that, trying to make her understand his lapses from past to present, sometimes even to minor precognition. Moving her hand to his photograph, Sarah wiped off the specks of dust there, her face strained thin. "But even if the location linked up to her abilities and she only saw a psychic memory that was imprinted there, I don't see how she could have made herself a part of it and interacted with it."

Mitch took out his pocketknife and began to clean his fingernails. After a moment he spoke. "And you really think . . . she saw the ghost of that man, Aliester C."

Sarah took a long drag on her cigarette. "There have been a lot of other sightings. Witnesses claim that his sudden appearance has caused several car wrecks. The place has got to be some kind of *psychic hotspot,* and that's another reason why it bothers me, Mitch. The deeper I dig, the more I find. Just like what happened to her *first* unborn baby. The doctors attribute his death to a freak accident of nature, possibly brought on by what had happened to her years before in the church—another freak accident of nature. But physiologically, they know that first accident had nothing to do with her reproductive abilities."

Mitch laid his head on his right shoulder, clucking his tongue again faintly. Watching him, Sarah tapped her nails on the desk. "If there *was* something, if his—ghost—could achieve true materialization *through* Vickie . . . God,

Mitch, you know how a sexual encounter takes up all of our senses and concentration—in the physical excitement of the act, we don't really *think*, we just react. It puts a person into a receptive state. *It's the perfect method of extended psychic contact.*" Sarah frowned, recalling the reports and the conversation with Vickie. "She said she *felt* him, Mitch, and she says he was *cold*—just as psychics feel 'cold spots' when they come upon psychic energy: like the suddenly frigid temperatures reported here and there in 'haunted' houses. If she truly had a sexual interaction with the psychic manifestation of Garcia, then that sharing may have given him *physical* substance . . . and she says she could actually touch him! It's unique, because these manifestations are only imprints detectable through the mind. The most that anyone ever feels is a *formless* chill."

Mitch stood, shaking his head. "I think you're grabbing at straws." He closed his pocketknife and dropped it in his pocket. "Come on, Sarah, I've kept you up late too many nights. Even if there are ghosts, how could they get someone pregnant?" His mouth twitched. "If you don't watch it, people here will think you're nuttier than they think *I* am—that your work is getting to you."

"But she *can't* have a baby. The doctors don't know what to make of it."

"But how could it happen at all, Sarah? *If* there are ghosts—if she could have actually seen, uh, *interacted* . . . what does it mean? What are you trying to find out?"

"I don't know." Smoke curled up from her lips. "Other things about this bother me too. The night of Vickie's . . . *incident* at the stadium, an elderly man who lived nearby died of such acute starvation that his body began to devour itself. His heart and lungs deteriorated as though he'd been dead for days and somehow—somehow he *collapsed* into himself. It's the same description of how her unborn child died."

Mitch clucked his tongue, and Sarah went to him and gently touched his arm. "Hey, are you okay?"

His lip trembled and he swung his head back and forth with a high giggle. "I'm okay, you're okay. Okay breakfast cereal. A-okay. Houston, we have lift-off. Warp factor two, Mr. Sulu—" Mitch stopped and held his breath, briskly rubbing his cheeks with his palms. He took three short breaths and dropped his hands to his lap, folding them tight. "Yeah . . . I think so, but it's all starting to make my brain buzz."

Feeling her face turn red, Sarah bit her lip, knowing her anxiety to put the knowledge in order was pushing her too hard—and him with her. The empty tone of his voice as he uttered barely linked words, the clucking, and the twitching of his mouth were all characteristics he exhibited when he awakened from his *own* nightmares. "Mitch, I'm sorry." She clamped her teeth together. "It just bugged me all night and I couldn't sleep very well. I know I shouldn't say things like that around you. I'm just trying to figure it all out."

"Hey." He pushed out a laugh, suddenly snarling with bravado and grabbing her hand. "I'm *okay.* I'm experienced, remember? *Rambo of the Nightmare World!*"

"Freddy Krueger watch out, right?"

"Right!" He shrugged. "Hell, I make jokes with the rest of them about the weird shit you institute people are into. If I hadn't recognized you from Drake's office when you were crying that day, I wouldn't ever have said two words to you."

"That's all you said then," she said softly, pressing his hand with hers.

"Huh?"

"What's wrong? That's all you said, and then you hugged me." She remembered it with a mixture of sorrow and gratitude. Out of everyone only he, virtually a stranger and full of his own despair, came to her softly and just listened to her talk. "That's all you said that whole night, Mitch. I remember it. God, I must have talked until you wished you were deaf."

"I made up for it," he said.

Sarah put her arms around him, holding him close in those memories. "That's why I had to talk to you about Vickie, Mitch. You help me to remember to care . . . because I care about *you,* Mitch, an awful lot. Even if you don't always agree with what I say, I know I can always tell anything to you, and I know you *care.* It helps."

His mouth twitched again, but Sarah just smiled this time and let him pull away. His face was as red as she knew hers was before. "I—I just understood what you were going through," he mumbled. "When you told me about Lesley, I *knew* what you were going through. You said you felt guilty. I sure as hell understood *that.*" Mitch put his hands in his pockets and turned to the door. "I gotta get to work," he said, then stopped. "But hey, I came up here for a reason."

"What's that?" she asked.

"Well, I was going to take you out to lunch to celebrate. His face wrinkled uncertainly. "I *was.*"

"Celebrate? Celebrate what?"

"I—I didn't dream last night." He kept his hands at his sides. "I—I thought I was cured."

Sarah took his hand again. "I'd love to go out to lunch, Mitch—thanks."

He clucked his tongue, but mildly. "Yeah, well, after that stuff you told me, the nightmares may be back tonight."

"No." Sarah walked him to the door. "But you do have to watch yourself and what you think too much about. You're a borderline lunatic, Mitch. You really are. You're just reaching out so hard for something real to grab hold of, and when you miss grabbing it, you just about go over the edge." She squeezed his arm before he could pull away again. "But I think that if you've managed to reject those dreams, you've rejected them. They shouldn't come back."

He stared at his shoes. "I hope not."

"If they do, you'll have to undergo some more of *my* therapy."

"Your place or mine?" He chuckled.

She laughed lightly at his feeble grin, nearly regretting the feelings between them that made her forget herself with him. "Does it make a difference?"

"Not as long as you don't mind getting into bed with a nut case."

"I love you, anyhow."

He gulped. "Anyway . . . how about lunch?"

"This early?"

"Twelve-thirty. I've got to check some animals they delivered this morning first. I'll meet you downstairs at the elevators."

"A real gentleman would come up and escort me out."

"I'll send up a ghost to do that. You won't see him, but he'll be with you." Mitch shut the office door behind him, and Sarah listened to his muffled footsteps as he walked to the elevator. When she heard its bell, she turned once more to the picture of her husband, Lesley, thinking how like him Mitch was. Both were childlike in their own ways, with their own special complexes and fears. In a sick sort of way she knew it was that frightened combination of guilt and innocence behind their eyes that had drawn her to both of them.

She made a face, restacked the phone messages, then pulled the top one off the stack.

"Good Lord," she murmured, reading it slowly. It told her that a man named Roy Boxton had called twice for her. He claimed to have come into contact with the supernatural—had seen a wildly painted van on a rural road near Stillwater, dripping with blood, which had then disappeared before his eyes. He wanted badly to talk to someone about it. He dreamed of it now.

Folding the note up, she dropped it into her purse and tried to put it from her mind. She could guess what he had seen, and it brought Vickie's problems rushing back to her.

Sarah picked up a second message, only scanning it, then laid it aside and dug through the rest one more time to see if the young woman had called yet. Although she feared the usual methods of psychiatry wouldn't have any effect on Vickie's problems, everything had begun for the girl with the death of her father. She had even linked her father to the baby she had lost. Using proven methods to let Vickie unfold her own past might not be the answer, but, Sarah guessed hopefully, it *might.* And even if the knowledge didn't result in a "cure," it certainly couldn't hurt.

15

As she entered the large dusky hallway, the green-and-white-tiled floor reminded Vickie of the hall in her high school, and that similarity gave her a peculiar comfort with the reminder of that time when her nightmares had been less frequent; when homework, the rare dates, and class functions filled her time.

She observed each wood door carefully, found one stenciled with a black number 28, then took the gum she'd chewed to a tasteless mass out of her mouth, walking back to an upright, bird-bath-style ashtray at the hall's other side to drop it in. Brushing a lock of hair absently over her shoulder, she went back and knocked, heard a voice, opened the door, and couldn't hold back a smile.

"Good afternoon, Vickie, I'm glad you called me." Sarah came out from behind her squatty, paper-stacked desk, laying down a notebook and pen. She went to a swivel chair in the corner and transferred a stack of books from it to a nearby file cabinet. The books caused a tiny cloud of dust and Sarah sneezed.

"Bless you," Vickie offered as she walked to the chair and pulled it back to the desk with high squeaks, liking the opposition to Dr. Drake's neat confines. Suddenly she noticed a skeletal man in a loose-fitting white shirt and baggy blue jeans sitting facing the desk. His spotted skin was shiny pale and his cheeks sunken. His bloated red eyes studied her silently under thinning black hair. "I—I'm sorry I'm a bit late," she continued slowly.

"Not at all," Sarah replied, wiping her nose with a tissue as she sat down again. She threw the wadded Kleenex in a wastebasket and wiped dust off her blue blouse. "This is Jim Whitten. He's involved in some experiments we're doing here in another part of the building. He's just leaving." There was strain in Sarah's voice.

"If I have to." Jim Whitten pulled at his lower lip sullenly, his eyes still on Vickie.

Vickie made herself look at him again, chilled by his blunt, lifeless pupils. "Are you a . . . doctor?"

"Huh-uh." Slowly, as though he were held together by rotting paste, he rose and turned his chair so that he faced her.

"I—I'd rather talk to Sarah alone, please."

"Very well." He didn't hide his disappointment as he reached forward to her hand. His touch was sticky and damp. "Pleased to have met you, miss." He lifted an aluminum cane and used it to stand, forcing a loud creak from the chair, then hobbled to the door, scraping his left foot along the floor. "Thank you, Dr. Sarah. Sorry to have been such a pain. I'll have a nurse take me upstairs to my room and enjoy my confinement and the use of the VCR you've provided me." He almost winked as he closed the door.

Vickie scooted her chair closer to the desk, and sat down, smoothing her baggy pink dress. "Did—did he have an . . . experience too?"

Digging in her purse, Sarah got a cigarette. "No." She kept her soft voice even. "We've contracted him to learn more in our area of study simply because of his . . . condition. I'm sorry, Vickie. He shouldn't have been in here—I apologize." With a frown, Sarah studied Vickie, and returned the cigarette to its pack.

Vickie glanced back at the door. "He looked like a very sick, old man."

"He's sick, but he's not old. He had his twenty-fifth birthday three weeks ago."

Vickie pressed her fingers against each other on her lap and managed to nod. "He looked terrible."

"The disease is aging him. Mr. Whitten has a rare and incurable case of cancer." She let the sentence stand. "It's an unusual study and I'm merely doing a weekly analysis of his psychological condition." She opened her pocket notebook with a brisk dismissal: "You said you slept better after our talk?"

"Uh, very well." Sarah's slight explanation of the man struck Vickie as strange, but she found it easy to put him out of her mind, remembering instead how soundly she'd rested the night before. "I slept better last night than I have in a long time. No dreams or *anything.*"

"That's what you said." Sarah flipped through the notebook and looked back up. "I have a few more questions to ask about your experience, Vickie. Do you feel up to that?"

Vickie nodded her head.

"Okay. Let's get on with it." The blond woman smiled with professional warmth. "First things first, okay? I need to go back over some of the background."

"Yes." Vickie closed her fingers tight. "All right."

"You told me you didn't know much about the death of Aliester C., but did you ever read about it in the newspaper or see anything about it on the news?"

"A long time ago. I heard about it when I was . . . little." Her voice was quivery as she stirred that part of her memory so near in time to her nightmare. "I—I think that was when I was sick. I was out of school for a long time and it's hard to keep it all straight. Sometimes people that I knew in Stillwater talked about it, but I never really listened." She tried to look apologetic and lowered her head. "I didn't know about it for a long time after it happened, anyway. I . . . wasn't allowed to listen to his music. Mom said it was bad. She said he was evil."

"You didn't ever read about him or see that TV special when you got older?"

Vickie chewed her tongue, wishing for a stick of gum. "I don't even watch news stuff now. I only read the funnies in the paper."

"Okay." Sarah made a note. "Have you ever studied parapsychological phenomena or are you aware of findings on the subject? Sorry— basically, have you ever read about ghost sightings or anything along that line?"

"I saw *Ghostbusters.* I started reading *The Shining* by Stephen King too . . . and I saw the movie on HBO." Vickie bit a nail, resisting that growing urge to chew another stick of gum. "But Mother found the book. I was seventeen then. I think she must have thrown it away."

"That doesn't count. I think it's safe to say that all you know of psychic investigation is what the word means—right?"

She tried to laugh. "I'm not even *sure* of that."

"Good. Then when you dreamed, you didn't know to structure the dream around supernatural laws." She moved the notepad to her knee. "So if your experience deviates much from those laws, it will lend credence to the supposition of their being imaginary . . . just very stimulated, but *normal* nightmares."

Vickie gulped. "I—I don't care anymore. I just want to be over *all* of this." She felt all the past tears of her marriage . . . and even before, all the way back to that horrid night when the minister tried to baptize her in water and did it in his own blood. She could only remember little things before those awful hours, and they were part of another life. A life without the fears that had crushed her since. "God, I want it all to be over so bad." Her voice fell and she wiped her fingers on her hem, trying to rub off the sticky dampness Jim Whitten had left on them. "I want to live a normal life so bad—"

"I want to help you, Vickie"—Sarah rubbed a finger along her pen—"but I have to learn how. We've got a lot to go over before I can know that." She examined a page in her notebook. "I've read the things you told the other doctors and the police, but I'd like to hear it from you. Do you mind telling me a little more about it?"

The words she'd repeated so often were tired, and she was almost as tired of them as she was scared of the memory they evoked. But Sarah wanted to help. "I'll . . . tell you," she said.

Sarah smiled cautiously. "It will help, Vickie. Okay. I think you mentioned that it was cold that night?"

"Yes."

"What kind of cold, Vickie? Was it an outer cold? An inner cold?"

Vickie returned again to the emptiness she'd known. "Both. I—I don't think I could forget that."

Sarah jotted down some words. "When did you first notice it?"

"I guess"—Vickie thought for a moment—"I guess as soon as I got in that van. It was warm in there, and freezing outside." She looked at Sarah confidentially. "But it was like that ice all soaked into me when I got inside, I think. I just wasn't thinking about it then. . . ."

You need me, said Garcia's voice.

Vickie frowned at the unspoken words in her brain. "Not until we were making love. *Making . . . love . . .*"

Need.

Sarah let her sit silently, then started to say something, and stopped. At last she spoke carefully: "Was it like . . . *ice?*"

"What?" Vickie nearly jumped as the word linked with her recollection. She had felt so renewed by his attentions. Her powerful orgasms had brought her back to life.

And then he'd shaken and exploded inside her, and she'd felt ice shoot into her . . . *and the hell began.*

Sarah's eyes narrowed.

"Yes."

She jotted something else in her notebook.

"I was so tired. It was like a dream—but it was too real! He—" She covered her face. "He—" Vickie choked and broke off, possessed by the terror once more.

"It's okay. Can you go on after that?"

She nodded, taking a deep breath.

"Do you want some water?"

"Yes. Please."

Sarah stood and went to the door. "Just a minute." She went out, leaving the door open.

"God," Vickie whispered to herself, fighting the wrenching memory of Garcia pulling away, tearing off inside her. She closed her eyes and bit her lip against it and sat as still as she could.

"Here you are," Sarah said, pressing a foam cup into Vickie's hand. Vickie took it gratefully and sipped the water. Her breaths were still heavy.

"Are you all right?"

"I think so."

They sat in silence for several moments as

Vickie finished most of the drink and set it down beside her feet. "I'm okay."

Sarah looked down at the notebook. "If you can't tell me something, Vickie, just skip it, okay?"

"Okay."

"Can you tell me what you saw when he stood up?"

"I think so." She held a breath, then let it out. "When—when he got up, a woman was just suddenly standing there. I saw her— G-Garcia was beside her and then blood was all over the place. She—I *can't*—"

"It's okay. What happened when you left, Vickie?"

"I—I had to open the door, and then I ran outside."

"Did you touch the woman?"

"No," Vickie said immediately. "No."

"Did she seem as solid as Garcia, then?"

"I . . . can't remember. Maybe not."

Sarah got up and walked around the desk beside her, then squeezed her palm. "I want you to know your baby is going to be all right, Vickie. And you and I can keep seeing each other. It won't cost you a thing. I'll see that the institute takes care of expenses."

Garcia. Vickie was afraid of the nightmares. She touched her stomach and stroked the baby inside, sighing as it moved. "My baby," she breathed.

"Yes. You were going to name him Samuel?"

The spoken name made her smile. "Yes."

"Why, Vickie?"

She shrugged, letting the other horrible thoughts drift away, and thought of how much she had wanted Samuel. How much he'd meant to her still unborn. She started to tell Sarah how she'd first thought that this new baby might be a replacement for him, but she knew that could not be true, and that no one would believe, not even Sarah.

"Who did you know named Samuel?"

The question jarred her and she jerked away. "N-no one."

Sarah leaned back against the desk. "Maybe your father?"

"No." Her features twisted. "I don't . . . know *why*. It's a special name to me." She took a deep breath and held still under the pressure of shadows. "I don't know *why*."

"What do you remember about your father, Vickie?" she asked quietly.

Clenching her teeth, Vickie felt a stirring in her belly, as if the baby inside her was sitting up to listen along with Sarah. It gave her a shiver.

"Vickie?"

With a callousness she knew she shouldn't feel, Vickie shrugged. "He—he's *dead.*"

Sarah walked back behind her desk and separated a box of paper from one of the stacks on her desk. "Do you remember the funeral?"

She laughed then. "God, I'm not having a problem with what I *can't* remember, Sarah." Vickie started to bite a fingernail, then picked up her purse and dug through it until she found her package of gum. She opened the last piece quickly, dropping the foil on the floor and blushing as she reached down to pick it back up. Trying to ignore the heat in her face, Vickie put the sugary piece in her mouth.

"When did your father die, Vickie?"

Her jaws clamped hard on the sweet rectangle as she began to chew, faster and faster. "Last . . . year," she murmured uneasily. The baby shifted again and her teeth worked up and down, then back and forth, breaking up the shape in her mouth into a lumpy glob. "But what does that have to do with what happened to me?"

Sarah lifted the lid off the box and took out a thin pile of papers. Laying it on top of her notebook, she began to turn the pages slowly, glancing at each one before she laid them to the side. Then she stopped and picked up the top sheet. Vickie's hands were jittering. "Vickie," she said evenly, "that was your *stepfather.*"

"My *what?*"

Sarah held up the white page and laid it on

the edge of the desk. "Your real father—your blood father—died in 1974 just before that accident in the church."

The paper was a photocopy of a short obituary. Vickie glanced at it, seeing a name that, even though she didn't remember it, was familiar: Samuel Winslow. Lips trembling, she mouthed that name and felt the piece of gum slip out of her mouth. The baby jumped inside her, making her grunt, and the framed plaques and certificates hung from suddenly spinning walls. She shut her eyes.

"Are you all right, Vickie?"

She couldn't hold her head up. She was falling again, falling through her past to the gap she knew was always there but avoided because it was even blacker and more sinister than that baptistry where the blood and water had drenched her hair and face. She felt inside of her childish body once more, felt the press of the big warm hands that made her feel secure, heard a deep, long-forgotten voice:

"I'm dying, Vickie. My heart is bad. I don't want to leave, but I won't be with you much longer."

"But Jesus died so we wouldn't have to die, Daddy," Vickie heard herself say in a squeaky voice. *"Jesus died for our sins. . . ."*

His strange, compelling face regarded her sadly. Then the big warm hands closed over her knee. And he spoke. *"Jesus died in our sins to set us free in the spirit, but we're never free of this kind of death. Death is part of life, Vickie, honey; in a way we all live for death."*

Death.

16

Though she had half expected some sort of strong reaction, Sarah was not prepared for Vickie to fall into a dead faint.

Sarah was already standing, cursing herself for not being ready, when Vickie's gum dropped to the tile and the paper slipped out of her fingers. She took two long steps toward Vickie before Vickie began to fall, knocking over the cup of water. Sarah caught her before her head slammed into the floor.

Angry at her own incompetence, she knelt in the water and lifted one of Vickie's eyelids. Her pupil rolled listlessly.

"Vickie," Sarah said firmly. "Vickie. Wake up."

Vickie sighed, then caught her breath as a tapping came from the door. "Come in," Sarah said, blotting the sweat on Vickie's forehead with her blouse sleeve.

The hinges creaked, and Mitch appeared.

"Am I glad to see you," Sarah muttered, straining to raise Vickie. "Come on—"

Mitch took one side and Sarah the other. "What in the hell are you up to now, Sarah?" Mitch whispered. Together, they lifted Vickie back into the chair.

Mitch brushed off her dress. "Who's this?"

Sarah tilted Vickie's head back. "Mitch, get the smelling salts out of my bag, okay?"

Mitch brought back a small glass vial and twisted off its top. "Damn," he yelled, wheezing, and held it over to Sarah. "Who the hell is she?"

Sarah hesitated. "This is that girl, Vickie, I was telling you about. I think she just remembered her father's death, Mitch." Sarah picked up another sheet of paper.

"This is a weather report. That sudden lightning I told you struck the church the night of her baptismal was part of the same storm that unpredictably began over Stillwater that same night—the night Aliester C. died." Sarah trembled as the knowledge solidified inside her. She laid down her cigarette. "Her hysterical psychic state that night in the church could have somehow left her open and linked her to Aliester C.'s death. During the coma, when she was technically dead, she may have been made especially receptive to the supernatural. Perhaps at each

crisis point in her life"—she ticked them off—
"her father's death, the baby's death, leaving
her husband—Vickie broke through that mental
fortress we build around ourselves, tearing a
hole through her learned reality." She clutched
the idea. "In Vickie the *natural* feelings for her
father and then her child could have crossed the
barrier into the *supernatural.*"

"Shit," Mitch murmured.

Sarah took his hand. "Don't freak, Mitch—
please. I want you to help me try something,
okay? I'm not sure, but I believe she really did
see Aliester C. and I believe there's a possibility
that she made up all the rest that she says happened out of some kind of need for attention. I
want you to talk to her about the things that
have happened to you, okay? Maybe that, on top
of the memory of her real father's death, will
bring her around to accepting that she made up
most of that incident in the stadium."

Mitch tapped his shoe. "Do you think that will
work?"

"*If* she made it up, yes. Just do it, okay?
Please?" Sarah held the vial under Vickie's nose,
and Vickie's head came up, her lip dripping
with spit.

"*Daddy!*" she screamed, her hands flailing.

Sarah grabbed her wrists. "Vickie!"

"*Daddy!*" she cried again. "Daddy's *dead!*"

She twisted back and forth, held in the chair by Sarah. "I want—"

"Vickie!"

Her lower lip trembled and bubbles of saliva escaped her mouth, dripping down to her chin.

"Vickie, listen to me. Your father died a long time ago, okay? *It was a long time ago.*"

Vickie's arms relaxed.

"A *long* time ago. You're grown up now. You got married . . . and then you got pregnant, and you were going to name your baby *Samuel.*" Sarah released Vickie, and Vickie wiped away saliva, tears, smearing her makeup until she looked like a drowning victim.

"That's . . . *Daddy's name,*" she whispered.

Mitch handed Sarah the Kleenex box on her desk, and Sarah began to wipe a tissue across Vickie's pale face. None of them spoke as the seconds passed, and then Vickie swallowed and held out her hand, taking the damp Kleenex from Sarah to finish the job. "You're Sarah," she said.

"Yes. I'm Sarah, and it's been a long time since your father's death. I'm sorry, Vickie, I didn't know how it would affect you, but maybe knowing what really happened when you were younger will help you now."

"My daddy's dead," she said. "I . . . *Why didn't anyone tell me?*"

The room was quiet. "After everything else,

Vickie," Sarah told her softly, "the doctors didn't want to burden you with it. But it's been bottled up inside you, way back in your memory, screaming to get out." Sarah threw the soggy tissues into her wastebasket, then held Vickie's hand. "Maybe that repressed knowledge made you see things sometimes that weren't real, or twisted things you saw into something that didn't truly happen. It changed the psychic impressions you might have had into some kind of *psychic delusion!* That's kind of what happened to Mitch." Sarah held out her arm. "Vickie, this is Mitch Lisciotti."

"Hello, Vickie," Mitch said.

"Hi," she answered, blushing and lowering her head.

Sarah returned to her desk and motioned Mitch to the second chair. "Mitch works for a kennel downstairs as a supervisor for the animals used in this building. I met him a few months back, and I've been trying to help him with some nightmares he told me *he* was having."

Vickie glanced at him. "What kind of nightmares?"

Sarah answered for him. "He dreams about his wife. They're dreams like you have."

Vickie's eyes met Mitch's and her legs shifted uncomfortably.

"His wife is dead," Sarah said.

Mitch rested his elbows on his knees. "Tabitha killed herself," he muttered gruffly.

"God, I'm sorry."

"It was over two years ago," Mitch replied.

Vickie wiped again at her eyes. "I had just gotten married then."

Sarah watched Vickie cautiously as Mitch's words began to sink into her and draw response.

She spoke into a silence. "Mitch had a pretty hard time of it, Vickie. When his wife died, it brought back a lot of memories about another problem he had when he was much younger. Something bad happened to him when he was about the same age you were when your father died. He and his sister were playing, and she had an accident that resulted in her death. His wife's suicide brought that back."

"What—what happened to your wife?" Vickie asked.

Mitch's mouth twitched, and he glared at Sarah. "We were . . . married for four years and talked about having kids, but I just wasn't ready yet. She knew it too." He paced back and forth, from Sarah to the door, to her. "But one night she told me she was pregnant. . . ."

Vickie watched as his face grew slack.

He clucked, clenched his fist, and smacked it against the other hand solidly.

"Mitch left her, Vickie," Sarah said. "His mental state wasn't strong enough to handle the pressure. His wife went to a clinic and got an abortion. She told him she had a miscarriage and when she begged him to come back to her, he did. Then she told him the truth and blamed him for killing the baby, even though *she* had made that decision."

Vickie shuddered. "Oh . . . good God."

Mitch stood up and shoved his hands into his pockets. "She said *she* was having nightmares." He sat again. "She started waking me up at night with her tossing and screaming. She said she was dreaming of the baby." His tongue made the clicking sound more rapidly. "She stopped going to work. I was losing sleep." The words became slower. "I thought she was making it up and trying to make me feel guilty, and I told her that I'd leave for good if she didn't quit. I knew she was trying to hurt me. She killed herself . . . while I was sleeping."

The room was completely silent.

"I—I'm sorry," Vickie said.

"A lot of it was my fault—and I knew it." Mitch looked to Vickie and saw compassion in her gaze, and understanding. "It made me feel like shit. Then *I* started to dream. Just like she said she had, but about *her.* I had to quit my job finally, and the only time it got better was when I was around animals. I started sessions with Dr. Drake and got a job with the pound, and then with a vet. The vet helped me go back to school, and later, Dr. Drake helped me get my job with the experimental animal program."

"And now that you've been through therapy," Sarah said, "what are your feelings now about contacting dead spirits? How do you really feel about it?"

Mitch cleared his throat, his tone becoming formal: "I try not to think about it at all anymore. I think I—everyone—has their hands full enough dealing with life." He picked at a thumbnail absently. "Dr. Drake told me that."

Sarah nodded. "But you know better than most how much harder life can be when death torments us."

"Yes," he murmured, looking deep into Vickie. "It's very hard."

17

"Hi."

Vickie stood silently in front of the elevator several seconds before she realized the hoarse voice was greeting her. She glanced over her shoulder, feeling much better since Sarah had brought her to the bathroom to clean up. She was trying hard not to dwell on the discomfort Sarah brought back by introducing her to that man, Mitch. She knew he and Sarah were trying to help, and that it had been difficult for him to say what he had. But at least his dreams weren't real.

"Hi," she said quietly, a tight knot forming in her throat at the presence of the sick man, Jim Whitten.

"Your name is Vickie, right?"

She returned her gaze to the elevator door, feeling his eyes on her back.

"Excuse me for living."

The elevator buzzed and the door slid open. Vickie stepped inside and raised her hand to select a floor button. He watched her.

"Bye," she said.

He smiled darkly, and as the door began to close stepped closer. "You have life," he said in a low voice. *"Life."*

The door shut.

Vickie leaned against the metal wall and tried to drive away the image of Jim Whitten's face. The sound of his voice echoed in her ears.

"God . . . I want to be well." Her hand searched the inside of her purse and squeezed the empty gum package with frustration.

Life.

Vickie closed the Oldsmobile's door quietly, standing still and letting the brisk wind lash her cheeks as Jim Whitten's voice finally began to fade into the long-lost recollection of her father. Sarah had told her that it would help her to be in the sunlight, but now big pillow-shaped clouds hid those warming rays.

Just like Mom had hidden the death of her true father.

Pulling the strap of her purse up over her shoulder, Vickie walked past the untrimmed evergreen bushes, along the porch with its long, swinging chair to the front door. She spread the keys in her hand and fit one in the lock. Sarah had offered to take her home, or at least call a taxi, but for once she'd wanted to be alone with her past.

Vickie entered the front hallway lined with pictures of her, Mother, and her stepfather—but none of her real father. She hung her coat on the closet doorknob with her purse and opened a new pack of Wrigley's.

Evelyn Timmons walked down the hall as fast as her weight allowed. When Vickie had first seen her after the hysterectomy, she'd been shocked that, since her last visit a year before, Mother had put on at least twenty pounds.

"It's about time you got back, young lady," Mother said. "You know you shouldn't be running around in your condition. I've a good mind to take your car keys from you." Her anger softened quickly. "A woman's got to mind her health when she's in the family way, Vickie. You're old enough to do that on your own, but if I've got to do it for you, you can be blessed sure I will."

Vickie worked her gum. "I went to see the other doctor I met at Dr. Drake's, Mom—Dr. Finley. I . . . talked to her last night. . . ." She tried to keep thoughts of her father from showing on her face.

Mother regarded her suspiciously. "Humph." The big woman shifted her weight, making her bright kimono stretch in the wrong places. "Are you wanting to go to another doctor now? I can't be paying every doctor that suits your fancy. Your father and I never wanted you to marry that boy, you know."

The hall seemed to echo the word *father* off its rough white walls. It reverberated and bounced from the light brown divan to the console TV, then back to the carved, walnut coffee table . . . then continued, reaching Vickie and settling deep in her ears, amplifying her resurrected memories. "My father," she breathed.

Mother frowned, her voice louder: "Dr. Drake says it would be better if you'd just get an abortion. If we had known early on—" She bit her lower lip. "It'll be dangerous now, but if you have it, Dr. Drake says it could— You don't really want to have John's baby, Vickie. You're still just a baby yourself."

Vickie exhaled a tired breath. They all believed she was crazy with grief and wouldn't accept that she was carrying John's child! Even Sarah believed it all due to grief—*grief for her long-dead and forgotten father.*

Vickie saw Daddy in her memories now. Death had taken him away. *Death had taken away her child.* She had knelt at Daddy's grave after school each day and prayed for hours.

Sarah said his sudden absence and the church disaster soon after had obsessed her with death and that horrid fascination had been reawakened when her son, subconsciously named Samuel after Daddy, had succumbed inside her womb, urging her into a *psychic delusion* when she left John and somehow arrived at that stadium. Sarah believed that Vickie might have really seen what she termed a *psychic re-creation* of Garcia's death, but that it had been separate from her, like a movie, and she had only fantasized herself a part of it.

But it had been *real.* Vickie knew the baby she carried now *wasn't* John's, no matter how impossible the truth appeared to be; and she wanted the baby—*she needed a baby*. She deserved *life* to make up for all the death she'd endured! She had spent every night since baby Samuel's death wanting a child. The child in her now was part hers. No matter who the father was, she was the mother.

"Mom," she whispered, trying hard to forget her irritation. She reached out and put her arms around her, chewing fiercely. "I—I *want* the baby. Maybe it's a *gift*. Maybe death took away Daddy and my other child, and this is—"

"You never cared about your father." Mother frowned haughtily. "Don't even talk like that. I'm the one who always took care of you."

Vickie pulled away. "I mean m-my *real* father. Sarah helped me to remember about him and she said she wants to help me."

"Samuel?" Mother's lips trembled as she stepped back. "She had no business talking about any of that with you!"

"He—he's my *father!*" Vickie shot out angrily. She clenched her jaw shut, holding back tears.

Mother took another step back. "Did Dr. Drake recommend this?"

"Dr. Finley's a psychiatrist he asked in for an opinion, but I— God, Mom, she—she wants to help me. She helped me to remember about Daddy—*my real daddy!*"

Mother folded her arms and made a throaty noise, stiffening her neck. "Then I guess we ought to call Dr. Drake and see what he thinks about all this, shouldn't we? Vickie, your father's death is one of the reasons you've had so many problems. For years the psychiatrists have said you shouldn't be shocked by that information. He was always letting you do anything you wanted. He was always trying to make you do everything for yourself—trying to make you grow up too fast! But you're *my* baby!"

Vickie scanned the photos on the wall.

"Vickie, don't smack that gum." Mother brought her hands to her hips. "You came back to me so I could take care of you, and I'm trying to do that as best I can. That woman shouldn't be telling you things that the other doctors

didn't think you should know, and I don't want
you to see her again. Dr. Drake is a good Christian man, and I can't believe he knows anything
about this. He wants to help you. You don't need
to go to some kind of quack who brings back the
terrible things we've already had to deal with
once. I know you thought you saw a ghost or
something silly like that, but Dr. Drake assured
me it was just something you dreamed up. It was
because of what that boy you married put you
through."

"Mother—"

She touched Vickie's hand and squeezed it.
"You were too young to get married. Now, you
know that, and we'll make it okay like it never
even happened, just like when your father died.
We'll get you well."

"Mother, why didn't you ever tell—"

"I'm not going to let you go through all that
again." Mrs. Timmons sighed with finality.
"Now go on and watch TV for a while while I
clean this place up."

Mother waddled to the long hallway. Vickie
watched and said nothing more, not even about
the strange coldness below her stomach. She
just pressed her fingers over it, feeling the forming baby.

Samuel. Her father was Samuel and her unborn baby was Samuel, and cruelly, death had

taken them both . . . but maybe her new baby
. . . "I want to be well," she murmured.

Mother opened the hall closet and began taking out the vacuum.

"I want to be well," she said to herself again.

18

Yawning, Sarah got out of the elevator and looked at the undecorated hall of the fifth floor. It was the institute's main work area, and it made her a little angry that she didn't have a room up here. She remembered Fowler's reason for having relegated her downstairs with barely concealed aggravation—that her research was such that it didn't require a close contact with the other institute experiments.

"Might as well be in another building," she muttered silently. No one else had an office lower than the fourth floor—except Mitch, and he wasn't really with the institute anyway. It annoyed and embarrassed her, and made her walk more quickly to check in on Jim Whitten. Mitch had left half an hour ago and she had promised him dinner. She wanted to be sure he was all right after his grueling meeting with Vickie.

But she was embarrassed by where her room was too.

"Damn you, Don Fowler," she muttered, and caught her breath as she saw him come through a doorway and walk toward her.

"I was about to come get you," he greeted her, reaching her side. "I'm damn glad you finished getting what you could from Whitten today."

Her nose wrinkled at his sour breath. "I'm never finished, Don—but you should have had me come up instead of letting him come to see me. I was going to check on him now. He hasn't got much time left."

The balding man shook his head. "Sarah . . ."

"I just hate this, Don—you know I do."

"None of us likes it, Sarah. But there's nothing that can be done to help him. Get on track, okay? I need you. No one else around here has the background you do in psychiatry, and I need you to keep track of all his mental anomalies." He sniffed. "Whitten is the only man we've been able to acquire for this experiment, and we're damn lucky to have him. You know about his unusual psychic receptivity, and no one else in the past year has volunteered to sign a waiver allowing us to—"

"*Acquire?*" Sarah shot back. "You make all this sound like some kind of damn Monopoly game!"

Fowler pursed his lips. "It's an opportunity

that eventually had to come. It's the chance to see how far we can record the *psychic* impulses of the mind beyond death, and how long. Just because it's not one of your pet projects is no reason to cut it short. It will give us understanding—"

"That's always our justification. That's the scientific justification for *everything.*"

Fowler cut her off. "You're as guilty of it as the rest of us. But let's not argue now, Sarah. Did you learn what you wanted from him today or not?"

"It . . . still seems like he's hiding something." She backtracked past her conversations with Vickie and Mitch to early afternoon, when she had endured the harshness of Whitten's faltering voice and stare. "I tried to talk about how his mother died and his relationship—if you want to call it that—with his father, but he won't cooperate. He won't even discuss how it hit him when he found out he was dying." She cupped her chin in her hand. "He won't say anything about the way his fiancée broke up with him when she found out, and I don't know if I can get that from him in the short time he has left. He's getting very close to the end, Don."

Don Fowler frowned. "Do you have enough to make a good analysis of the state of his mind now?"

"I . . ." She blinked, remembering their dialogue uneasily. *"His state of mind?* He acts like he *wants* to die. He's looking forward to it like a Christmas party. Today he just rambled on about how death wasn't even real anymore. He said he used to be afraid to die, but that death was so much a part of him now that it was becoming his friend. He started singing some old song about loving the dead."

Fowler glared impatiently, tapping his foot on the tile. "It's hard to watch yourself die bit by bit, Sarah—the cancer is slowly spreading up into his brain."

"I know," she muttered. "But he's getting so much worse that I'll need to update his file every day now. He's getting sicker, and his mind is getting sicker too. He told me that death came to him in his dreams . . . kept saying he *wanted* to be dead." Sarah frowned, concentrating. "He said that death was like immortality, because you could only die once."

"Is there anything else you want to ask him?"

The flat words were almost threatening, and she took another step back. "At the actual point of death I—"

Don Fowler grabbed her wrist and pulled her recklessly down the hall in the direction he'd come from. "We may be at that point now. Whitten has taken a very sudden and unexpected turn for the worse."

Cold fingers brushed her spine and she

stopped, almost falling as her arm wrenched out of his grasp. "Oh . . . oh, God . . . but you were letting him walk around this afternoon."

"Nobody knows what happened to him." Fowler grunted. "Everyone thought he had at least two more weeks. He was strong and he's been stable these past days. But he collapsed after his visit with you two hours ago. The nurse who was supposed to be with him found him unconscious in the elevator. Sarah, *come on.*"

Her eyes were damp. The uneasiness of being around Whitten's increasingly bizarre behavior had joined her anticipation of meeting with Vickie and made her hurry through her questions today, cutting him off when he rambled, just wanting to finish and get him out of her office.

"Come on!" Fowler's clammy, pudgy fingers pulled on her wrist again, dragging her with his weight.

Whitten's open door crawled nearer, and she forced her legs to move with Fowler's, ashamed of how she'd acted to the dying man.

Jim Whitten opened his dull eyes as they stopped inside his doorway. He grit his teeth against obvious pain.

The nurse was at his side, bending over him. "Do you need something to make you feel better?" she was asking.

"No," he managed between gasps.

She turned on a machine to which he was connected, creating a noisy hum, then faced Sarah and Fowler. "We need to get him ready," she said softly.

Fowler nodded. "Hurry with the questions, Sarah."

19

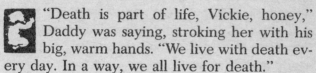"Death is part of life, Vickie, honey," Daddy was saying, stroking her with his big, warm hands. "We live with death every day. In a way, we all live for death."

"But Jesus died so we wouldn't have to die, Daddy," Vickie said in her squeaky voice. "Jesus died for our sins." He started to nod, then folded his hands over one knee, his breath a dry rasp. She reached for those hands that always made her so secure, tugging at his little finger.

"Jesus died *in* our sins, Vickie. He died in our place." Daddy made a face. "He died to set us free in the spirit, but we're never free of this kind of death."

"Death," she repeated, tilting her head to the side.

"Yes." He looked at her sadly. "I'm dying, Vickie. My—my heart is bad. I don't want to leave, but I won't be with you much longer.

That's why it's so important that you be strong. You have to learn to go on by yourself and make your own decisions . . . just like you learned to walk . . . like you learn new games and things now."

The words were scary and she shook her head. They made her wish for the happy endings of the bedtime stories he made up and told her each night—and made her think of the shadows in the closet that would reach out until Daddy closed the door so she could sleep. She had one time dreamed that death must be those shadows, and that some night, when Daddy reached into them to shut the door, they would pull him inside and— *"N-no."*

He touched the sideburns kept trimmed to earlobe length, then hardened his mouth and slipped those comforting fingers down to hold her smaller fingers in his. She held back with all her strength, not wanting the hand to ever let her go. Outside the window a bluebird flew by and twittered loudly.

She squinted in the bright sunlight and felt its joy of life. "Why couldn't Jesus die to make us *really* live forever? Why couldn't He die for our bodies and not just our s-s-souls?"

He didn't say anything, and she memorized the dark circles under his eyes and the new wrinkles. *Death,* she thought, and had a longing to be like the Virgin Mary in her children's Bible. She wanted to bring her father's life back to him so he would never leave her. She wanted a child like Jesus—except one that would take away the death she was more and more afraid of. *All the death.*

She had prayed so hard . . . and Daddy was almost dead. Death was taking him away from her.

Through her tears she shut her eyes and prayed silently for a baby that would take away the pain and death, but when she looked back up, Daddy had stopped crying and was holding his chest with clenching fingers, his eyes closed tight.

"Daddy?" She slid off his legs and backed away.

He moaned.

"Daddy?"

He wheezed, slobbering, trying to reach his hand back to her.

"Mommy!" she screamed, running toward the tiny kitchen. *"Mommy—it's Daddy!"*

Mother emerged from that doorway, biting her lip and wiping shivering hands with a ragged plaid towel. "Samuel?" she whispered, her chubby face puckered in fear. She hurried into the living room, knocking over a lamp, rushing to Daddy's chair and bending over it.

Vickie stared silently, then heard the whimpering sorrow tear from Mother's throat.

Slowly, frightened, she followed, edging around
Mother and looking into the slack, sallow face of
her father. He wasn't moving at all now, and his
eyes were all white and rolled up in his head.

Mother didn't say a thing, but made a noise
deep in her throat—a horrid, sucking sound, like
galoshes in slimy mud.

Vickie stared at Mother's glassy eyes, and felt
the ball of fear that had been growing since she
first heard the whispers that Daddy was sick.
"God killed him!" she blurted out. *"He t-took
Daddy away!"*

Mother turned quickly, tears in her eyes. "Oh,
Vickie," she cried, reaching out to her. "Oh,
darling, I'm sorry—"

"God killed him!" she repeated, staring into
the horror of death.

"God didn't kill him, darling," said Mother.
"God just let the spirit of death take away his
soul so he wouldn't hurt anymore." She held
Vickie close, stroking her hair with fingers still
damp from the kitchen sponge. "Daddy had to
die so he could be with Jesus. . . ."

Vickie pulled away and wiped her cheeks. "I
don't want Jesus. I w-want to make death *live!* I
don't want the soul to live. *I want my daddy!"*

"Oh, Vickie—" Mother shook her head and
squeezed her so hard, it made Vickie gasp. "God
won't do that, darling. *He* is the master of our
spirits . . . *but death owns our bodies. Death*

grows and grows inside of us, and we have to die before it eats away our souls. Our sins destroy our bodies, honey. . . . Daddy's sins have eaten away his body now. We have to sacrifice our sinful bodies. . . ."

"To D-Death?"

Mother nodded, wiping Vickie's face tenderly. "Death is the master of our bodies."

Vickie didn't listen. She felt hatred for the uncaring God that took away her father, and when mother sent her to her room, she sat there and thought, afraid and stimulated by the memory of Daddy's death . . . and of salvation . . . *of souls and life.*

Death is the master of our bodies.

Tears were hot in her eyes for a long time, and slowly, she made herself stronger. She prayed to Death. She prayed to Death for a baby that would bring *real* eternal life, and she offered her *spirit* as a *sacrifice*. . . .

20

The tiny observation room was full of her fellow investigators when Sarah Finley went in. Their presence overheated the room. Already perspiring, Sarah edged toward the one-way glass that stretched from waist high to a foot from the ceiling, still hearing Whitten's rasping answers in her ears.

"Hey, Sarah," whispered a short, pudgy bald man in black-framed glasses.

"Hi, Brett," she replied, then peered through the glass. Jim Whitten lay on a shiny steel operating table in the center of the room, his body almost an extension of the humming machines that were hooked into him by a colorful mass of wires and tubes. An orderly turned a video camera this way and that, recording these moments. A blue plastic mask covered the lower half of Whitten's face.

"Is this really it?" a shrill, unknown man's voice whispered near them.

"Everybody seems to think so," Brett answered with anticipation. "They're filling the room with a high concentration of oxygen so they can take his mask off."

Sarah watched as Whitten's emaciated arms struggled feebly with the white sheet covering the lower half of his torso and bony legs. "God." Her voice trembled. "Why don't they just give him something to knock him out?"

Brett shrugged, edging close to her. "Research Grapevine said he wanted to stay awake . . . but I don't know. Sometimes with the pain it doesn't work anyhow."

Whitten's chest heaved with every breath, making his long, wispy frame appear more frail than it was. The ivory-clad researchers, doctors, and nurses in the room all wore their own breathing masks and weren't even looking at him as they monitored the information being displayed and recorded by a dozen machines. At last a blond nurse nodded at another nurse near Whitten, and the latter turned to remove his mask.

Jim Whitten's wretched, pale face stared at the observers, as though he could see straight through the two-way mirror hiding them. The pain was livid in his dying, red-rimmed eyes, and only a small spark of life remained. Yellow saliva dripped down his cheek onto the sweat-marked sheet under him. He blinked furiously.

"This is it," murmured Brett in excitement, and Sarah heard similar murmurs from the others surrounding her. She remembered the same air of expectation when she'd watched the first man land on the moon with her parents and friends years before. An excitement at a "leap for mankind"; but this time that leap was being made at the expense of a man's life, *and nothing was being done to help him.* It jarred her as she recognized the excitement in her own feelings . . . and was saturated in guilt for the others and for herself.

"This is history being *made*," Brett said loudly, to mumbled assent.

Whitten's face screwed up like a piece of paper being crumpled, and he lay back on the flat pillow, then closed his purple eyelids. Embarrassed, Sarah closed hers as well, realizing her intrusion in this moment the dying man should have spent alone or with the love of family. But instead, Jim Whitten was dying before an awe-struck and anxious audience, eager for the moment of his end. The only thing missing from this modern Coliseum was the smell of rancid popcorn.

The whispers and murmurs became infrequent. Jim Whitten wasn't moving.

Three more minutes ticked by as the researchers in the room bent over their instruments and read their screens silently.

"He's dead," said a mask-muffled, uncertain voice over the intercom after another five minutes had passed. "But we're still getting readings. *We're still getting readings!*"

A twisting in Sarah's gut made her gulp, and she began to backtrack through the crowd, recoiling at the tremors of their sick excitement.

"Good God, he's opened his eyes!"

Whether the voice had come through the intercom or belonged to one of those within the room, Sarah didn't know. She glanced up unwillingly as Jim Whitten sat upright on the table, a curious and cold expression on his face. His eyes were dull and icy, and his flesh seemed more pallid. He wheezed hoarsely.

"I'm getting readings that he's still dead . . . and conflicting analysis showing he's alive," came a man's muted, quavering words through the speaker.

The bright lights in Whitten's room blinked. "My machine has stopped," gasped the blond nurse. Whitten thrashed sluggishly.

Sarah closed her eyes, not wanting to believe —not wanting to see—

"God damn," said someone. "God damn! I—I saw it. Life from death—God . . . God damn."

Life from death. Sarah caught her breath and let it out unsteadily, remembering Whitten's words this afternoon. He'd smiled crookedly and muttered that death was really like birth— its pain self-contained pangs of labor. . . .

Life from death.

Suddenly, Vickie Laster was on her mind.

21

Vickie dreamed. Past and present slipped back and forth in confusion until she didn't know one from the other. Daddy held her and died, and Mother held her close, too, not letting her run when the face of Garcia came close . . . and replaced Mother's . . . and then he became that sick man, Jim Whitten. She could not stop remembering and imagining, the past memories and present images merging.

"Vickie."

The voice startled Vickie, and she let out her breath as she woke into stark blackness, startled by the weight of something heavy getting into the bed beside her. Something—someone—*cold.*

"Vickie . . ."

Panic iced her veins, and she couldn't stop a trembling spasm. *It was a dream.* She was still asleep, and Garcia—the memory of what had happened—was back once more to invade that rest. She denied the dream hands touching her, fondling her. "No," she whispered, fighting to awaken.

A shadow lay beside her on the coarse sheets . . . greenish glow around wild, greasy hair and whiskery cheeks.

Garcia.

A scream caught in her throat. *He couldn't be here!* Sarah had told her, *almost promised her, that this thing—this occurrence—had happened due to where she'd been! It couldn't follow her!*

"I want you, Vickie. I need you, and you need me. You asked for me." His voice was a dry, singing chuckle. "You prayed to me. Death on earth, Death's Will over men—bring us back to life again!"

His damp body moved on top of her, and she felt his naked skin against her thin nightgown, pushing into the swell of her abdomen. But it was just another nightmare! He could not be here. *He could not have followed her!*

A sandpaper hand slithered down her leg and pulled the cotton gown up her distended body to her small breasts, then up past the nipples savagely, covering her face with the heavy material. She shut her eyes and made herself lie still, trying not to scream as he forced his legs between hers. She grit her teeth, denying the vehemence as he pushed inside.

But the pain made her gasp. *It had to be a nightmare. Another nightmare.* She knew that if she reopened her eyes she would be in that horrible shack: the shack of her nightmares, surrounded by empty, gaping lockers. *She knew she could not control the dream.* With despair she ignored the shiver of his pulsing muscle inside her and the feel of his rough hands on her breasts. She reached up and pulled the gown from her head, opened her eyes.

It was dim, as it always was in her dreams. But with a pounding shock she saw glimpses of her old playthings—the furry teddy bears and dolls —*and knew she was in her mother's house. Not* in the shack of her nightmares, but here in her mother's home—*her home!*

Vickie turned to jelly. "N-no," she moaned. Inside she cried: *Not here! God, not here. Stay away! Go back!*

Garcia drove inside her desperately, harder and harder. His sweat rubbed onto her face and arms, slithering over her goosebumps.

Vickie swallowed a shriek, panting in blind terror, and the air exploded frigidly all about her, making her gasp. She clawed at the body on top of hers, trying to push it away.

But the body had changed now. The weight became lighter and the shape of her attacker thinner as his suddenly sharp hipbones rammed into her taut thighs.

The gaunt, shadowed face laughed, spraying her with rotting saliva, and she stiffened as she tried to force her petrified lungs to scream—*to scream*—

"You have *life*, and Death has *heard* you. Death is the God of *Truth*. Death's Will over men—*bring me back to life again!*" Jim Whitten grunted hoarsely, his voice as abrasive as his dry and shriveled flesh. Icy wetness exploded from him—*just like*— Her teeth chattered and she felt the chill coating her . . . mixing with her own juices—

In the name of Death.

Vickie squeezed her eyes so tight that the black nothingness of her vision became yellow . . . red . . . *green*.

Life.

The shape on top of her lurched, moaning. Her veins pumped frozen acid through her body. The baby jerked and shuddered inside her; her body wouldn't stop trembling.

Her inner self—her *soul*—froze, bringing shivers as that fiery chill spread deep. At last the desperate shock forced its way through her throat.

22

Sunlight.

The warmth woke her up. Vickie knew it was morning at last.

She raised her aching head, relieved by the dusty rays slipping through the pink window drapes . . . and *nauseated.* The horrors were still heavy in her thoughts—dark shades that encompassed her in a sticky spider web. Garcia . . . and Jim Whitten. And the forgotten light of a time long past when she sat on her daddy's sturdy knee, held by his comforting hands.

Vickie prayed the visions were all gone now. She had closed her eyes hours ago with the nightmare body still heavy on top of her and counted to a number well over a thousand. At last, she had drifted into a sleep within the dream. She knew it *had* to have been a dream: the body was gone now, even the sticky blood she felt falling all over her.

She had to try to *forget* all those evil shadows, shadows of Garcia as he became Jim Whitten, as he *raped* her.

Fucked her.

Garcia.

Just as Garcia had done before.

It was too real. She had been through nightmares all her life, and nightmares almost as bad as this last one every night since—Vickie shook her head. But not with these same sensations, not with such a hideous transformation. Only the night that this had all begun was as wretched.

It was too real.

Her heartbeat felt fragile and uncertain. Cold sweat covered her body. *If the first time hadn't been a nightmare, then this last might not be one either.*

Her heart beat quicker.

"No," she whispered. Sarah had told her that these—phenomena—could *not* reappear at will. They were attached to certain places. And Jim Whitten was *alive*.

It had to have been a dream. A horrible, ghastly dream. It was all an insane nightmare.

Insane.

Her body shuddered, and she closed her eyes, ignoring the rip she could feel in her gown and the pain and bloody stickiness of her pulsating vagina. With all of her strength she sat up and pushed herself off the damp mattress.

"Oh, God," she cried with welling tears. Cramping stitches sewed themselves into the walls lining her stomach and she dragged herself to her feet, finding her knees would not hold her. Fighting the building cramps, she eased to the floor and stretched her hands to the door and hallway.

As she crawled toward the door, nausea overpowered her and she began to retch. A thin, watery spit came from her mouth. "G-G-God . . . Mother!" she shrieked, suddenly desperate to break out of this solitary world. *"M-Mother!"*

Vickie moved away from the clear, gooey slobber before she collapsed on the carpet. *"Mother!"* she screamed.

In the silence she listened for the slow and heavy steps.

She waited.

"Mother?" she called weakly, wanting help. *Needing* help. For once, she *wanted* Mother. "Help me." Her weakness increased the terrible panic. *"Mother!"* she cried hoarsely.

Silence.

"Mother? Where are you?" She stared down the hallway, seeing only the furniture and the silent vacuum cleaner. Putting her hands beneath her, she pushed herself up to her knees and crawled toward Mother's room, listening for a sound in the quiet.

"Please?" she rasped, her throat raw. "Mother?"

The curtains were still drawn in her mother's room, and it was dark. Under the blue blanket, she could make out Mother's shape still in bed.

Vickie begged: "Mother, I'm sick. Help me. *I'm sick!*" She began to cry with self-pity, her head dropping to the floor. Time passed without meaning and shadows changed. Her cramps faded and returned. Pushing and pulling. The heat in her forehead clashed with the cold sweat forming on her body, and her vision shrank.

"Help me, *please!*" She grabbed the blanket's end and pulled herself up with it. But Mother lay unmoving on the mattress. *"Help me!"*

Mother didn't move. A rotten smell overcame the stale odor of the carpet. The skin on Mother's face was like oozing sponge, her head deformed—caved in, the bones splintered and crushed in tiny pieces that powdered her formless moist flesh.

Like her baby, Samuel.

Wanting to retch all over again, Vickie climbed upon the bed, afraid, but drawn with ghastly denial to the still, mutilated form. She breathed with fever. Was this yet another dream?

"Help me!" Vickie grabbed the remnant of an

exposed, shrunken arm and pulled, abruptly
hating her mother in this ghastly, overwhelm-
ing horror—*hating everyone and everything*.
All she could think of was how life was betraying
her—driving her insane. *"Mother!"*

Time stayed still, but hours passed. Vickie
cried, but could not stay awake. When she finally pushed herself up to her knees, her throat
was so ragged she could not even scream with
the despair welling inside her—that this dream,
nightmare, was true!

Mother's shriveled eyes still stared up va-
cantly, blobs floating on the skin that was cold
and loose and pooled over her shattered bones.
Her face was drawn and pale in a wide puddle.

—like Samuel—

Another violent attack of dry heaves ripped
her stomach and throat, and she fell back on the
bed, trying to ignore the stink of death tugging
inside her nostrils and wanting to turn her inside out. She knew the sun was low in the sky
now by the light that filtered through the blinds.
Its red illumination affirmed the destruction and
lifelessness in Mother's deformed, empty face.
She *was* alone now.

Forcing all the strength she could into her
arms and legs, Vickie pulled herself to the edge
of the bed and dropped her feet over the side.
The fever that had distorted her thoughts was
ebbing, and though weaker than she'd ever

been before, she had to try to get help. In her dreams Daddy had told her she had to learn to go on by herself . . . *and she was really by herself now.*

Touching her stomach and feeling a strange uneasiness at its hidden life, she swallowed and choked.

The carpet was rough to her bare feet and she grimaced as she put weight on them. "God," she murmured through a dry mouth and throat. She stood, crouching to keep her balance, and supported herself with one hand on the mattress.

The doorway wobbled, miles away, and she counted the paces that would take her to it. Her emotions were suddenly focused on the bad feeling about the baby.

Her baby.

She had to get help for her baby.

Slow. One foot forward. Her legs were jelly, and she feared they would crumple under her weight. She let herself down to her knees and crawled, the green carpet of Mother's room magically changing into the aqua-blue of the hallway. Her fingers groped, sliding into something moist.

"Oh, God," she whimpered miserably, seeing the remaining bubbles of her spit. She jerked back and crawled through endless, plodding time to her own room. The bright red fabric of the carpet reassured her and she reached toward her wooden dresser for the line that led up to the phone resting there. "Please . . ." she mumbled, no longer able to ignore the gnawing emptiness in her soul.

Sarah. The doctor's name turned over and over in her mind. She stopped and felt for her purse overturned on the floor, fumbled past keys and through her billfold, at last clinging to Dr. Finley's card.

Rolling to the dresser with hellish pangs, she wrapped her fingers around the phone wire, and pulled, gasping at the glancing new pain when the receiver crashed down on her shoulder and the rest missed her face by inches. Trembling, she managed to hold the receiver to her ear. Her wavering vision made her touch the buttons slowly. She hoped that Sarah was there. The line rang.

"Hello?" a tense voice said immediately.

"Sarah?" she croaked.

"Yes? Who's this?"

Hope exploded in Vickie. "Vickie Laster. Please . . ."

"Vickie? What's wrong?"

"Help me," she pleaded, fresh tears sliding over her cheeks. "Please help me."

"Where are you?"

Exhaustion fought her words. "M-my home . . . *H-help me.*"

23

 "Vickie?"

The word echoed in a huge cavern.

"Vickie, wake up."

The sudden light from somewhere above made Vickie blink. The pink face approached, and she felt firm fingers tighten around her wrist.

"Her pulse seems to be stable."

"Sarah?" she gasped.

"Take it easy, Vickie. You're going to be all right."

She didn't have the energy to raise her head. Her thoughts were morbid. She was exhausted, as she had been when she'd burst into that far-away gas-station office months before.

Sarah touched a cool hand to Vickie's forehead. "How do you feel, Vickie? Do you know where you are?"

"T-tired." Her eyes opened wider. "Mother . . ."

"They're taking care of her, Vickie. We'll do all we can for her, I promise."

The baby shifted inside Vickie, bringing a cold sweat. It felt a part of her, *but no longer a part. Like something unnatural implanted inside her. Like a cancer.*

Jim Whitten.

"Vickie?"

Her eyes groped, at last finding Sarah's face again.

"I'm going to stay here with you, Vickie. Do you understand? You've had a high fever, but it's broken. You're weak, but there's nothing wrong with you and no need for you to go to a hospital." Her words were tender. "I want to stay with you and make sure you're all right. Would you like me to do that?"

The blockade that had been holding the horrid experiences from her thoughts crumbled a little, but Vickie tried hard to keep control of herself. *Mother was dead.* It wasn't a nightmare. Mother was *dead. Perhaps none of last night was a dream.*

"Do you want me to stay, Vickie?"

She nodded. "Yes . . . p-please. Could I have a drink?"

"Of course." Sarah stood up. "I'll be right back."

When Sarah left, Vickie closed her eyes again. Images were waiting for her, but she refused to let them through. She was afraid to admit them.

Afraid.

A long time seemed to pass, and then a faraway door creaked open and, moments later, closed.

"Sarah?" she called out, fighting the returning terror of loneliness.

"I'm here." Sarah hurried to her side and knelt, holding a glass of water. "That was the paramedics leaving. I'm going to stay with you."

Vickie let Sarah raise her to a sitting position, and sighed when the glass touched her lips.

"Easy."

The refreshing water cleansed her throat. Too soon, she had to breathe and pulled back.

"Is that better?"

Vickie nodded, not having the strength to answer.

"More?"

In reply Vickie licked her lips and Sarah brought the glass back. At last it was empty, and though her throat was still sore, Vickie knew she could stand it. She was remembering Daddy now, and how he told her she had to learn to stand it . . . *on her own.* Daddy had taught her things . . . how to fly a kite, how to fish and swim. The memory of them splashing water at each other in the pool and him helping her reel in a big bass gave her strength.

"Do you want me to try and get you into bed?" Sarah asked. "I can make some soup and help you eat. Then I'll clean all this up while you sleep. After a good rest you should feel much better."

But then Daddy left her. Death took him. And now, Mother too.

"No," she whispered with the new strength ebbing quickly away. "I don't want to stay here."

"Where do you want to go, Vickie?"

The strange fear increased. "I don't know." The smell of Mother's decay hung in her nostrils. "They—*they know I'm here.*"

"Who knows, Vickie?" Sarah lowered Vickie back down to the carpet, but didn't take away her hand.

"They do." She tried to think of Daddy and closed her eyes again. *"I can't remember parts of it, but Garcia and . . . and . . ."*

There was a long silence. "What, Vickie?"

Vickie stared into the darkness of her eyelids. "That—that *man.*"

Another long silence. Unconsciousness tugged at Vickie and she forced it away, trying to hold on.

"Do you want me to take you to my place?"

"Yes."

"Okay," Sarah said slowly. "Do you want me to clean things up first?"

"No." She peered into Sarah's features. "Where is Jim Whitten?"

With a blank expression Sarah stared back. "What?"

"Please," Vickie said, shaking her head. Sarah's expression made her shiver. "Please, let's leave."

24

Vickie was still dizzy when she stumbled out of the steam lingering in the tiny yellow bathroom, but at least she was clean. She could barely remember getting into Sarah's car. She passed out as they drove, and was grateful she hadn't dreamed. But when she awakened in the heavy, sweat-soaked blankets of a strange bed, she shrank with terror, screaming, seeing her mother's destruction over and over.

She fought to blank her mind—to keep the terrible memories pressed back in her subconscious. Sarah came in, soothing her and half carrying her into a hot tub of soapy bathwater, stroking a warm washcloth over her tear-streaked face. *It was over now.* Over. Sarah was helping her and it was over. Vickie stood stiffly against the wall of the apartment's front room. A twenty-gallon aquarium half filled with water and empty of fish stood next to her on a wrought-iron stand, its glass coated with the smears of evaporation. Across the room the white walls were nearly hidden by three four-by-eight bookshelves stuffed with uncat-agorized books: ancient, brittle hardcovers stood side by side with creased paperbacks. Even the dusty console TV in front of the blue divan bore a burden of books. Sarah sat in an armchair, one of the paperbacks in her hands as she thumbed a page.

"The bath helped, I take it?" Sarah asked, meeting Vickie's gaze.

"It felt good," she managed. "Thanks for help-ing me clean up."

"I'm glad it helped." Sarah put the open book down on the floor to keep her place and came to Vickie, leading her to the divan. "You needed it too."

Vickie leaned back into the soft cushions, shifting in discomfort. "I did."

"Do you want something to eat now?"

"Please," she answered immediately, her stomach an empty hole. She was starving and needed strength to separate herself from the horrors in her mind.

Vickie watched Sarah go into the adjoining kitchen. Mother was really gone now. All she had was herself, and her precious unborn baby.

Mother was dead.

Daddy had told her she had to do things on her own.

"Here's a glass of milk. If you can keep that down I'll make some eggs and toast."

Vickie took a sip.

"Vickie?"

Unhampered by the walls of the uterus she no longer had, the baby moved inside her, sending a chill up her spine. It vibrated with a peculiarity she had never known with Samuel. It made her tingle with an increasing inner chill, like the chill she'd felt in the renewed contact with Garcia . . . with what he had *become*. But she hadn't told Sarah much about what had happened last night and didn't really want to, because it proved she was crazy. "I'm okay."

Sarah nodded and sighed. "God, I wish Lesley were here."

Vickie bunched her legs up on the couch. At least she was more comfortable here. "I *do* want to understand what's happening to me, Sarah," she said. "I need to understand." Mother's wasted body crushed her thoughts. *I'm insane. I made it all up. I'm insane.* "Is Mother—my mother—really dead?"

Sarah bowed her head. "Yes, Vickie."

"Oh." Vickie closed her eyes and huddled in her own darkness, letting the moments pass, wanting them to pass until she could awaken to find this was all a dream.

Sarah cleared her throat. "Vickie, why did you ask about Jim Whitten last night?"

The name made her flinch, and Vickie cringed again from the terrors of insanity. Or even worse . . . the terror of *sanity*.

You have life, Whitten had said, *bring me back to life again*.

"Vickie? Do you feel okay?"

"He—he was . . . *there*." Her mouth was dry and sour as she forced herself to say it. "Garcia . . . and then *him*." She began to hope that this would prove her dreams a lie, a fabrication of her crumbling mind. She suddenly *wanted* to be insane.

Sarah was startled. "He—came to you?"

"I know." She wailed uselessly. "I know, Sarah. It was all . . . It was all just *me*, my nightmares." Vickie covered her face with her hands. "I dreamed of Daddy, too. I'm insane. I know I'm insane."

Sarah stood. "What time did it happen, Vickie?"

She shook her head. *Insane. She was insane. It was all in her mind*.

"Vickie, what time did it happen?"

"I was asleep. God, I don't know."

"What time did you go to bed?"

She gasped for breath, as though the air were being torn from her by unseen forces. Insane. "Nine o'clock."

Sarah's face was ashen, and she slumped. "It doesn't prove you're insane."

"It proves I made it up." Vickie set her jaw, ready to be crazy, really wanting to be crazy. The possibility of what happened being true was more terrible than insanity. "It proves that I'm cracking up. Like Dr. Drake and the others said. I made it up because of what I'm really so scared of."

"No."

Vickie kept talking, letting the words flow without thinking, "I'm afraid of people dying because of Daddy, right? So I was afraid of Jim Whitten, and so I dreamed about him. They said I dreamed up Garcia because—"

"No."

"But—"

"That's wrong. They're wrong!" shouted Sarah. She took a step forward. "They're all *wrong,"* she whispered. "You dreamed about Jim Whitten," she said, *"because he died."*

Vickie jerked up with wide eyes. Her legs crept together.

"He died that night."

Holding her hands out defensively, Vickie shook. *"No."*

"Stop it!" Sarah grabbed her shoulder and stopped her. "Stop that, Vickie! He died last night. And then he—*he came back to life."*

"Please." Her hands flailed against Sarah. The milk taste on her tongue turned bitter. "Please."

Sarah jerked her hard. "Vickie, I want to help. *I will help you!*" Sarah released her then and leaned in close. Her breath was harsh . . . hot. "You must answer me. *We have to learn—*"

Vickie doubled over and vomited the sour stinking bile bubbling up her throat.

The soft Mozart piano concerto from the stereo lulled Vickie as she rested, lying flat on Sarah's divan in the warm sunlight. She was glad Sarah had opened the curtains. Her hysteria was finally past, and she refused to think about insanity. The sun had melted away the shadows. She *had* to try, for the baby's sake. *Her baby.*

"You've managed to keep down the toast for an hour," Sarah told her, checking her watch. "Do you want to try another piece?"

"Yes, please." Vickie lay with her back and head propped up by pillows as Sarah went into the kitchen and made the toast.

"Could I have more butter?" Vickie called.

"It's just margarine," Sarah replied, "and no, you can't." She imitated a stiff, older lady's voice as she carried the toast out. "A very light topping of it when you've got the 'tacky tummy.'"

"Okay."

Munching the toast, Vickie relaxed, touching her oversize stomach with a light hand and pretending it was the toast that made her fat. But the firm shape inside made that imaginative pretense slide away quickly, giving way to strange pride. The baby was hers, and she couldn't let anything happen to it. It was hers and she knew the doctors had to be wrong about its supposed deformity. It was her second chance and she must protect it. Sarah would help.

But it felt so different—so unlike Samuel.

Sarah stood. "You look pale. Do you want to go back to sleep?"

"I'm okay." She stared into Sarah's blue eyes. "Why is it me, Sarah? Why am I seeing these things? Why did Garcia come to me again? How—" She rubbed the bulge of her waist. Garcia had to be real, and not just something in her mind. He was the father of the child within her. She refused any thought of her husband, or of Jim Whitten. "You said Garcia couldn't—"

Sarah shook her head. "He shouldn't have. I don't understand it at all. It's unlike anything that's ever been recorded. His point of contact to this plane should be that stadium area."

The words of the nightmare teased at Vickie, mostly forgotten. "Mr. Whitten said . . ."

"What?" Sarah scooted forward.

"He said I had life. He said that to me when I first came to see you." She shut her eyes to the ominous, straying visions of her memory. "He said I had life."

Sarah frowned. "He was alive then."

Vickie lay back on the divan. "I think that milk's bothering me."

Sarah bit her lip and nodded. "I should have known better than to let you have it. My mother always told me that nothing curdles a 'tacky tummy' faster." Sarah tried to sound flippant. "Like, sorry, Vickie."

"Your mother, huh?" Vickie tried to pursue this safe subject. "What was she like, Sarah?"

Sarah brought her hands together primly at her waist, striking a pose. "Supermom, actually. She was an honest-to-God full-time mother and housewife—I couldn't get half the things accomplished in a day that she could." She gave a sly smile. "And I'd never want to."

"Sounds like my mother."

"Well," Sarah said, "moms are basically the same within their generations—or were, anyway. Mine was a little put off by my desire to be a 'professional lady' rather than follow in her footsteps, but when she got over it she and Dad were very helpful in letting me go to the schools I wanted. I really owe them a lot. I wouldn't be doing what I am now without their support."

"Your mother really wanted you to be a . . . parapsychologist?"

"I didn't say that, and I'm a psychiatrist, not a

parapsychologist." Sarah made a fist and grinned. "But once she saw I was determined, she helped me all she could. The parapsychology work came later."

"Mother wouldn't even talk about anything supernatural." Vickie's stomach was finally settling. "She said it wasn't Christian and it wasn't real. She wouldn't even let me watch horror shows on TV. I was fifteen before I saw Frankenstein—the one with Boris Karloff."

"Christianity is made up of the supernatural itself. The Christian God is supernatural. *All* religions contain the supernatural within them. And many of the things parapsychologists study are even acknowledged as real outside of the field, Vickie." Sarah shifted in her chair and sighed. "Some of our investigations do prove to be hoaxes—hallucinations brought on by mental instability—but many aren't, and they're not something to be frightened of any more than we should be frightened of any other manifestation of the unknown. The media is responsible for that kind of feeling. TV gives anything supernatural splashy coverage, and people all start seeing spooks for a while. If there's a report of one person seeing a ghost or UFO, we hear from a hundred more who saw the same thing an hour later, but that interest soon dies down."

"Do you . . . get a lot now?"

"How's that?"

Vickie shrugged.

"If you mean the experiment with Whitten, nobody's really sure what we've proved there." Sarah shook her head. "The institute's trying to keep it quiet until we can figure out what did happen. When I called in this morning, they still didn't have any idea what was going on, and we worked our tails off yesterday."

Vickie sat up straight. "That night you met me in the restaurant, you said something about getting a lot of strange reports."

Sarah started. "Did I? Probably just overwork," she explained hastily. "I'm sure it's just overwork. You know it seems there's more of everything when you get behind." She looked back through the bedroom door at the portrait of her and Lesley on the wall. "My husband always said that."

"That's the truth." Vickie picked at a scab on her arm. "You were married?"

The apartment's heater started up loudly. "Yes." Sarah swallowed hard. "His name was Lesley. He died eight months ago."

"I'm sorry," Vickie said quietly.

Sarah continued to stare at the portrait.

"Was your husband a parapsychologist too?"

"He—Lesley was a gifted and very talented psychic. He could see things like you do, Vickie. I met him when I took a couple of classes dealing with parapsychology." Sarah smiled vaguely.

"Lesley was the subject of some research. He had volunteered to help my teacher in some experiments, and because of the interest I'd shown in his class, Dr. Lan-Tai called me and asked if I'd like to assist him." Her smile broadened, and to Vickie the purity of that smile made her look years younger. "I took the opportunity, of course." Fondness continued to relax her features, melting the hard lines around her mouth and eyes.

A sense of belonging began in Vickie and she held it close, wanting it to drive away the loneliness that waited all around her. She grinned. "You wanted to be a *ghostbuster*, right?"

Sarah laughed. "I told you that ghost is an overused word, Vickie. I personally do believe that some are surviving personalities, though." She slipped out of the humor and her eyebrows pressed together. "I think they're people who've died, and in death their essence—what they *were*—has been transmuted into an intelligent presence on another plane." She spread her hands, palms up, then giggled at herself. "I talk a lot when I get going, don't I? Sometimes I lie awake in bed at night and talk to help myself understand things."

Vickie laughed. "I used to do that a lot, but not just when I slept. It really pissed John—my husband—off."

A long look passed between them, and Sarah's

face grew a little sad. "I didn't used to do it. Not until after Lesley died. We talked in bed before we went to sleep, and he helped me learn a lot of what I know now."

"In bed?" Vickie couldn't help grinning again.

Sarah burst out laughing. "Kind of kinky, huh?"

"Kind of." Vickie drew one leg up in front of her, wrapping her arms around it.

"I don't do it as much now," Sarah said. "It's better to talk with someone else. That's why I like Mitch, the man you met in my office. He's a good listener."

Vickie nodded. "Did you ever work with your husband at the institute?"

The mildness left Sarah abruptly. Her lips tightened. "Yes," she breathed.

Vickie regretted her words.

"We tried to communicate with his father after he died. Lesley had been close to him and it seemed like a good chance to make a contact, but it was exhausting him. Then he wouldn't stop. The pressure he put himself under would drag him down. He would use up so much energy just trying. . . ."

Vickie remembered Sarah explaining that the energy was taken from her and that was the reason her experiences made her so weak. "What happened?"

A heavy breath flooded out of Sarah. "He killed himself. His father killed him."

Feeling Sarah's hurt bitterness, Vickie went to her, touching her shoulder gently.

"I needed Lesley." Sarah made a strange choking sound and closed her hands together. "I needed him." A sob tore from her lungs. "But he left me to be with his father."

Vickie stared at her, feeling Sarah's tense shiver.

"And he can't come back!"

25

"Sarah?"

Sarah looked at Vickie on the blue divan and shook her head, not ready to say anything.

"Sarah?" Vickie held her arms out. "Sarah . . . I'm dizzy. . . ."

Her high, fatigued voice broke into Sarah's thoughts. She forced her mind to the present with difficulty. "What's wrong?"

"I'm getting dizzy, Sarah."

Responsibility won the day and Sarah wiped her eyes. She stood. "Do you want something to drink?"

Vickie shook her head. "I hurt." She rubbed her oversized abdomen. "The baby keeps moving. It's *hurting* me."

The unstructured impossibilities of Vickie, Garcia, and Jim Whitten that had been rising dangerously in Sarah broke into her thoughts without warning, but she kept her mouth shut, denying them. "Not enough evidence," she muttered to herself.

"What?"

Sarah's head moved briskly. "Nothing. Are you tired again?"

"Yeah, I think so." Vickie's grin was feeble. "I —I'm sorry."

"No." She took Vickie's hands and helped her up. "I'm sorry. I talk too damn much. I've always talked too damn much." She remembered Mitch guiltily when she realized she'd broken their dinner appointment the night before last, and she'd never called him.

"Let me help you back to bed," Sarah offered in apology. "Rest will help, Vickie."

Vickie's fingers tightened painfully over Sarah's, and she resisted, pumping her head back and forth as Sarah led her to the hall. "I'll dream."

"No." Sarah tried to keep her voice aloof and strong. "No, you won't. I've got some medicine to make you sleep so deeply you won't be able to, and I'll be right here with you. I'll be right *here.*"

A few more steps brought them into the cluttered bedroom, and Sarah helped her into bed, then fed her some of the sleeping tablets she used off and on when Lesley's absence bothered her the most. She straightened the blanket and pulled down the hot quilt. When she looked back at Vickie's face, the young woman was already asleep.

Had Vickie really broken through to the other side?

Though Sarah could consider the idea theoretically, there wasn't enough evidence to prove it possible. She backed out of the room and turned off the light, sagging against the wall in the hallway. *It was impossible by everything now known.* The very thought of the chaos such a vicious reality would create made her forehead hot. She tried to dismiss it. Her ideas were just the hysteria of these past months and the awful burden Lesley's death had shifted onto her.

A headache blossomed, and her legs went hollow. The past months were finally catching up to her. It would have happened much sooner if it hadn't been for Mitch. His concern and vulnerability had made him the perfect person to help her overcome her frustration. He gave her the will to go on. The hours of their talking opened him up to her, and she forgot her losses in order to help *him.* That had helped her more than anything else.

She was sweating now, her skull throbbing. She'd never had a headache like this. "God . . . damn . . ." She forced herself to the bathroom and looked at the deep circles under her eyes.

She searched through the medicine cabinet, grabbed the aspirin container, and shook it, almost crushed by her pain as she realized it was empty.

Her brains were splitting with the sudden pressure. *"No!"* Sarah staggered back to the living room, bumping the aquarium, grabbing her purse with deranged purpose. She found her car keys through the tears of agony. A groan came from the bedroom. Sarah pulled open the door to the outside hall. Bits and pieces of knowledge closed in on her.

She stopped, knowing she shouldn't leave Vickie even for the few minutes it would take to get to the drugstore and back, but she was hurting and scared—very scared.

She couldn't help Vickie like this. She hesitated, then moved slowly into the outside hall. She had to help herself first, so she could—

Like with Mitch.

It almost stopped her. But she *had* helped him, hadn't she?

Sarah closed the door and hobbled to the stairway, refusing to notice that the pain became less acute with each step she took. She had helped Mitch, and she would help Vickie too.

And Vickie would help her to understand.

When she got to the store, Sarah picked out a large aspirin bottle, then walked back to the cashier, hardly noticing the greasy, short-haired punk in a jeans jacket eyeing her from the next aisle. She refused to meet the gaze behind his dark sunglasses, paid, and nodded when the young woman thanked her. Sarah picked up the crinkly plastic sack and stepped back out into the sunshine, wanting it to melt away the chill of the bizarre ideas that slipped through her mind.

Aliester C. had come to Vickie and a man was found dead nearby. Jim Whitten had come to Vickie . . . and her mother died, in the same inexplicable way.

Sarah walked faster, struggling not to admit her fear. The punk was watching her as she shut the car door, revved the engine, and turned out of the parking lot. A cigarette helped to calm her nerves.

The buildings passed her quickly. When she arrived at her apartment building, she saw the orange-white-and-blue ambulance out front with a dread that froze her heart.

"Oh, no," she cried, hurrying through the door ahead of the white-uniformed men and their stretcher. Her heart pounded as she hurried up the wide stairs to the crowd of fellow tenants outside her next-door neighbor's apartment. Two younger men were trying to calm down the old wrinkled woman who lived there with her husband. She was crying hysterically.

The sound drove ice into Sarah's spine. "Oh,

dear Lord," she said, moving quickly to her own door.

She didn't ask what had happened, and closed the noise out quickly. She *knew,* and knew that her deep, subconscious fear had helped her to escape death.

She didn't understand, but she *knew.* And she knew she had to try to tell Vickie.

26

The street outside the old brick building housing the Observer Institute rooms was packed with news cameras and reporters carrying portable computers, tape recorders, and old-fashioned pens and writing pads today. The cars identified them as belonging to local news stations, CNN, magazines, and the papers . . . even local radio broadcasters.

And now the green-shirted policemen surrounded each entrance.

Mitch Lisciotti put his hands in his pockets and watched them all with a sinking feeling in his stomach from across the street. His tongue wiggled against his teeth because he knew why they were here. He had first heard the rumors of what had happened when he'd tried to get in yesterday and take care of the animals. He'd planned to go up to Sarah's floor and find out why she hadn't met him night before last. He had called her place late into the night until he fell asleep.

When the police barred his way, he called her office and was met with a busy signal. His ghastly dreams were full of the paranoid belief that she was avoiding him, that she had turned against him at last.

And what he was hearing, even on TV . . . wasn't . . . *wasn't* possible.

The entire institute building was off limits. He couldn't do his job, and he couldn't find Sarah so she could give him the reassurance he desperately wanted—

Needed.

The only thing that made him feel any better was the understanding that Sarah must have had her hands so full she had honestly forgotten their date—that maybe she was still here and had never left, so caught up in events she didn't even have time to call him.

His tongue was clicking fast against the roof of his mouth as he saw Brett Wilson, one of Sarah's friends, dart out of a taxi, nearly tripping as he ran into one of the TV cameras. A woman in a brisk business skirt, carrying a microphone, crossed his path and trapped him. Brett was shaking his head angrily, trying to move to a cop.

Mitch moved nearer into the confusion of

raised voices, crossing the street full of immobile traffic and honking horns.

"Is it true that you people here at Observer have made an earth-shattering breakthrough in your research?" the woman's pitched voice was asking. "We've heard several rumors that a man died here of a serious illness but miraculously regained consciousness, free of his disease—"

Brett's face was fiery red. "There are a lot of rumors running around here right now, but all I can tell you is that a statement will be made by Dr. Fowler shortly. I do not have the authority to confirm or deny—"

A burly man decked in a blue business suit shoved another microphone at Brett. "The people have a right to *know*—and we're going to follow this up and make your lives hell until you give us some answers!"

"A statement will be made by Dr. Fowler within the next hour!" Brett shouted. His voice was raw and strained to the breaking point. Mitch was close enough now to see the dark circles under his eyes and knew he had been awake all night. Even if the stories he'd heard were a lie, *something* had happened.

"The Surgeon General has issued a statement that this institute is to be investigated. Is Dr. Fowler aware of that?" asked the woman, pushing close. "There is a confirmed report of a patient in St. Paul's Hospital dying only thirty minutes ago and returning to life in perfect health. That has been *confirmed*. The—"

"I don't know what the hell you're talking about," Brett spoke louder.

"You don't seem surprised." She smiled darkly.

Brett flushed a deeper red and pushed his way through the dozen people. A young police officer took his arm and kept them away from him. "We have no comment at this time," he kept saying hoarsely. "No comment." He got to the door and unlocked it as the cameras drew up behind him, barely escaping inside and slamming the door closed. The officer stood outside with an unreadable expression.

Mitch trembled, listening to the reporters mutter and exchange information and sour curses. Their words were so interlocked they quickly became meaningless except for their direction. Somehow, the rumor had gotten out that Sarah's patient, Jim Whitten, had been resurrected from the grave like Lazarus.

A miracle. Everyone was saying that.

But Mitch had met Jim Whitten. He knew the way Sarah talked of him and of the crazy, sick things he told her. She said that he *wanted* to die.

Mitch tried to see around the cop into the lobby for a sign of Sarah one last time. He was worried . . . afraid. This place was in an uproar that would probably spread through the whole town with the new report from the hospital. Something was happening. Something that appeared to be wonderful news.

So why all the secrecy?

More commotion from the corner made him look that way. National Guardsmen were taking their places inside and outside the building, and Mitch saw a growing number of civilians gathering beyond them.

His tongue clicked.

27

Vickie was screaming.

Her head throbbed, and the ghastly horror of the recurring nightmare was alive in her. Sweat splashed around her like the blood in her dreams, and she tried to rise out of its dark smears. It was bleak and endless, and she screamed, wanting to be free.

Inside of her the baby vibrated.

"No." She didn't want to remember. *She just wanted to have her baby and be free. She had to do whatever she could to be free.* She panted as the baby leapt inside her harder and faster. It was hers. *It was hers!*

But it had become like a deadened and useless limb—part of her but not. It was attached to her, and she could feel it, but more and more she knew that it was no longer hers. Tears poured out her eyes as she opened them, like the dream's blood water against her face. . . .

"You have life," Whitten wheezed in her mind—those words of days before and the guilty feelings making her heart thud hard in her chest. She needed to tell Sarah. Sarah would know what to do. *Sarah would understand.*

"Vickie," Daddy's long-forgotten voice said from far away, *"Jesus was born and died so we could live again."*

"But, Daddy—"

"Our lives here are ruled and owned by death."

Her child's logic had figured it out quickly. If spiritual life could be brought from physical death, physical life could be brought from spiritual death. Jesus had died as a sacrificial lamb, and brought spiritual life.

But she had wanted to overcome physical death.

"Death owns our bodies," said Mother.

Death. She prayed to death. She prayed to death and accepted it as her savior.

"God," she wailed, struggling to get out from under blankets that covered her like that preacher's blood. "Oh, God." Vickie dropped back to the spongy mattress that tried to surround her. She cringed at the thrashing death she was baptized in. Love, loss, hate, and despair churned in her. The baby was grappling and growing even now—no longer part of her. It was already taken away, like Samuel, filled by the death she had prayed to and accepted before she was even pregnant. Like her father, the life of her womb had been stolen from her.

Her baby.

At last Vickie began to understand: *it was the child she had prayed for.*

Sarah was barely able to awaken Vickie, and before Vickie could understand the meaning of Sarah's frantic words, she passed out. Still, Sarah did her best to put her thoughts together as fast as she could and to explain to Vickie what might be happening. Vickie opened her eyes again as Sarah hurried to tell her about the baby she was carrying, but she nodded off to sleep again and again as Sarah spoke. Finally, Sarah could not draw a reaction when she pinched Vickie's earlobe, and her words dropped off in futility. Vickie had no control, and explaining what might be happening wasn't giving it to her.

But it reinforced Sarah's own understanding, and once again she knew she was only using someone else to clarify her knowledge.

Yes. Though she wasn't even sure she was right. Rationally, she knew she couldn't be right. *But it all fit.*

"God." She sighed, and pulled the blanket back up over Vickie's shoulders. "God help us, Vickie," she whispered.

God. Sarah shook her head and backed out of

the quiet room. *If there really was one.* But until He made an appearance, it was just her and Vickie. "If you're coming, Jesus, now would be a good time," she muttered. Bits and pieces from the psychic manifestations so often reported these past months and even the mystery of Lesley's death made the possibilities hold together. It was all intensifying crazily, rapidly.

Death.

Finding her purse where she had dropped it inside the door, she carried it back and sat down heavily, opening it and picking out her small looseleaf notebook. With Vickie in the other room, she thought it would be safe to have a cigarette. As she lit up, her eyes moved briskly over her previous jottings. Then she began to write.

The front door suddenly rattled in the middle of her third page, and Sarah was torn from her thoughts. She paused briefly to compose herself, put out the cigarette, and returned the book to her purse. As she reached the door, she was suddenly filled with reluctance to open it. She wanted another cigarette, wanted to back away and hide, but made herself twist the knob and pull the door open. Cool air circled in from the hallway.

"Hello, Sarah." Mitch's voice was emotionless.

"Wha—" She stood back to let him in. "What's wrong, Mitch?"

"I should ask you that. You stood me up the other night." His manner seemed strained.

"Something happened, Mitch."

"I know. I saw the news." He huffed impatiently and nervously. "The institute released their report on Jim Whitten this afternoon."

She stared at him, then lowered her eyes. "I—"

"Did you know about that?"

"They told us not to say anything about it."

Mitch swallowed, barely controlling his voice as his words shuddered under his clucking tongue. "They let out the report after someone else died in the hospital across the street from the institute this afternoon. They said that a man who had just died sat up and started screaming." Mitch's voice cracked. "The machines they hooked him up to went *crazy* and some kind of bizarre surge wiped them out—fried every chip and circuit in them. I tried to find you at work, but they've got the building blocked off! *I can't even check on the animals!"*

Sarah shifted her eyes to the bedroom door, thinking of the events of the afternoon. "When did this man come back to life?" she asked.

"When?" He laughed sarcastically. "What the hell difference—"

"When, Mitch?"

"Around three, maybe three-thirty."

Sarah turned and walked slowly into the

kitchen. The timing proved her right beyond a doubt. Clenching her teeth, she opened the refrigerator and took out the bottle of daiquiri mix, then heard him behind her.

"What happened at the hospital was fully documented, Sarah."

She closed her eyes. *She knew.*

"But . . . it's impossible."

"But it happened, didn't it?" She poured some of the mix into a glass, then took out a bottle of 7-Up to follow. Mechanically, she opened a cabinet and took out the rum, topping the mix off, then brought out a bottle of whiskey and offered it to him.

"A double," he muttered.

She measured the whiskey into another glass, finished it with water and stirred, then brought the drinks to the table and sat down, shutting her eyes against the dread she'd felt when she had watched Whitten open his mouth and speak.

That was already two days ago.

"You *knew*," he accused her, red faced. *"You know what's going on."* He took his glass and drank most of it. "It's *insane!"*

She stood and went into the living room, turning the TV on to CNN. He followed her.

"—still don't understand what happened in either case," the newscaster was saying. "The Observer Parapsychological Institute has been asked to forward duplicates of all their studies in this and related matters to the Surgeon General's office immediately. Officials at the institute claim to have confirmed and verifiable proof that Jim Whitten died Tuesday night of a cancer that had spread up to his brain, but an examination of Mr. Whitten Wednesday after his apparant miraculous return to life, and the ensuing biopsy, prove him to be completely free of cancer—"

"Sarah, look at me!"

She turned. "What do you want me to say?"

"What in the fuck is happening?" His pupils were dilated with fear. He grabbed her arm, and she felt him tremble. "Why?"

"I don't know." Her eyes wandered back to the newscaster as he dissolved to a flattering picture of Jim Whitten before the sickness had taken hold.

They were both glued to the television now, and Sarah felt Mitch's confusion in the tense air between them. His face was sheet white and even his nervous tongue was still as he listened to the commentary. He sat on the divan. "God—"

"Do you think so?" Sarah said.

Mitch bit his lips. "I . . ." He finished his whiskey. "Can you— Would you—get me another . . . please?"

As the newscaster went down a list of scientists who denied the possibility of what had happened, Sarah made Mitch another drink and brought it to him. "Vickie saw Whitten in her dream that night—the night he died. I brought her here."

Mitch looked toward the closed bedroom door.

"She didn't know he'd died, and there was no reason that she would dream about him." Sarah took a quick swallow, then pushed her glass away. "Her mother was dead. Vickie knew it and had been in that house with her all day."

"What sort of sense are you trying to make now?" His tongue clicked against the roof of his mouth. "Good God, Sarah."

She stared at his angry disbelief and threw her half-full glass against the wall, flinching at its loud, splintering shatter. *"Damn it,"* she said, "I *can't* cover it up and explain it away for you anymore, Mitch." She looked away from him, and sighed, bending over to pick up one of the big broken slivers of the wet glass on the floor. The bits and pieces tingled in her thoughts loudly, and now she was certain she guessed correctly at what had occurred— *Bits and pieces* . . . Her eyes held him, though she saw far beyond him into her own thoughts. "Vickie Laster was the apparent catalyst for physical phenomena."

"Physical phenomena?"

"Why the hell do you want me to tell you when you won't even listen?"

He stopped another question. "I—sorry. Go on."

Bitterness at the ridicule she had lived with—that Lesley had lived and died with—stung her, and her voice became a hard lecture. "Briefly, souls or ghosts take on a physical presence and re-create their memories of what has *already* happened. They use someone receptive on our own plane of existence to reenact something that has already occurred." She tried to stop the anger, but slowly, deeply, understood she didn't want to. She wanted someone to know what she knew and was still trying to comprehend. "In ways it's like a psychic photograph that can only be seen by certain people. It happened to Vickie. But I only understand *how* it is happening. I can't fully understand *why.*" She broke off, breathing with uncertain excitement.

"Okay." He bit his lip. "How?"

"We talked about this ability when we talked about your dreams, Mitch. It's what makes them come to you. Vickie is a powerful physical medium with the abilities of a mental medium too. Physical manifestation is presumed to be brought about by the medium's willing, though often unconscious, *acceptance* that the psychic forces are *truth.* Your inner need for Tabitha was so strong that your dreams of her became a truth. The psychic dream rarely expands beyond the mind of the medium—usually someone unusually sensitive or in an area where psychic vibrations are very strong. With Vickie's ability, that truth is not limited to her own mind or even an immediate area. Her *belief* seems to give these forces a *reality* in this world. My studies indicate that belief creates its own truth. It's what makes crazy people stay crazy. *To some extent we can all create our own truths.*"

Mitch frowned.

"Look, Mitch," she went on, her words tripping over each other, "mediums are those of us with a powerful gullibility. Their open minds can sometimes give the psychic forces physical presence. Your dreams of Tabitha occur because your extreme guilt won't let you accept her death. Until you can deny that guilt her memories will keep her alive in your mind, especially when you're most vulnerable and gullible—when you're *asleep.*" Her words faded into silence, and they stared at each other. "But Vickie's belief made the phenomena so real that she actually interacted with it."

Mitch's face was full of hope and despair. "What do you mean?"

"Her belief was so strong that she did much more than observe phenomena, Mitch. She didn't just see something or hear it speak. I think it became so real to her that she *experienced* it and it did become physically *real*. And she became a part of its past, just as it became a part of hers. She brought something already dead new existence on this plane. She did cross over." Sarah felt beads of sweat on her forehead. She recalled Vickie telling her that she had prayed to death and that her call had been answered. "Or—or it crossed over through her."

His face twitched.

"Mitch, she's pregnant, but it's physically impossible. I can't see how. How can physical phenomena draw their material reality from her?"

"You don't know—"

"I don't fully know why." She wiped her forehead. "But Vickie told me that she prayed to death like some people pray to God—and maybe that overpowering desire to connect with death became so strong in her that it opened some kind of door to the death inside us all. The moment anyone is born, they begin to die. It's a biological fact, and it's the only damn thing that makes sense, Mitch. Most mediums use prayer or meditation to settle themselves into a state of receptiveness. Her prayers to death could have served that purpose, letting spirits of the dead use her for materialization, allowing them to *impregnate* her with that death. It would break the laws separating death and life. It would explain what's been happening."

His eyes were wide and his mouth opened soundlessly.

"It—"

"No." He put his hands up as if to ward off her words.

"If the dead come back to life, Mitch, no matter *how* it happens—there must be some kind of an exchange. I don't see how that law could be overcome. For every action there must be an equal and opposite reaction."

"Sarah, it's impossible." Mitch stood. "It's crazy!"

Sarah went to him and took his hands. "I think it was Vickie that brought about Garcia's reappearance. Her grief and meditating prayer resurrected him." Desperately she tried to hold on to the train of thought. "I think the phenomena followed her here. That couldn't happen by the rules we know now. Such things require a *contact point* between the medium and the location of memories. But I think she's become a contact point—a very powerful breach between the two existences." Sarah caught her breath.

"What is it?"

Everything was fitting together as she spoke —what had bothered her since the beginning: "People use up a lot of energy in that kind of a trance." Sarah thought of Lesley. "It can *kill* them. But Vickie doesn't weaken when she's in contact. I think she's some kind of a—a transformer of psychic energy, Mitch. Her mother died inexplicably when Whitten came back." She squeezed his fingers forcefully. "And around three o'clock today, a man died in the apartment next door. And I know they died in the same way. *An impossible way. It's part of the exchange!*"

"What?"

Sarah shook her head. "I don't know. *I don't know.* Vickie is unlike any psychic ever recorded." She stared at him earnestly. "Vickie Laster presents a potential for breakthrough almost unthought of."

Mitch broke contact and took a step away. "What in the hell—"

"I'm afraid, Mitch." Sarah's hands dropped to her sides. "I know she can't control it. She doesn't know. Her imagination, her prayers, have touched beyond her own perimeters. Like her ability to draw on other people's strength— their lives. It still goes against every known law, but maybe not the *unknown* laws." She said it with a strange mixture of a triumph and base fear. "I tried to tell her. She has to learn to be able to—"

"Sarah," Mitch said, his head turned away.

"Mitch, it's so fantastic. Her own will has opened the door between life and death."

"Sarah!" He grabbed her wrist.

"Vickie is pregnant with a deformed, impossi-

ble baby—fathered *by an apparition or ghost.*"
Her words came fast with the excitement of understanding. "Her experience was sexual. The
sexual act is basically the giving of life, and was
used for that purpose in early tribal rites of necromancy. Such rites were used in the defense of
necrophilia up to our current age—*the use of
the sexual act to bring life to the dead.*"

Mitch's breaths were labored. "I don't believe
it."

A muffled scream from the back of the apartment drowned out his words, and Sarah froze.

Mitch's eyes went big. "Oh Jesus," he whispered.

Sarah pulled Mitch after her. "Come on."

28

Vickie looked up as the door swung open and a shaft of light fell over her cheek.

"Vickie, what's wrong?"

She jerked around to face them, and her tongue fell out of her mouth, drooling slobber onto her chin. "I . . ."

"It's all right," Sarah whispered. "It's all right, Vickie."

Vickie shivered as Sarah sat on the mattress and pulled her close. Sarah's tobacco breath surrounded Vickie like a protective shield. "What's wrong?" Sarah whispered.

Raising her arm, Vickie pointed at the portrait on the wall of Sarah and her slender husband in a forest setting. Her hand trembled.

"Lesley." Sarah said. Sarah's eyes were in hers and they stared into one another. "It was . . . Lesley?" She laid Vickie's head back on the bed and almost tiptoed to the portrait. Her fingers touched the slick metal frame briefly.

"He wants," Vickie told her. "He *wants*—"

Mitch helped Vickie stand. The room roared in silence as he led her after Sarah.

In the portrait Lesley held Sarah's hand in that captured memory of the past. "He came to you?"

"He *wants*—"

Sarah's face screwed up with hostility, and she ripped the portrait from the wall. She threw it into the corner, where it crashed and splintered glass on the floor loudly. "No!" She searched the room with an intense, fearing stare.

"Sarah . . ."

The familiar voice pricked her and she thought she saw a glimmer of him in a faint blue glow across the dusky bedroom. "Lesley?" she whispered.

Mitch rubbed his arms in the suddenly clammy air. Sarah's mouth moved silently.

Mitch grabbed her shoulder. "What is it?"

"Him."

Mitch looked at the smashed picture on the floor.

"He—he's here."

"It isn't possible." Mitch's tongue clicked and he shifted defensively, tucking his thumbs into his pants pockets. "Sarah—"

She was looking right at the ghostly vision of

her husband, tall and lean, the deep circles under his eyes from long, sleepless nights. He stood naked before her, and Sarah knew that Mitch couldn't see him—or *wouldn't* see him. She was afraid, she wanted Mitch to hold her, but she pushed him away. "Take Vickie out," she said.

"Calm down, Sarah." He held Vickie's limp body close. "It can't be—"

"Take her out of here!"

Lesley's misty image smiled in that old, lopsided way, his shiny teeth showing on the right side, and he walked nearer. Icy air preceded him. He wrapped his skeletal hand around Mitch's. Mitch cried out and tried to pull away. "It's freezing! God—there's something—"

"Lesley, don't!"

The wispy form closed its long fingers with a snap. Bones cracked like the clatter of falling icicles.

"Help!" Mitch screamed.

"Sarah," Vickie cried.

All at once, Sarah was revolted by Lesley, even in her memories. "No." She forced herself between Mitch and the thing that had been her husband. "Now, Mitch. Get out. *Get Vickie out!*" Her eyes were red and wet.

"Sarah!" Vickie was screaming.

"Goddammit, take her out of here!"

Lesley was laughing shrilly, his gaunt face stretched, and suddenly Sarah didn't feel repulsion as much as fear, or fear as much as horrid curiosity. His frigid breath was in her face. He was solidifying, his continued materialization weakening Vickie as she trembled in a near trance. Mitch was barely able to hold her up. Vickie's special ability would begin to drain Sarah's life soon, or Mitch's.

"You"— Sarah covered her mouth, shuddering at the form flowing nearer—"you're *dead.*"

Mitch remained nearby, pain etched clearly on his face. His hand was ruined, his thumb hanging limp. His mouth twitched, but he still held Vickie up. She felt strong love for him for that.

"Go, go *please,*" she whispered.

Lesley stepped closer, freezing her with his body's temperature.

Sarah's jaw trembled, muffling her words: "Take my notebook in—in the purse." She was frightened of Lesley being here more than anything had scared her in her life, but it would not overcome her need to understand—not now. "I wrote the ideas down. Read it—please. *Try to believe.*" She swallowed. "I'll . . . call. . . ."

He edged toward the door. "I—I'll come back."

Her heart beating faster, faster, wanting for a brief moment to go with them.

But Lesley would follow, and she knew she had to stay. She had to stay for them, and for herself to know what death was. She had to *know*.

Mitch pulled Vickie into the hall. The door closed by itself behind them. The air around Sarah grew colder and colder.

She closed her eyes, heard the front door shut.

She was alone with a ghost—the ghost of the man she'd lived with and made love to and wanted back for so long, holding all the dark secrets of death she sought.

"Sarah . . ." The gravelly voice beckoned her and she searched for its source.

"I'm still here."

Her heart caught, and she felt the familiar closeness. It seemed she could even detect that unforgettable timberwood cologne scent.

The wispiness reappeared beside her. "Lesley?" she whispered. "It can't be. . . ."

An awkward smile floated on his lips. "So after all these years, you don't believe in ghosts." His tone was a teasing, cruel memory.

"No." She was ill. Her study of Vickie and her obsession with Lesley's death had brought this on. "No," she said with a tremor.

"You do and I *am*," he replied, and came closer.

Sarah held her breath, electricity dancing on her flesh and deep inside her. All her horrible memories of Lesley's death flashed back. His naked body became more solid. "No," she said.

"Didn't you want me to come back? Didn't you beg for me to come back?"

Sarah was forcing herself away from him, and felt the wall behind her. "Oh, God." She shook her head. "God, not now. Why *now?*"

"Your need and desire has become in Vickie . . . Your desire for me draws me."

"No."

"She is our contact for now. The forces that separated us are disintegrating, Sarah. *She has rescinded the laws.*"

Feeling the electric tingle of his fingers, she gasped.

"We have waited. We have followed the laws and overcome them." Lesley grinned hollowly. "What we all searched for has come to pass." His gray eyes delved into her soul. "Give yourself to me, Sarah."

Her heart beat faster, faster. "I—I loved you."

He touched her lips lightly with icy fingers. "Love is empty."

Her mouth was dry.

"You have life, but no understanding—only its *want.*" He did not smile. "I have *death.* Death is knowledge and understanding, Sarah. Death shows the *truth.* Give yourself to me and you will have that knowledge."

She swallowed, afraid.

"Guilt is our bond, Sarah."

She brought her hand to him weakly, actually

touching the bristles on his unshaven face. He looked like he had when she watched him die—unchanged. He was dead. It was impossible.

"You . . ." She took back her hand and held it over her mouth. "No . . . you're dead. You're *dead*."

Lesley clutched at her hand. "You can be my life. Give yourself to me, Sarah."

Her throat was tight and her long greed for the understanding he promised compelled her. She reached to touch him. "I wanted you so. I needed you."

"You *wanted* me—yes. You always *wanted* what I could give you. You wanted the knowledge I could give you and you called that want love."

The words crawled over her, forced themselves into her, just as he pressed his hard nails into her hand. Though the truth stung her, she still clung to him with the long need: the need of understanding for her self.

Her self. She needed. . . .

Acid burned in her heart.

Sarah was trapped, paralyzed. She couldn't scream. Her heart was crumbling inside her, tearing. "Lesley, I loved—"

"No," he replied, almost in cruelty. "Not love. You admit it was not love. You wanted me—you needed me." He held her closer without passion, driven as if by hunger. "But I have *you*. I have your *life* and you have my *knowledge.*"

He was against her, solid now. She couldn't move as he pressed her into the wall, and the weakening that enveloped her made her know it was all *true*. She gasped, and her legs turned to mush. She opened her mouth to cry out, but could only gasp again.

"You prayed for me to return, Sarah. You prayed for the understanding of death."

"N-no," she whimpered, not able to stay on her feet. His arms let her down to the carpet. Her teeth chattered.

"You have worked so hard to contact death, and your prayers were heard—*by death.*"

One for another. Her desire and guilt had willingly bound her to death—just as it had Vickie—and now her life was to be exchanged. She wanted to scream, wanted the fullness of life, even the life she had just given up.

The gateway to Hell had been unlocked.

It made her want. But it took away hope—

The pressure inside her built and she could not refuse it. She was cresting in the vacuum. Her inner body shuddered and shriveled. It was torn into pieces and pulled from inside her. And then her self—her very soul—was ripped out of her as she screamed—

29

Jim Whitten felt powerful. He was beyond death and past the borders of physical pain. Others were dying and returning to life even now, but he was the first of them all to pass through the realms without pause.

He had the life he only dreamed of during those tear-filled nights when he'd first learned he had cancer. Sitting on his bed at home alone, he had feared death, even more when death raged through his stereo with those old songs by Aliester C.

Death into life.

The songs lingered into the dreams he had that night, though he kept them a guarded secret. He, who was dying without hope of a cure, had volunteered his life and death to the music of Aliester C. And those lyrics hummed over in his brain as he became more and more attuned to death. As it spread through him he'd seen the truth in that girl, Vickie, and the hybrid creature she bore in union of life to death. He offered his death to her, too, and now she had returned immortal life to him, freed of death's physical threat. She bore his death and agony through the one inside her, whose birth would give complete freedom through the destruction of all laws.

Freed of death—and he was the first, rightly the first, to experience it truly—straight from that final moment into this new being. The music he listened to had directed him through a thousand foggy visions: the knowledge—the perfect sight—of death was his.

He watched the white-suited researchers leaving the room. They plagued him with their endless questions, examinations, and proddings. Their voices were formless noises to his ears. They were alive and feared the death he'd undergone. But he was alive, and had surpassed death. He'd experienced what they only dreamed of in nightmares.

He was their master.

The door closed and they were gone.

"Can you talk, Mr. Whitten? How are you feeling?"

The big-hipped red-haired nurse had stayed behind, and he reached out to her, feeling an amusement as she shied away. "I— Are you hungry, Mr. Whitten? Can I get you anything?"

He reached toward her again, felt her hand this time as she didn't back away. His quickly answered requests these past hours proved he could have anything—anything at all. He could even have *her*. The life that denied him so much was his now. He could have *anything*. Without the fear of death, nothing stood between him and any craving.

He could not be denied.

The nurse frowned, and he transfixed her with his eyes. She stood, instantly hypnotized by his death-given authority as he touched her inner thoughts and felt her hideous fascination for him. Anger pulsed through him and he visualized killing her.

But that action would be pointless. She would come back as he had. The law of death was broken, and upon the birth of the death-child growing inside of Vickie, this nurse would be reborn as well.

Death was no longer an end, but rather a means to an end.

The awareness caught him by surprise, and he considered it slowly. Then he pinched himself hard, gasping at the pain.

At least he could hurt—and that meant he could hurt others.

"Would you like to sleep?"

Whitten realized he'd dropped his gaze and the nurse had regained herself. He followed the fullness of her curves and examined the urging inside himself. "Perhaps you could sleep *with* me."

She looked uncertainly at the machines surrounding them and back into his pupils. Again, he held her with them and touched her thoughts.

Her foremost desire was to find out what had happened to him. She envisioned herself talking to reporters and on late-night talk shows, divulging discoveries to Dan Rather and Johnny Carson that she hoped to be credited with, at least partially.

"Perhaps we could talk," he said seductively, using his voice as he might a machine he mastered. He would exploit her as she and the others here used him. They promised him money they never expected him to use for the right to be a part of his life and death. They exploited him selfishly for their own purpose of fame and discovery—and to satisfy their desire for eternal existence.

In the same sense he would use them now to satisfy himself.

"Okay. What did you experience? Do you know what happened?"

He yawned with exaggeration. "Lock the door."

"I can't. We're not supposed—"

"They said I could have what I wanted, within

reason." He grinned and looked at the thirtyish woman, visualizing her naked, her wide hips rubbing into his. "What's your name?"

"Candita."

"Candita," he said. He rolled over in the bed, spoke with disinterest. "My life before was like being in jail, and what happened is like seeing the door open and knowing you're free, and then knowing you've only been released into a bigger prison cell."

"You're saying that life is a prison?" she asked.

Whitten considered his growing despondency. Despondency he hoped he could ignore through the saturation of experiences. "Life," he told her sourly, "is death."

Her eyes went big until he made himself grin. She laughed in relief. "Come on." She nudged him, her eyes sly in the anticipation of his secrets.

He touched her leg and chuckled without feeling. "Life is fucking and getting fucked." Words flowed into his throat and he spoke them: "To know true life you've got to fuck death."

"Oh?" she asked cautiously. "That sounds like a rock star my big brother used to listen to all the time—Aliester C."

Whitten slid to his feet and pulled her skirt up, exposing her hose and the soft skin underneath.

She stared, openmouthed.

"Take off your clothes and I'll fuck you with death."

Her wide eyes shot to the closed door, and he heard her gulp as he transfixed her with his stare and sank his will into her. Her own base needs were very much like his. He pushed her back to the bed.

"N-not here," she said.

"Why not?" Whitten felt a stirring of excitement twist in him unexpectedly. "You won't care."

Under his will she lay back on the bed and fumbled breathlessly with the white uniform buttons. Whitten went into the bathroom. He felt the frost-tinted walls and used his new strength to tug the gray, two-foot-long paraplegic bar beside the toilet free with a noisy crack. He studied the end and knew it would suffice. It was heavy and its rounded point nearly perfect.

"What did you *feel?*" she called, almost naked now. She rolled the panty hose down her milky ankles, dropping them onto her shoes, and lay back, her hands hiding her body as best she could.

"Close your eyes and I'll tell you."

"I could get in a lot of trouble. Do you promise to tell me what happened to you? I shouldn't be in here and—"

The pole felt good. Powerful. He felt the

surge of expectation. "Close your eyes and I'll tell you."

She hesitated, staring at him almost fearfully. "What's . . . *that?*"

He moved back to the bed and touched her forehead with his fingers. "Close them for a moment and tell me what you see."

The woman's eyes darted to the door and then back to him. She shut her eyes. "This better be good," she muttered.

"What do you see?"

She sighed with exasperation, but kept her eyes shut. "Nothing," she replied. "Darkness."

"That is death, I think. That is what I was afraid of."

Jim Whitten stepped between her dangling feet and held the thick rod level with the bed. "Keep them closed, now." Her big, pale legs were spread slightly and he smiled, positioning his weapon. Hate-filled lust burned through him as he thought of the miserable life he'd known, the way he'd been used by others—rejection by his fiancée. "The secret," he told her softly, "is that death has lost its grip." He slid the metal pole up until it nearly touched the hair where her legs met. His arm tensed, shaking in anxiousness. "The secret is power. Power over others. The power I have over you." His heart pumped loudly. "The power of using."

She opened her eyes to see the end of the

metal pushing slowly inside her. Her mouth opened in terror and a high sound slipped out. The rod kept disappearing, stretching her skin, tearing into her. She tried to rise up on her elbows and push away, but his will froze her in immobility, only allowing her to scream wretchedly as her hot red blood gushed onto the sheets with the splash of draining water. She shook—flailed—uncontrollably as the cold metal tore viciously into her uterus. Deeper—

"No!"

Feeling a unique thrill, he watched as her screams became a gurgle and the blood pooled on the sheets, soaking them and dribbling down to the floor around his bare feet. He shoved the pole harder until she was convulsing and showering the room's walls and himself with her life, then he hummed Aliester C.'s "Back to Hell." "You'll be back," he told her writhing body with glee. But he frowned with annoyance at the warm blood still splattering his arms. *Death was messy*.

The momentary excitement subsided as she became still, and Whitten felt the boredom again. He didn't bother to look up as the door crashed open behind him. Someone shouted, and he closed his eyes as hands pulled him back.

"True power," he murmured, "is the power over boredom."

30

Mitch closed Sarah's bedroom door behind them and tightened his grip around Vickie. Though his hold was too tight, Vickie didn't resist. Mitch led her into the living room and set her down on a chair. Sarah's purse was on the divan and he dug through it with his uninjured hand, coming out with the notebook.

"Damn it," he muttered, and turned back to the bedroom. He tried to flex his limp hand with a helpless moan. At last he grabbed up Vickie's purse and one of Vickie's suitcases, got Vickie up, and urged her out into the hall. He closed Sarah's front door, and as they went down the steps, he began to move more quickly. He led her outside to a blue two-door Chevrolet and helped her get in. A young man in a jacket was watching them from the front door. Vickie shut her eyes and huddled on the cold vinyl passenger seat and tried not to think of anything.

Time passed, and only the sound of the engine and the awkward one-handed turns Mitch made proved to her she was awake.

Sarah.

"Vickie, your . . . prayers . . . have somehow opened a door."

Sarah's clouded words of that afternoon rolled back through Vickie's thoughts. The other psychiatrists had believed her experiences to be dreams, not real. But dreams were like watching TV—never so vivid that you could taste, smell, and feel them.

These were not dreams.

—opened a door—

She sat up and studied their surroundings, trying to get it all out of her head by gazing at her own reflection in its mirror—but the hell she'd already passed through was strong in the circles underlining her eyes.

She was afraid, and saw her tears glisten in the streetlights.

—you've opened a door—

Her baby.

Another chance. It was what she wanted, and she grasped it blindly. She'd wanted a baby more than anything for as long as she could remember.

Now she was pregnant.

She did not dare think of it.

Minutes passed like hours, but at last Mitch

zigzagged into a parking lot crowded with pick-ups and late-model cars. Vickie had found the gum in her purse, and chewed a piece while she examined the two-story red brick apartment buildings. Mitch slammed his door and came around to open hers. Hushed by his grimness, she climbed out. She found she could stand on her own now. He retrieved her suitcase and she followed him up the sidewalk. Her teeth chattered with the cold.

He glanced at her. "Freezing out here. As bad as—" He broke off and looked away.

"B-below zero," agreed Vickie.

"It's been a cold winter." His lips were tight, making his face seem thinner than it was. "Let's get upstairs. I have to bandage this hand. I may have to go to a doctor."

She didn't say anything.

"I'll make some hot coffee too. We both need some hot coffee."

"I . . ." whispered Vickie.

But he was already starting up the nearest building's outside stairs, swinging the scuffed suitcase. She staggered after him, climbing the stairs at his heels. On the second floor they passed the numbered doors in silence. "What about Sarah?" she finally asked.

Mitch put down her suitcase and unlocked the door. "Come on," he murmured, moving his hand to a light switch. Inside, the walls were naked of decoration and personality. A frizzy yellow armchair with a newspaper crumpled on it and a brown vinyl couch filled the living room.

Vickie shut the door and sat out of the way on the couch. Mitch disappeared down the hall, and Vickie heard the squeak of a medicine cabinet opening.

Sarah.

Exhaustion made her eyes heavy. Her stomach was burning and only fear kept her going—fear of the shadows that wouldn't leave her alone until they became real.

"Mr. Lisciotti?"

Mitch came back into the living room. His hand was bandaged and he popped some aspirin into his mouth. He stopped beside the TV and stroked the gray-and-white cat sitting there. "If it's a question, don't ask it. I'm not even an animal psychiatrist." A high meow sliced the room as the big cat arched its back into Mitch's hand. "Sarah shouldn't have—" He clenched his fist. "I hope she'll call soon."

Vickie nodded, smacking fiercely on her gum. Her head ached with ghastly and inconceivable visions. *Even the baby was infected.* She tried to shut out the bone-chilling cold and gruesome bleakness of the bedroom they left and that surged to overcome her mind until now, the new life inside her vibrated the nightmares . . .

"How do you feel?" Mitch asked her more gently. "Can I get you anything?"

"We left Sarah behind."

"I know."

Looking at the lines in his face, Vickie knew he was frightened, too, and it made her apprehension worse. She covered her cheeks thinking of Sarah, the only one who had understood.

Taking one of her hands, Mitch sat on the couch beside her. "Believe me, Vickie, I understand. I understand that we have to do something." He squeezed her fingers. "God. I shouldn't have left." He held up his bandaged hand. "Nothing was *there*."

She returned the pressure of his good hand. "I only wanted my daddy back. I wanted my baby back. I prayed to death because it's so powerful, and I—" She looked Mitch straight in the eye. "Because *everyone* dies."

Mitch's breath was shallow. "It's not possible to just wish someone back from death, Vickie. Look, maybe I don't know what happened, but I do know that there's a difference between dream and reality." Mitch shook his head.

Vickie remembered Sarah telling her that Mitch had dreams too. That he dreamed his dead wife was alive. "But you refused your dreams," Vickie said. "I *accepted* the death, Mr. Lisciotti. I *wanted* it."

"A dead person *can't* come back to life." He released her and stood.

Vickie shut her eyes and bit the gum between her teeth, trying not to think of what she'd seen. *The baby was one of them. It was not a living gift at all. The baby was not really alive. It was dead, just like its father.*

But she was the mother.

"No." Tears welled in her raw eyes. She didn't want to believe that the death she had prayed to had come to her in the form of her child.

"Vickie?" Mitch stood in front of her. "Hey— Vickie." He bent over her and she heard his tongue cluck behind clenched teeth.

"I want to talk to Sarah."

Mitch glanced toward the phone. "She said she'd call."

"We have to go back."

Mitch shook his head. "You can't. Sarah told me to keep you out of there, and I'm not going to take you back."

"You—you don't know what's going on."

The words had an effect on his face. He backed away to the opposite wall and rested against it. "No."

"You don't know—"

"It's not possible, Vickie. None of it is possible." He wiped his face but could not remove the fear from it. "It can't be."

"Mr. Lisciotti . . . What about *Sarah?*"

His hands shook.

"Don't you understand what's happening? Jim Whitten died. Didn't Sarah tell you? I . . . dreamed of Garcia that night. I f-felt his drops of blood, and he *changed* into Jim Whitten. I knew I . . . was *insane.*" She crossed her arms over her round stomach and lowered her head. "All the doctors say I'm insane. I knew they were right and he had to be a dream." Tears slid down her cheeks. "B-but he *wasn't* just a dream. He was *dead.*"

Mitch crossed the room to stand over her. "They just thought he was dead. The machines all broke down, and he's alive."

She stared at him. "Sarah said he died and came back."

"No. He almost died. They thought he died. But he came out of it. I saw him on TV."

The baby throbbed inside her. *You have life.* Mitch's features blurred. *You have life. Death's Will over men—bring us back to life again . . .*" Mr. Lisciotti, I prayed to death and it heard me. Death answered my prayer!"

Mitch took a step back, holding up his bandaged hand, his voice almost frantic. "How can you know?"

Vickie wiped her eyes. Her breath caught, and a wrenching wail tore her lungs. The weariness made her shake.

"Hey!" He grabbed her arms and held her steady.

"It's not just me! I— Look at your own hand!" She was exhausted—her throat dry and hot. "I have to do something. *It's my child and I—I can't stand it.*"

"You need to rest. Come on." Mitch put an uncertain arm around her, helping her stand and leading her down the narrow hall. He guided her to a simple bedroom that held only a waterbed, a small pine chest, and a straight-backed chair.

She shook her head uselessly, but her eyes closed as he helped her lie down. The mattress bulged soothingly around her. Still, peace would not come. She was aware of some horrible direction being brought to full bearing inside her, something that sought to bind her between the life she had thought was hell—*and Hell itself.* She had brought it about herself, and maybe only she could stop it. Her voice was a whisper: "He's real, too, now."

"What do you mean?" Mitch snapped. "Who? Who's real?"

"That man. Sarah's husband." The shadows in the room seemed to be leaning toward her. "They want so much." She clutched the sheets in both fists. The deep shadows crept nearer.

Mitch sat down beside her. "What do they want?"

"Life." Her lips quivered. "They take life. I can feel it. I—I couldn't at first. I didn't know. But now I—I . . . they want to be alive." Her words were thick and terrible in choked emotion. "I can feel the need and want inside them. They want so badly. They want to come *back!* They use me to come back! They use my baby! But it's still mine!"

Violence jarred her mind and she reached for Mitch, but he and the bedroom disappeared into sudden darkness . . . and she was falling.

31

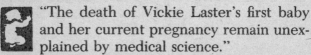"The death of Vickie Laster's first baby and her current pregnancy remain unexplained by medical science."

Mitch pushed away the notebook Sarah insisted he take, stood up from the tall bar chair, and stretched. His hand pounded with pain. He knew he would have to go to a hospital tonight. He had to do that, and he had to go back to Sarah's.

The instant coffee he'd made was already cold, and after a final taste he dumped it over the dishes cluttering the sink. Sarah told him to get out and he had obeyed—fear and pain drove him to obey as that familiar warning buzz of uncontrolled lunacy sounded in his mind.

His good hand wavered over the phone. He had abandoned her like Tabitha. Sweat broke out over his body. Finally he picked up the receiver and dialed. A connection was made.

It rang ten times before he put it down. Then he refilled and stirred the mug and reached for a cigar. He rubbed the brown wrapping with a thumb, then sat down.

Tabitha.

He swallowed, remembering. He hadn't felt this near to losing control since she died. It was this incredible situation. He just wanted to get out. He was losing control.

But Sarah was alone.

Mitch stared at Sarah's journal, then at the dark TV set.

Impossible.

Vickie was ill, and maybe Sarah was, too, and maybe the world had gone berserk—making his own minor lunatic excursions pale in comparison. But it didn't make him feel better . . . or saner.

How could two men come back from the dead?

Slowly, he let his eyes drop back down to Sarah's book.

Though these are only my own unsubstantiated ideas, there seems a method to the madness; it appears that Vickie unconsciously draws upon the very life of the person or people nearest her. This explains the uncommonly rapid recovery from her trances and the deaths around her from totally unknown causes. Since this sudden mayhem around Vickie appears involuntary, I am inclined to believe that all the grief she has gone through has brought it out. Her unique ability allows phenomena, maybe astral projections of a force never guessed at, to project their materialization into her memory, causing her to become their bridge between this world and the next. If this should prove more than theory, then the baby may actually be a part of both worlds.

The rest of the page was blank, and Mitch turned to the next page slowly. "Sarah," he muttered, "you're nuttier than I ever was." Other entries detailed some of the ideas she'd explained to him: how Vickie had been made barren by her operation, how the baby inside her couldn't receive nourishment in the usual way. That knowledge churned hot in his brain, throwing up the wall of impossibility once more. He strove against it. Sarah said the baby lived within Vickie as a parasite, taking life from her. Sarah said that Vickie weakened in her trances and became a parasite herself. Death took, and she took.

She called Vickie a gateway, and as the baby grew unchallenged inside her, so it seemed that the potency of the impossible grew.

He found himself wondering how difficult it would be to give Vickie an abortion, then fought self-disgust. Hadn't he learned anything with

Tabitha? The very notion brought back that past pain.

"God, I'm cracking up again," he murmured.

Yet even the television news could find no way to explain all this away. No one present at the "events" came forth to do so. This didn't prove the veracity of Sarah's piecemeal reasoning, but it showed that something beyond ready explanation had occurred.

"No way," he said, rubbing his stubbled cheeks as he kept his tongue still with difficulty. "No damn way."

But what had happened to his throbbing hand?

Gripping a chair arm, he picked up the notebook with a wince, struggling with belief. Sarah described an ability in Vickie that was beyond rational possibility. She theorized that death had outguessed the laws of existence and was being reborn through the young woman in his bedroom.

And whether he believed that or not, something was going on and Sarah needed him.

He started for the front door, then thought of Vickie in the next room. She didn't need him, but she needed someone, and he would be leaving her alone too. "Jesus," he groaned.

He couldn't focus. His thoughts spun like a wheel of chance. Sarah was near insanity—nearer than he ever had been. His hand had been crushed by air. And Vickie, a girl he barely knew, was lying in his bedroom, beyond insanity.

He felt dizzy, crushed by responsibility he didn't want. Steadying himself against the wall, he took a deep breath.

"Help me," he whispered, feeling the grasp of reality slipping away like years before. "God, help me."

Then he went out the door.

He'd found himself first at the hospital. The intern had unraveled his makeshift wrapping, prodded the limp thumb into position, then circled it with plastic and gauze to set it. The pain had been incredible, but the young doctor had made no acknowledgment of it, saying only, "Bad fracture." Mitch shuddered. His vision darted from the doctor to the clear plastic emergency curtains enclosing the tiny cubicle. He grunted incoherently.

While he'd waited for the X-ray and examination, he'd overheard several nurses and an orderly whispering about the man who died and came back to life that afternoon. Without thinking, he'd come to St. Paul's, where it had happened. The choice had been automatic, as close as it was to work and home. The orderly expressed doubts, but the nurse refuted them. Her voice had made his hair stand on end.

The nurse had said the man died from a severe throat laceration—something not reported by the newscasters—and when he began to breathe once more and his heart pumped anew, the wounds disappeared.

"But keep it to yourselves, okay?" the nurse had warned.

"Right," Mitch said to himself, steering his blue Monza toward the streetlight at the corner, then turning right to Sarah's apartment. He wished Sarah had told him more, or that he had taken the time to read more of her journal.

More than three hours had passed since he and Vickie left her, and the phone call he made from the medical center's lobby twenty minutes ago had gone unanswered. A chill grew under his jacket.

Pumping the gas pedal, Mitch barely looked at the silent, single-level houses and the cars parked for the night in their driveways. It was after eleven when he drove into Sarah's parking lot and found an empty space. The gutter was filled with pieces of newspaper rustling in the wind. Mitch stopped for a moment, struck by their powerlessness against the forces that were tugging them and sweeping them away, piece by piece. Then the breeze picked up and scattered them all. He squeezed the collar of his coat tight around his neck.

"Chicken," he scolded himself aloud. He tried to be calm. But Sarah had been acting so strangely. He was closer to her than he was to anyone these days, and he'd never seen her like that.

Breathing deeply, he made himself walk to the apartment building. Mitch touched his bandaged hand and sucked in a breath of the cold air.

He was terrified.

Mitch opened the front door and entered. His mouth went dry. "It's crazy," he told himself. Yes, but wasn't that right up his alley? Hadn't he gone insane once upon a time too? He mounted the suddenly unfamiliar stairs and thought he saw the hall lights flicker.

No. Illusion. Delusion. Not happening. As he denied fear, the illumination seemed to steady.

He had escaped with Dr. Drake's and Sarah's help. He had put the pieces back together again. But he could feel the bedrock cracking now, his sister's scream inside the broken freezer fracturing his thoughts. Tabitha's scream, Sarah's scream.

He left the slick bannister, wanting to go back. The lights dimmed through the building again when he reached the door, knocked.

The door sprang open. Clammy, foul air came from inside. "Sarah?" He crept inside and flipped on the lights. *"Sarah?"*

The sigh of the heater vent was his only answer. He gulped, moving into the living room. The foul odor intensified. He followed it toward the open bedroom door. The air grew colder. "Oh, God," he said.

She lay twisted in the doorway, and even in the dark of that room, what he saw made him gag. Her stained clothes were draped around her crushed body. The melted pink skin of her arms, legs, and face was shiny and shriveled, bubbling and still spreading over gray, pulverized bone. Her hair and scalp hung loose, like a bathing cap, and patches of hair had dropped out around her. Her eyes were wrinkled and oozing slimy fluid.

"Oh shit."

Her eyes were moving fantastically in their decaying sockets. Mitch backed to the other side of the hall and clenched his teeth. A sweet, barbecue scent mushroomed. Blood dripped like tears from Sarah's flaking eyes onto sunken cheeks. Her gory, mutilated lips moved but made no sound.

He couldn't breathe, paralyzed by his thrashing mind. Then the smell overcame him and he coughed violently and turned away, barely holding back the stomach cramps that wanted to pump vomit up into his throat. He swallowed the bad taste as cold sweat made his face wet. "Goddammit!" he screamed as some of the

stinking saliva dripped over his chin. *"Oh . . .
Goddammit!"*

"M-Mitch . . ."

He heard the faint whisper with horror, and
his heart hammered so hard, it hurt. He twisted
to face Sarah's almost unrecognizable, stretched
features, at the awful mouth that still moved,
knocking loose blackened teeth. Fighting his
stiff limbs, he knelt beside her and made himself
reach down to what was left of a seeping, rubbery wrist. "M-my God."

A cracked, pale tongue slipped over raw lips
and her high inhuman voice crackled with agony: "My hus . . . band . . . came."

"Sarah." He trembled, choking again as her
rotten breath brushed him. He saw her hopeless
pain and shut his eyes in tears. He didn't want to
look at her. *She couldn't be alive—she couldn't
be dead . . . like that!* He knew he had gone
over the edge. *He wouldn't look.*

"Mitch . . . it . . . was . . . Lesley."

He had to look, covering his drooling mouth.

"Death . . . ends hope," she whispered, and
her lips crumbled before his eyes, sucked into
themselves.

Mitch felt the lump in his throat burrow down
to his heart. His eyes moved to the picture of
Sarah and her dead husband shattered on the
floor. "Oh, Jesus," he gasped.

She gazed at him from ruined eyes, festering pupils dripping down a torn cheek.

It wasn't possible. It couldn't be possible.

Mitch screamed.

32

Vickie held the baby joyfully in her arms, inhaling its newness and captivated by the soft tenderness of its skin. She smiled at its gurgle and cooed at it. She had wanted a baby so long. If only Samuel . . .

But she couldn't think of poor Samuel anymore. She had hurt and hurt over him, and now she had to think of the new life that had come to her. She had a baby—a sweet, cuddly baby. It was the change she had craved, the meaning she had sought for so long. She had given birth to a new life, and so had entered into a new life for herself.

She sighed in the bright sunlight, smelling the fresh air of the summer. Life . . . Her baby.

Holding him in one arm, she opened her shirt and sat down on the old porch swing at Mother's house. He had a pink, pudgy middle and short arms and legs. A cold wind blew and she shivered, but didn't stop her duty. She raised him to her breast and felt his lips surround her nipple hungrily, suckling her life.

"I need you," she told him. "I don't have anyone—anything—but you." She tilted his face up toward hers.

The eyes were blank, lifeless.

Vickie screamed, and the baby disappeared. The sun turned black. The wind blew ice. *"Vickie . . ."* whispered Garcia into her ears. Jim Whitten repeated the call, and it was echoed by others:

"Vickie."

Her blood turned cold. Dim, horrible shapes floated noiselessly through the black rooms in her mind, bodies that strangled one another and tore into each other with fingernails and teeth, spraying blood, surrounding her. They all had Samuel's pink prune-baby face.

Behind them Garcia jeered them on, stabbing himself but not dying, killing the woman he was dancing with, and hooting as she rose again and again.

"Vickie."

The baby clawed inside where her uterus once had been. It pressed and pulled restlessly against the healed inner scars, and her limbs twisted jerkily.

"Someone, help me!" she wailed, jerking upright and clasping her fingers around the nearest bedpost. Betrayal haunted her. She was responsible for Mother's death. She was responsible for death itself.

When she was young she prayed to death.

"Help me," she whimpered, shrinking back. That truth gnawed at her and she couldn't reject it.

A thudding began in her ears, erratic and wet. The presence and smell of Garcia, Jim Whitten, and the others closed in around her . . . the dozens destroying themselves—

She burrowed into the sweaty blankets. "No!" she pleaded.

"Life."

The voice came from someone very near, and she looked up, her heart beating madly. Shudders burst up from her abdomen, as though a hurricane had erupted inside her. She tried to rise but could not hold herself up. Instead, she rolled off the side of the sloshing bed. Her arm wrenched under her as she fell to the floor. She kept on, slamming finally into the wall and digging her fingernails into its hard plasterboard.

"Shit." With that exclamation Mother hated, she ground her teeth, then slid her feet beneath her. Her arm throbbed, and she moved it with a sharp intake at the shocking pain that ran up her elbow. Thick saliva gagged her.

Vickie leaned against the wall. "God, is it too much to ask?" Sarah had said it. She was the point of contact between life and death. She could no longer deny it. She was the point chosen by death. She had died herself and was touched by death so often now that it was the central part of her. She bore the only child she could—a child of death. It was as she was. And she had been forced to endure so many shocks that she no longer felt human. *She no longer felt alive.*

"Oh, Daddy," she murmured, and squeezed into the wall, resting her head on her right shoulder. Pain mounted in her skull. All she had wanted was to start to live again, to have Daddy back. To at least have her baby, Samuel, back and to never die herself. Vickie shivered.

Instead she had an ability to harm others, and worse, it was an ability she couldn't control.

She was death.

The apartment's central heater clanked loudly. The sound made her flinch and she looked around the room warily.

Nobody was there. The visions had disappeared.

If only she could undo what she had unwittingly done . . . but it was too much a part of her. She hated what she was, but even though she bore a baby of grisly nightmare, she could not help but love it. No matter who or what was its father, she was the *mother,* and she could not help loving her child. She could not help loving it any more than she had been able to stop loving her baby, Samuel. He had been dead too. She'd never even gotten to hold his still body in her arms and tell him that she was sorry.

Her baby needed her, and she loved it.

But he would destroy.

Tears welled in her eyes. Was it the baby's fault that she had brought all this on? Could Adolf Hitler's mother have destroyed him before he was born if she had known his future? Vickie was ashamed of her wavering desires. She had to do *something,* even if her ebbing strength would not allow her to do much, and she knew that the listlessness would only get worse. She would grow weaker and weaker and people would die all around her, like Mother had. Daddy had told her a long time ago that she had to make her own decisions.

It was not the baby's fault. She knew none of it was anyone's fault but her own. She had been used and was being used now—but she had allowed it!

The only answer was death. She had to go back to death to find peace and to protect others. She had to make her choice, and maybe it was time for her to go back to death now, taking her baby with her. At least that way she would not be alone, and would not let *him* be alone.

Vickie took an unsteady step toward the hall, grabbing the slick surface as hot tears of resignation slid down her cheeks. Her legs cramped, but she knew she had to go on like Daddy had once said, even though the helpless feeling in her made her want to scream. She forced her steps on endlessly and into the bathroom, closing the door with a hard swallow. The sour odor of her sweat clogged the air. Vickie crossed the white, tiled floor to the medicine cabinet and found a razor blade in a plastic box. It was like the razor that woman had used on Garcia. She slid the cold steel out, fixed on the shower, and limped to it breathlessly. Vickie held the faucets for balance as she stepped in. She turned on the water, removed her sweat-soaked clothing. The spray beat into her without mercy.

"God," she cried, not knowing what or who she was praying to anymore. "Please, God." She backed closer to the nozzle's spray to increase the pressure, but even that could not clean away the filth she felt covering her.

It coated her insides. The life was being sucked out of her. Her own child reached out to take more.

A low wail wrenched itself from her. She didn't want the terrors that visited her. She didn't want any part of any of this. She only wanted to have her baby, and for it to be normal. She didn't want to die.

She pushed into the fingers of driving water, her heart in her throat. She probed her distended stomach, feeling its hurt in a need that was so much the same as her own. Memories of that baptistry and of her long-ago pain poured onto her in relentless waves. Her legs trembled, and suddenly she collapsed. Her wild grappling couldn't stop her fall. The razor blade dropped and she smacked the wall, hitting her head against the wet, solid floor.

Minutes passed as she lay there, blinking in the shower's storm. Her mind was filled with spinning blood memories of the preacher's life raining down on her like this water. Her buttocks slid this way and that on the slippery tile flooring and she reached out to grasp the slippery razor blade beside her, clenching it until its sharp end cut into her thumb and she whimpered. She scooted back to cradle herself in the mildewed corner between the walls. Her fingers reached up and found a gash in her scalp. Her hand came away smeared with more fresh blood. She must force the sharp blade into her wrists, and add the rest of her life to it. She brought the blade to her wrist. The steam lingering in the air seemed suddenly to thicken. Shuddering, she held the very crevices of the wall, raking them with her nails and the metal sliver, and nearly slipped again. She stared into the steam, then squeezed her eyes closed and tried to cramp herself into a smaller and smaller ball as the steam began to take a form—a man's form. She moaned.

"Vickie."

The voice was deep with unhappiness. Vickie recognized it. She looked up with impossible hope. *"Daddy?"*

The water clouded her vision, but she still recognized his tall, thin body under a clean work shirt and blue jeans. His big hands reached down toward her, and she dropped the razor with a tiny splash as her hands rose unsteadily to meet his.

But there was nothing there.

"Daddy?" she whined, surprised that she could still see his foggy silhouette. "I can't feel you." She shook her head and it throbbed harder until she had to stop. She wanted to feel his warm, secure grasp. She wanted to be with him! To just *touch* him!

"No," he whispered. "Because I'm not coming back, Vickie. Only the ones who *want* do that. I am at peace, and I want you to be at peace."

She felt herself shrinking back into her little girl's body, like in her dreams. "I want to be with you. I want you to hold me!" She wanted to become the baby inside her so he could lift her tiny body up into his hands and hold her close. His hand reached to her cheek, but she felt nothing. Still, somehow, the very mist vibrated with a sense of him. "Daddy, please—"

"I can't make your decisions, baby-girl. I wish I could. I wish I could take you with me now, but you've got to do this on your own. If you try to come to me by your own hand, you won't ever reach me. You're grown now, and I know you can find the answers and do what you have to— but it isn't *this*. Life can be hard, but it isn't over for you yet, Vickie. Just remember I love you. You cannot defeat death through suicide, and you can never escape it if you try to." His hollow voice shook inside the room. "Remember Love," he urged tearfully. "Remember Love for life."

"But, Daddy—"

The steam's structure wobbled. "I love you, baby-girl."

She thrust her hands forward to hold him as his steamy shape billowed and filled the shower, breezing her with his essence. She cried out in an ecstasy of hope that he would still grab hold of her. *"I love you, Daddy!"*

But he wasn't there. Nothing was there. She slumped forward until her face touched the wet floor beside the razor blade.

33

Turning the steering wheel with his aching hand, Mitch watched the two-lane street dully, only half listening to the commentator speaking on the radio. The horror of what he'd seen was lodged in him, and he doubted it would ever leave, but even worse was the awful knowledge that Sarah was gone. She was dead, and he couldn't help but place on himself a part of the responsibility.

Like Tabitha.

". . . Whitten died. The tapes and data recorded up to the time of the machine's unexplained failure have still given no clear indication of what caused the massive power surge. Strangely, the latest report shows that the surge was concentrated on Jim Whitten and the machines connected to him, and had no effect outside his room, or on the machines not connected to him. Reports from St. Paul's are nearly identical and witnesses to both phenomena felt a drop in temperature and a mild electric shock. Whitten, meanwhile, has been examined by the federal agents who have taken over the case. On their order, the patient from St. Paul's has been moved to the Observer Institute. It is reported that both of these revived inmates have been restrained due to incidents of violence, though the only detailed report we have so far is the still-unconfirmed story of Jim Whitten killing a nurse in the Observer Institute's rooms. It's a riddle that grows more puzzling every hour."

Turning off the radio, Mitch drove the car into a space between a Volkswagen and new Ford pickup at the edge of his apartment's lot. He was too drained to do more than wipe his face on his shaking, bandaged hand. After several moments he got out. Drops of moisture made his face slick. It had begun to drizzle, on top of everything else.

Mitch passed a teenager sitting by the stairs in his jeans jacket and ignored his glance. The weight of Sarah's notebook in his coat pocket pulled at him as he climbed the stairs. Sarah was dead. Something unknown and unbelievable had happened, and Sarah was dead.

Though he didn't understand it, he was beginning to believe that it was all somehow connected to the other impossibilities, and that

Sarah's written theories might be at least partially true.

The thought made his tongue click against the roof of his mouth.

His fingers clutched the cold, undecorated rail tensely. It was raining harder, and the uncertainty of his past years consumed him as drops pelted his tingling flesh. He remembered the muffled cries from his sister, Tammy.

Tabitha. Sarah.

He stopped at the top of the stairway and looked out at the lights of the misty, sleeping city, past the rows of houses to the skyscrapers far beyond. The rain sounded in the tree branches. "It can't be!" he shouted, hurting.

Mitch entered his apartment. He reached to the notebook in his pocket, barely aware of the splashes from the bathroom. "Vickie?"

He shut the door, flipped on the living-room light, and looked down at his watch. It was after one now. He knew he should call the police.

He should. But he should have done a lot of things.

Yes, and he didn't want to call and try to explain *anything* the way his head ached. Nothing. He pulled Sarah's notebook out of his pocket, took off his coat, and dropped it on the couch. He retrieved his empty coffee cup and went into the kitchen.

"In the midst of life we are in death," he said,

and tried to chuckle at the dark humor. Instead hot anguish pierced him.

He measured a spoonful of instant coffee into the cup and filled it with hot tap water. He wanted to relax in familiarity and forget it all. This was a nightmare, and when he woke up, he wanted everything to be back to normal.

Sarah.

He set the mug on the table and went to a kitchen cabinet to take down the bottle of brandy. Unscrewing the cap, he poured a shot into the mug and watched it spill over the sides. "God damn," he whispered.

The water still ran at the back of the apartment, and he picked up a cigar while he listened, then lifted the mug, spilling again, and sipped. The alcohol boosted him a little and he sat down, lighting up the cigar.

"Death is death," he told himself. "Sarah is dead."

The shower ran.

He passed the minutes impatiently, waiting for the water to stop. He wanted to get Vickie out—to be here by himself. He wanted to be alone to think and cry.

He opened Sarah's notebook, feeling the sad ghoulishness of reading his dead lover's words. He peered at the scribbles that were so sloppy, it was almost as if they'd been written by a differ-

ent hand, or as if Sarah had been in a terrible
hurry.

Vickie's just told me that she has prayed to death
and that she believes those requests were answered. This may be the reason I was overlooking.
While I don't believe in a God of death that might
have answered those prayers, I can believe that in
her meditative state, she connected her ability to
the psychic realm beyond, inviting them into our
dimension. You can even make it work from a religious standpoint if you want to: I have studied
many faiths, and if one assumes a spiritual God
behind the creation of the physical universe and of
life, that act of creation would have forged a connection between the two realms that could not be
severed except through total destruction. The creation of nature through supernature would forever unite the two, making the natural world ac-
cessible to the supernatural, and vice-versa.

In the Old Testament there are stories of a God
that cut a covenant with the Jews. Christians believe God fulfilled that covenant and made a new
one with all humanity. They believe that their God
changed the laws governing man through the ful-
fillment of the Old Covenant. In their view, the
laws governing life can be *changed*. With her
background Vickie would know this and agree
with it.

Going further, and using the idea of Christianity
as Vickie unconsciously would, if we assume this
God had once transposed His "eternal life" into

the mortal life of this world by a human manifestation—had allowed those given parts of Himself to be born as one of his own creations into mortality —it could be assumed that this precedent would prove the capacity of the supernatural to live within the natural. With everything crazy that's been happening, why couldn't Vickie Laster's rejection of God and her blasphemy in the sanctified water of a church cause this holocaust of exchange? Our own belief in things gives them their basis, and with Vickie's religious background, the events in that baptistry may have been all it took to unleash her incredible ability into a new reality. The only way to cure her and end what she has started may be to somehow make her reject that truth she created or maybe even to use her own beliefs to reject it. If she could be baptized once more, and accept the ceremony's meaning of life rather than death

The words ended abruptly and Mitch closed the notebook. Baptism. The baby. Vickie was pregnant despite a hysterectomy. The baby was forming in a wombless, sterile body. A "dead" body.

"Vickie!" Mitch called out with sudden urgency, pushing back from the table. Coffee splashed on his hands. He stood, dropping the cigar, and shouted her name again.

The shower was still running in the distant room.

He ran toward the bathroom. Forced wobbly legs faster. "Vickie!" The hall seeming to rush up around him, he passed his bedroom.

He crashed through the bathroom door. Wet spots pooled before the open stall around a soggy shirt and jeans. The shower filled his ears and he pushed his hand into the hot water to turn off the nozzles. As the steam cleared, he saw Vickie cowering in the farthest corner, her back to him, her head smudged with dark blood.

He stood in shock, muttering a low exclamation. After some seconds he saw her faint movements.

At least she was still breathing.

He caught a glimpse of metal beside Vickie's leg, then bent down and picked up the razor. He closed his eyes briefly. He was relieved she was whole, but the razor blade showed him how far gone she already was. He threw it in the toilet, trying to hold back the rushing memory of Tabitha. "Fucking hell," he whispered. What should he do? Should he do anything? Was any of this even real?

But if anything was real, this had to be, and now it was up to him to help her . . . for Sarah.

But what could he do? Hadn't Sarah told him he had to protect *himself*—didn't he know that from years' experience?

He took a washcloth and wiped at the wound on Vickie's skull. Though it was swollen, the bleeding had stopped. Mitch took her pulse; it seemed okay. He wrapped a towel around her shoulders, then flinched at the oozing slash in her thumb. Putting his good hand under one of her arms and keeping his embarrassed eyes averted, he lifted her. She stood groggily on limp legs, and he dragged her past the rumpled bath mat into the hall and to the bedroom. He brought her to the bed and used the towel to dry her off. Ignoring the pain in his hand, he found a T-shirt in a drawer and got it over her. He eased her back until she was lying flat. With a disturbed glance at her distended stomach he pulled the blanket over her.

Vickie lay on the wadded linen, shivering.

"Hey, Vickie." Mitch touched her forehead, feeling warm sweat. He clenched his teeth and took a deep breath, looking over the solid reality of his bedroom. He reached to the lamp on the side table and clicked it on, then took her hand in his.

She blinked, then lurched at him, pulling the sheet and blanket with her, and wrapped her arms around his leg, squeezing so tight, it hurt. "Mr. Lisciotti?" She pressed her face against his pants. "H-help me."

Prying her away, he sat on the bed and moved the limp hair out of her face. Her pupils were dilated. "Vickie? What happened?"

She was crying. The sobs wracked through

her body and he felt his own, full of the fear of
the unknown that had done this to her, and
Sarah, and him.

At last their sobs waned, and in the quiet,
Mitch felt he could speak again. "What happened?" Her hand clutched his wrist, and he
didn't let himself draw back.

"I woke up. I . . . God. I'm with them when
I sleep." She shivered. "It's like I'm one of them,
but—"

"One of who?"

"It—it's like being a part of nothing, and
knowing that you're nothing—that there's nothing ahead for you. It's inside me." She drew back
cautiously. "They're inside me. I had to try to
get away." She closed her eyes and took a long,
deep breath. "I was going to kill myself, but
then . . . my daddy came back to talk to me."
She looked at him. "I need to tell Sarah! They
want life. They *want!* That's all I can feel from
them is their want. Daddy said they come back
because they want!"

Mitch bit his thumbnail and remembered Sarah's body, empty of life. "Who are they?"

She shook her head. "They know me," she
warned. "I—I can't hide. You can't help me.
Daddy said I had to do it myself."

The edge behind her words made him realize
the extent of what he was volunteering. There
was no protection he could offer her. No protec-

tion for her, or for himself. He shuddered, fearing what might happen to him now. What if Tabitha came back to him?

It made him want to leave again—to just get the hell out! But Sarah had given Vickie to his care. He shook his head, no longer wanting to listen to her words.

Vickie pulled away. "Sarah needs to know what Daddy said. I need to talk to her." She slid to the edge of the bed and stood, looking ridiculous in the large T-shirt he'd put her into. "We've got to go to her."

She pulled against him, but though his hand was on fire, Mitch would not let loose. He pulled her close and stared into her eyes, only half an inch from his. "Tell *me* what happened." She stared back at him, terrified, and at last Mitch released her. She dragged her nails over the cotton quilt. He held his cheeks and began pacing . . . His tongue made its clicking sound. "I saw Sarah," he said.

She sat on the bed.

"Something—something happened to her, Vickie."

"What?" Vickie raised her fingers to her mouth.

He avoided her eyes, seeming to smell Sarah's soft scent. "She's dead," he whispered.

Vickie's eyes were big and staring. "Sh-she—"

A painful sob ripped his lungs in half. "She's dead!"

"Oh . . . Oh, no."

She wept and bent to the sheets, holding her face in her hands. Mitch watched her with pity, feeling the same pity for himself, and he cried with her.

34

 She felt alone. Daddy had come to talk to her, but he wouldn't even touch her. He didn't want to come back. And now Sarah was gone too.

Vickie went with Mitch into the living room and sat on the floor to drink bitter coffee with him, listening to his account of what had happened to Sarah. Everything had been taken away from her now. Her daddy, Mother, her baby Samuel, and Sarah, and this new baby . . . It was all part of a past she could never have again. Parts of her life had been taken away—life itself was taken from her.

She was already dead.

She could not even cry. Her emotions were as barren as her body, filled like it by death.

Death that was alive.

But Daddy said she could do something about it herself. He told her she had to go on alone.

And she was more alone now than ever. Everyone she sought help from died.

"Sarah wanted me to help you," Mitch said.

"No," she blurted, afraid for him. "It's too late. I wanted my daddy and my child . . ." Her voice tapered off to almost nothing. "I prayed. I prayed to death." She remembered the steam of the water and the electric odor, the minister's crumbling flesh. "Jesus took my daddy away. Momma said so and the preacher said so. Momma and the preacher said that death controlled our bodies." The past was so near. She could taste the stale water of that baptistry. "So I prayed to death to give me a baby like Jesus, who would give *real* life. I couldn't breathe!" She shut her eyes but couldn't close out the images. "I was in a dark place and felt so empty." Her tongue slipped over dry, hot lips and she felt the blood drain from her face. "I was dead." Mitch reached out to clasp her hand and she crushed his fingers with the ghastly, hideous recollection. "I was dead, and I came back to life. Then Death came to me, and f-fucked me! I was baptized in the blood of death. And my prayers were answered."

"No," Mitch said.

"Death made me pregnant."

"No!"

Vickie giggled insanely. "I will bring life to death and death to life and life to death and

death to life and life to death and death to
life . . ." Vickie put her arms around him hope-
lessly. "God, Mitch, I didn't realize what I was
doing. I didn't know what would happen! And
Daddy came back and said it was all *my* decision. But I don't know what I can do."

He fought the desire to pull away. He knew
he should listen to her as Sarah had listened to
him, with her thoughtfulness and understanding. But Vickie's words dragged him into a
whirlpool of uneasy fright, making him want to
block out the words, the madness.

Mitch groaned and pushed away from her imprisoning hold around his neck and shoulders.
"Look, there's got to be a way." He tried to
think. "There's *got* to be."

"An . . . abortion?"

He looked at her, the icy word reminding him
again of Tabitha. "Maybe."

She shook her head. "I can *think* of doing that
now, but I know it won't work."

Mitch paused as an unknown tenant's footsteps sounded on the landing outside his front
door. "I guess we should try it."

"I think it would only kill *me*, Mitch." Vickie's
fingers raked through the carpet. "I think it—
sometimes I want the baby so bad, and I think
it's been keeping me alive, just like I'm keeping
it alive. But maybe it doesn't need me anymore!
In school they taught a class about parasites.

Sarah said the baby was a parasite. Sometimes, when a parasite becomes so big, the teacher said that its removal can kill the host."

Mitch took her hand, held it.

"I'm afraid of death, Mitch. I know it's terrible. I'm halfway there now. I thought it would help if—if I killed myself, but I'm afraid. Death is horrid and empty and hopeless. I don't want to die." She scooted back, leaning against the end of the couch. "They used my emotions. I needed someone. I was so alone, and they knew it. They tricked me, Mitch. God—they killed my baby! I want to take it all back, everything they took, everything I gave." Her own tongue fumbled inside her mouth and a deep blush filled her cheeks. "I . . . I gave them life. I don't know how. But I know I gave it to them. They used it. *They used me.*" She held her hands together bitterly.

"Okay," Mitch finally said hoarsely, "but how can you take it back, Vickie?"

Tears were gleaming in her eyes. "I don't know how to take it back."

They both fell silent, and Mitch thought again of Sarah, of Sarah dead. He pulled out his penknife and began to clean his nails. *You have to know when to believe,* she had said tonight. *You have to learn what to believe. Belief can make things real.* Minutes passed. His head throbbed. He closed the penknife, opened it. Closed.

Opened. "We've got to try *something,*" he said, looking up at her. Her head had fallen onto the couch. "Vickie?" Her eyes were closed and she was still. "Vickie?" he said loudly, shaking her shoulder.

Her breathing was soft, steady.

She was asleep. Mitch jerked to his feet. *"Vickie!"* he shouted.

Her snores were slow and labored, as though she were in the middle of a brisk, unconscious workout. *Shirley MacLaine's Sleep Dream Exercises* his mind flashed— But even that could not break his rapidly disintegrating mood of dread. Viciously, he wrapped his fingers around Vickie's upper arm and shook her again. *"Vickie!"* he screamed. *"Wake the fuck up!"*

But the loud rasp of her sleep buried the echoes on his panicked cry, and though he shook her again and again, she did not hear him.

Finally, Mitch put his arms under her and heaved up her heavy form. He guzzled his own deep breath and forced himself up, lifting her unbalanced form and barely believing her incredible weight. The feel of her tingling flesh swept into him quickly, making his heart pound. He moved on Jell-O legs, carrying her back into the hall, walking as best he could between the narrow walls to his bedroom and sliding her onto the mattress. He laid the blanket over her and stood back, wanting to be proud of himself for still functioning. Fear clutched his soul.

He knew by the way her eyelids shimmered that she was dreaming.

"Sarah, I need you," he whimpered. He went to open the window facing the second-floor walkway. He hoped that a few moments in the cold air might help clear his thoughts and keep him from being so afraid. He leaned out over the frame, staring up and down the walkway, and wrapped his arms close to his chest as he peered over the city lights, down to the parking-lot trash bin filled with discarded cans, pop bottles, and newspapers. The man in his jeans jacket sifted through the garbage, then looked up and met Mitch's eyes, grinning darkly. Mitch ignored him and forced the bad feelings away with icy discomfort.

But it was too fucking cold.

He dragged himself back inside and pulled the glass down, locking it. He turned.

The bedroom was blacker than the night outside.

He shivered again. The hallway light had burned out.

"Damn." He felt his way through the unlit room, bumping the corner of the bedframe with his knee. Vickie's form was visible on the bed, the blanket bulging over her middle as it moved up and down faintly with each breath she took. Mitch groped for the light switch and flipped it.

Nothing. It was burned out too.

Mitch cursed, then moved out into the hall and shut the bedroom door behind him. He felt his way toward the closet to find new bulbs. A wave of ice met him and he trembled, feeling himself being watched. He smelled a distant rose fragrance, musty and damp, and swallowed hard. It was the smell of Tabitha.

"Oh my God." He wheeled around, feeling his bowels try to loosen . . . his throat going dry.

"Hello, Mitch. Hello, my love."

His heart stopped dead. He was held still by Tabitha's green eyes. She stood at the hall's end, naked and glowing with a faint blue and yellowish hue, her long arms reaching out to him. *His nostrils filled with the electric pulses that mixed hotly with the decayed rose scent—*

She took a step forward. "Yes. I can come to you outside your dreams now, Mitch. You believe in me again, it's been so long. I thought I could never get back. You denied me."

"No," he breathed, staggering back.

"You *left* me, Mitch. I needed you and you didn't even believe in me when I lived. You never believed in anything but yourself. But now you need me. Only I can give you life everlasting and the meaning you never had."

"N-no—"

"You see me because you *do* believe in me, Mitch. You already accept me and your own blame. I loved you so much. I only wanted to give you our child—"

"No!" he screamed. He edged farther back into the hall's protection. He was not guilty— not— But her voice crushed him.

"You owe me life." She came straight at him as though she were a mist floating through the air, and her frigid aura slapped him hard. "You killed me, Mitch. You killed me with your selfishness and you must owe me life."

He backtracked and she followed, chasing him through the hall's shadows. She was still coming nearer, and not like in the dreams. He didn't dare look away. He sucked in a deep breath and let it out raggedly. "You killed *yourself,*" he told her, trying to believe it. "Sarah said . . . it was not my fault. *You* made your choice. You killed yourself."

"*You* made me. *You* forced the abortion." She frowned. "You *left* me."

His mind grabbed desperately at the lessons Sarah taught him. Sarah had told him he was using guilt as a crutch to keep from facing up to life and his own limitations. The pressure of having a child, of fearing that it might die like his sister, had been more than he could handle. Tabitha's forcing fatherhood on him might only have endangered them *all* as he slipped further into insanity.

"You tormented me," Mitch struggled, "and —and I'm *sorry*. I'm sorry for what I did. But I didn't kill you. I didn't kill the baby. I didn't want—" He shuddered, finally face-to-face with the truths he'd battled for so long.

Tabitha had killed their baby and then herself.

You must choose what to believe, Mitch, Sarah had said. His breath caught in his throat as he understood that accepting *was* belief.

Mitch clutched at the wall dizzily, knowing that his awareness was too late now. The strength of his life began to slip out. Faster and faster.

"I will drink your life and make it my own. I will take it in place of the love you never gave," Tabitha whispered, her stare driving into his heart. "Even if you don't want to accept me, I can take you now. There is no way out."

She slid closer, flowing over the carpet. His tongue clicked when she touched his bandage. "Death is so *empty*. As empty as you are now. As empty as your life's always been!" Her fingers moved up over his bandage to bare skin, and he gasped as energy drained from him at her greedy touch. Tabitha—the solidifying dream of Tabitha—laughed shrilly.

"No," he moaned, fighting to hold on to the

strength she was draining from him. Her icy fingertips touched his cheeks and forehead, bringing him hopelessness. He dropped to his knees.

Death ends hope. Sarah's words struck him with their truth.

Tabitha's voice made him shake. "You killed me and our baby. You only thought of yourself, and how you had hurt your sister. You killed your own child, me, and yourself with that guilt."

"Forgive me!" he screamed with dissolving hope, feeling his insides begin to melt . . . disentegrate. The guilt he had lived under for years smashed his brain into a million pieces, feeding him its endless death.

Tabitha caressed him. "You are still so afraid, but only for yourself. You killed us for your fear. You're so afraid. You only believe in your fear!"

But in his memory Sarah looked into his eyes: *"Until you reject the guilt, until you refuse to accept responsibility, your belief of Tabitha will keep her real to you. She will be real. Vickie is doing the same thing, but through her bizarre power Vickie can give the phenomena—the dreams—physical reality, making them as real in truth as they are to us in our heads."*

Vickie. The baby. Though he was empty of will, Mitch forced himself to think of Vickie and the child she was bearing. They were even now giving his life to Tabitha. He lurched up and fell farther into the hall, struggling ahead until he grabbed hold of the bedroom doorknob. *"Vickie!"* He screeched and staggered inside the black room, stumbling to the bed.

He touched Vickie's round stomach as Tabitha's iron-cold fingers crushed into his shoulder. Vickie didn't move. He groaned, falling to the floor, torn by terror and doubt. Maybe his guilt *was* all true. Maybe Sarah was wrong. Sarah . . .

As he struggled against Tabitha in a hurricane of spasms he thought of Sarah and how she'd died, wrestling in guilt just like him.

"If only you could believe in something besides your guilt, Mitch," Sarah once said. *"You will never be able to make up for the things you may have done until you can overcome it."*

"Sarah," he wheezed, feeling Tabitha's fingers sink deep into his flesh.

She laughed. "Not even Sarah."

"I didn't kill anyone!" he screamed terribly. *"Not you. Not the baby. It was you! You're not real. The guilt is not real."*

Tabitha's chuckle stung him. "Then *you're* not real, Mitch, because all you have left is guilt." He clawed the air while his thoughts gained momentum, like a dark maelstrom at whose center stood the impossible, taunting figure of Tabitha.

As he was dragged into stifling darkness, Mitch screamed out uncontrolled, lunatic laughter, and felt his thoughts fill with every endured madness. He had to refuse his guilt, because it was not real. Sarah had said it was the guilt of ignorance and panic, the same feelings that had caused Vickie to cry out to death for life because she was so overwhelmed by her pain.

His guilt was not real.

And Tabitha said he *was* his guilt and so *he* was not real. His guilt was *him,* but Sarah had said it was only his imagination, and his imagination didn't exist if he didn't exist, *so nothing at all was real. He was only a figment of his own warped, nonexistent imagination.*

His thoughts whirled frantically and he let them push on, not even trying to stop the whirlwind sucking him faster into its deep, black abyss. The smell of roses overwhelmed him.

"Mitch?"

The voice was billions of light-years away, garbled by the leaden walls that surrounded him in the nothingness of unreality.

"Mitch?"

The voice was louder, and he jumped when he felt an impossible *something* touch him.

—no— He did not exist—

"Oh, God, Mitch. You're scaring me! Please, get up."

Guilt did not exist and could not exist because life could not exist because death could not be real and people could not come back to life that did not exist . . . and his imagination could not exist because he could not exist if life did not exist.

A slap jarred him fully awake and he blinked, staring into his sunlit bedroom. The blankets had fallen on the floor. "No, there are no Klingons, Captain," he rasped.

"It's me, Vickie. Don't you remember?" She was holding his . . . *hands*—his bandaged hand and his unhurt one.

But he didn't exist.

"Look at me—"

Vickie squatted beside him, her middle like an enormous beach ball under her T-shirt and robe. She was full of bleakness, and the very sight of her bulbous, ghastly body made him want to get away from her. He jumped when he felt the hot flesh of her hand squeeze his.

Sarah smiled in his mind. *"You're a borderline lunatic, Mitch. You reach out so hard for something real to grab hold of, and when you miss grabbing it, you go right over the edge."*

"I'm supposed to be the one who's sick—" Vickie said. She shook his shoulder.

He tried to allow reality to seep back into him, letting her fingers slide over his, wincing at the feel of her sweaty palm. "Guilt is not real," he said. "I'm not real." He felt his swinging thoughts steady. "But I'm *fine.*" He wished Sarah were here so she would know.

"What happened?" Vickie asked. "I had a horrible dream that you were dying. I woke up and you were here on the floor. I thought you were dead."

"Near enough," he said weakly. "But I'm—I think I'm okay. I just don't want to smell another goddamn rose for the rest of my life." He forced himself up and sat so he wasn't facing her. It seemed incredible that Vickie, who had enabled Tabitha to appear, had no knowledge of what had happened. He knew he'd survived only because his guilt complex had nearly driven him insane again. It was years since the last time he went over so violently, and he had protected himself well since then, but this time— He had doubted his own existence. That doubt had torn physical reality from Tabitha, because she could not take from him what wasn't there.

Yes. His mind felt clearer and cleaner than he remembered it ever having been. Sarah had said there was no physical connection between the world man lived in and the world beyond except through acceptance. Tabitha had tried to persuade him to accept responsibility. The other world tricked and persuaded Vickie. He made his rapt eyes link with hers, but still kept them off her body. "My God," he whispered softly. "My God." He touched his forehead. Sarah had guessed it. A contract of nature. An equal and opposite reaction."

Vickie stood. "What?"

"She wrote it down. Nature works under laws, alongside supernature. The two can't mix except through our own agreement. She said that the supernatural can't physically contact us except through our *invitation.*" He touched his shaking fingers together. "They trapped you."

Vickie crossed her arms over her enlarged stomach. "They hate us for what we are. They want what we have."

"Death ends hope," he said with a shiver.

She shivered too. "It's vibrating inside me all the time now, Mitch. It—it hurts."

Pacing the room moodily, he could see the shine of sweat on her forehead, and it made him more afraid. "Goddammit," he whispered with frustration, breaking off. Sarah's written thoughts finally sank in hard. "Sarah said that maybe all we have to do is get you baptized again. Really baptized this time."

"No," she whispered.

Squeezing her arm, Mitch felt his control increase in the absence of the guilt that had dwarfed him. He stared at his hand and felt as if he were seeing it for the first time, as if he could do something with it maybe, besides just wipe tears from his eyes after nightmares late at

night. This new strength of will made him guess
that he had only exchanged his previous insanity
for another, more dangerous form of madness.
There was an urgency inside him that wanted
now to make up for his failings, and he clutched
it blindly as a symbol of his penitence and new-
found freedom. As Sarah had foretold, for every
action there *must* be an equal and opposite reaction. "It's all totally insane," Mitch murmured.
"Like death. I touched death last night and it *is*
madness. It drove me back to insanity, and that
stopped it from taking me. That madness has
been born in you, Vickie. Death is coming to life
in you." He got to his feet slowly, knowing that
Sarah was right. "We have to get you baptized
for real."

"N-no."

Mitch forced himself to look at her, at all of
her, with strength and commitment. "We have
nothing to lose," he said, barely believing the
stand he was taking.

35

The church was modern, plain, and uninspiring in design. The white walls glowed with candlestick fixtures. Men and women in drab Kmart dresses and slacks surrounded Mitch, enveloping him in warring scents of cologne and perfume. Beside him, Vickie wore a yellow blouse that stretched over her stomach. He shuddered as her leg grazed his on the pine pew and quickly looked toward the silent, seated choir in their purple robes. In front of them the minister pounded his fist on the redwood pulpit as he spoke on and on of the terrible occurrence brought by science—of the way God was blasphemed in the resurrections of the dead . . . Mitch barely heard the words that underlined his being here. Growing in him was a feeling of usefulness that almost overcame the fear of what he was doing—what he and Vickie were facing.

"We need your seed offering to stop this onslaught by pseudo-science!" the minister said. "If you want to do your part, give freely. God wants you to give until it hurts. Pain is part of life! Look at the way Christ suffered."

Mitch squirmed, not liking the preacher and the way he was twisting his own religion. It was one reason he had stopped attending church. He shut his eyes and snoozed off and on.

The organ keys suddenly blasted loud. Mitch jumped, bumping Vickie's tense form. Her features were tight—wired.

"Now who would give themselves to be baptized on this third night of our revival?" cried out the big red-faced evangelist. He gestured behind him to the white plastic tub as high as his pulpit. "Let's make the devil *cringe* tonight. How many of you want to get into this holy, sanctified water and wash off that sin and death Satan has bulldozed into your lives?"

Mitch blinked, nudging Vickie nervously. A wrinkled black man in a plaid sport jacket stood up in the front.

"Hallelujah!" shouted a woman's voice.

"We should have a dozen standing now!" boomed the preacher with slicked-back Revlon-black hair. He held up a big leather-bound Bible with a threatening gesture. "Let's really make God know we're His—that we want eternal life!"

Mitch nudged Vickie again. "Come on," he whispered sharply.

"No." She pushed him back.

The force of her shove made him bump the man in a gray polyester suit beside him and he blushed his apology, then scooted closer to Vickie. He felt her nervousness but knew he mustn't let it stop them. She had to do it. "Vickie," he muttered.

"I'm afraid."

He was too, but Vickie had to go. For him, for herself, for everyone . . . *for Sarah.* He grabbed her hand and jerked her awkwardly to her feet.

"That's two," the preacher shouted. "Now, come on. Didn't I preach hard enough for you other lost souls?" He chuckled. "Nothing to be afraid of, you know. Baptism will wash away your sins, and you all know you've sinned. One look at the nickels and pennies you throw in the offering plate proves that."

"Amen!" blurted out the woman again.

Mitch squeezed Vickie's arm hard to keep her from struggling. Her eyes accused him, but she kept silent.

"Come on up front. Everyone who wants to be baptized into the life of Jesus, come on up front!"

Vickie didn't move. "Go," he urged, dragging her sideways toward the aisle.

"No, Mitch." They reached the gold-carpeted aisle and she faced him. "Sarah—"

"Sarah said this is the way, Vickie." He pushed her toward the preacher with a deranged humor he wouldn't have believed himself capable of. "This is the Way, the Truth, *and the Life.*"

Vickie stopped. "What if it happens again?"

Mitch took her arm and pulled her toward the group that had formed around the minister. A loud "Amen" hurt his ear. He squeezed her with reassurance. "Just do it, Vickie. Don't think about death, think about *life.*" His body was trembling.

"I don't know."

They both stopped and noticed the preacher's blue eyes on them. Mitch blushed.

"You sound like you're after my job, son. Just remember to give your ten percent, too." He chuckled, laying a hand on Mitch's tacky brown-and-yellow sport jacket. "Now, I want only those of you who're going to be baptized to come with me now. I'm going to take you to the dressing rooms and you can put on a choir robe so your clothes won't get wet." The minister gave them his TV smile. "Don't want none of you saying that me or Jesus made you get pneumonia, you know."

As he pushed her toward the others, she grabbed his hurt hand, sending an unexpected lightning jolt up his arm. "G-go on." He winced, prying at her hold with agony.

"Mitch—"

He got her fingers loose with relief, but the pain brought him nausea and he had to stand very still. "T-trust me," he said feebly. "Trust Sarah."

One of the women down at the very front came forward to take Vickie's arm and Mitch saw her speak softly. Vickie shot a sudden frightened stare back at him, and then they disappeared through a door.

His heart was pounding and his nausea was growing. With a sharp breath he turned back up the long aisle. He continued past his pew and pushed open the door into the paneled lobby to find a bathroom. He was barely able to hold back the sickness.

A familiar man in a concert shirt and jacket nodded at him as he found the door reading MEN, and Mitch jerked his head in return, then hurried inside. As soon as he made it to the stall he was sick, losing all of the dinner he'd eaten with Vickie. He crouched there on the floor for several minutes as his vision began to clear, reminded of the last seconds of Sarah's life . . . feeling the guilt of that try to overtake him once more.

He tried to ignore the nausea that was again gaining strength with his fear. The porcelain bowl was cold on his face. "God help me." He waited until his breaths became even, then pulled up and shuffled to the sink. Mitch looked at his pale complexion in a smudged mirror. He held a paper towel under a dripping faucet, then he wiped it over his pale face. Vickie was facing her own moment of truth now, just as he had with Tabitha. But he knew he could not help her do it even if he wanted to. He *knew* that. He wanted to feel brave when he talked to her, and his words were brave, but he knew he could never face anything like Tabitha again.

The lights fluttered.

Mitch gasped, his flickering reflection a mask of fear. The fixture was buzzing above him.

The lights went out.

36

Vickie could not stop trembling. The older woman who had held her hand and prayed with her was with someone else now, helping her to change into a purple choir robe as she had Vickie.

But neither of the other two women was afraid.

The baby was like a burning ball of wax inside her, shooting its decay into her soul, rejecting the care she even now wanted to give it.

"Who's first?" asked a woman in a knee-length pink dress. She stood in the doorway leading to the baptismal pool behind the pulpit. She held out a hand and smiled, three silver bracelets clinked together on her wrist. In the sanctuary the choir sang:

"Redeemed, redeemed—"

A hand prodded Vickie forward. "She's ready."

"Come on, dear," invited the woman in the pink dress. Her wrinkled hand seemed to stretch toward Vickie.

Someone pushed Vickie forward.

"No," she begged.

The woman's hand closed around hers. "Nothing to be afraid of. You can't drown in the living water of Christ." Her smile was pleasantly superior. "I was baptized when I was barely old enough to swim, and *I* wasn't scared." She pulled Vickie out into the church and led her to the frame stairway against the waist-high plastic tub of water. She urged Vickie up the creaking stairs to the top, then backed away.

Vickie shivered; the stairs were cold to her bare feet. She could not close out the visions of years before. "Daddy," she whispered.

The song came to its end.

"Praise the Lord!" shouted a man's voice, with muttered assents of "Amen."

A warm, damp hand took hers and she realized that the middle-aged minister was standing below her, already in the water that licked at his crotch. He smiled easily, urging her down the stairs into the tub. "What's your name, young lady?"

"No, I . . ." She gasped, the tepid water rising up around her ankles, her legs, then, as she reached the bottom of the tub, her hips. She was petrified with memory.

"What's your name?" the preacher asked.

Somehow she managed to answer. "Vickie."

"This is Vickie," the preacher announced to the church members. "She's come to take another step toward Heaven, for herself and her unborn child." He touched Vickie's swollen stomach and grinned. "Now, if anyone else out there has accepted Jesus as their Savior, and hasn't already been baptized, and isn't on their way down here to be baptized right now, I want you to know that the Almighty is going to be real disappointed."

Vickie couldn't speak. She had *not* accepted Jesus. She did not *want* Jesus. Despite everything that had happened, Jesus had still taken away her father. The water suddenly chilled her like ice, and her heart was a jackhammer against her ribs. Death had been her savior when she died before. Death had brought her back to life. She had prayed to death.

Death had answered her prayer.

"Now, are you ready to be baptized in the name of Jesus the Christ, Vickie? Are you and your baby ready for that magnificent fullness of the spirit that will come down on you like that wonderful dove that came to Jesus himself when he was baptized by John?"

"Back to hell is where we'll go," a loud voice screamed out, echoing shrilly through the sanctuary. *"Back to hell to burn real slow."*

Vickie twisted around, sloshing water. She struggled against the preacher's heavy grip. Among the choir stood Garcia. His brown whiskery face seemed to jump out from among the others. He wore a choir robe, except that his was *red. Soggy red,* dripping its color onto the floor. The men and women in the choir were humming his melody. Vickie pulled frantically against the preacher, the sloshing of the water against the tub making her attempts sound like gentle, futile things.

"Use life now and stake your claim," hollered Garcia, meeting her eyes with a grin. "Do what feels good—*and take no blame!*"

She stared, frozen by the cold, dark tendrils filling her up from inside, reaching into her heart and soul, promising her a warped version of eternal life.

Garcia cackled, and Vickie stared at the minister's soundless, moving mouth. Garcia sang louder and walked to the pulpit beside the tub. The congregation was staring at him, but no one moved, and when he turned to her, she felt the power of death. *"Come back from your shadowy grave. Come, let us be your willing slave! Death on earth, death's will over men! Show us how to steal and sin."* Garcia wiped his nose with his hand and then wiped his hand on the minister's Bible with glee. He loped toward her like a deformed John Cleese as the minister of silly walks, his right leg stiff and unbending, his limp left leg dragging behind. He was laughing as he bent and peered into her eyes. *"Bring us back to life again!"*

"No," she cried, pushing at the minister's solid chest. Where was Mitch? Her baby fidgeted and scraped at her insides, clawing to get out.

"Death will be, but not for free." Garcia tore his choir robe open down the center, splattering her with cold blood. " 'Cause you've got to fuck the dead for eternal bliss. *You've got to fuck the Father and His ghost and Son . . . to piss!"*

Garcia dropped the robe to his feet and stood naked in front of her. He paraded back and forth in front of the congregation as if he were performing a concert. *"Everyone!"* he shouted.

"Fuck the dead for eternal bliss! Fuck the Father and His ghost and Son . . . *to piss!"*

The congregation rose to their feet, clapping their hands to Garcia's rhythm and echoing his chant with their tuneless voices.

"Praise the Lord," hollered a man in the front row, and others followed as Garcia waggled his fleshy baton, grinning back at Vickie with his shining, pearly teeth. The voices of the congregation faded out, then back in, but they were singing another song, an old familiar tune Vickie hadn't heard in years.

"He's got the whole world in His hands, he's got the whole world in His hands."

Garcia's teeth seemed to sparkle more brightly. "That's me, Vickie. That's *us! My Will and your baby.*"

"He's got the itsy-bitsy baby in His hands—"

Garcia's presence charged the words with a new, bitter blasphemy, challenging life, God, and the very structure of the universe. She trembled, the world graying out. "My baby."

The vague shape of the minister spoke, the congregation theatrically halting its song. "I baptize thee"—he put his arm around Vickie and pressed her into the water—"with my power in the wonderful name of our Savior, *death.*"

At the word her body collapsed. The water slid up her neck, over her mouth, nose. Like years before. As the water brushed at her eyes, Garcia loped toward her, his body twisted and distorted in the refracting light. He reached the edge of the tub and stood over her, a wavering image whose outstretched arms seemed to encompass the world. The image suddenly swelling, he shoved his face into the water, molding his rough lips over hers. His icy tongue plunged into her mouth; his shriek exploded into her throat, renewing the baby's vibrations inside her.

Death!

She could not help herself.

In the name of death.

Garcia laughed and disappeared.

"Je-sus!" the minister screamed. He spasmed as though struck, and dropped her. The water was suddenly boiling. It scalded Vickie's throat as she opened her mouth to scream. She broke the surface with a screech and blinked her vision clear. Before her the minister's flesh turned red, and his skin blistered and popped, splattering her with yellow pus mixed in blood. As his skin disintegrated in a rain of blood, the tissue beneath began to boil. Vickie covered her mouth and fought against the water toward the steps, her mind overloaded, recalling these sensations from another time, flashing as she became nine years old once more, fighting to pull herself out as screams tore the air around her, lights exploded into night. Garcia stood on the steps above her. He reached out to her and dragged her out of the stinking pit of boiling blood.

Vickie.

She moaned and recognized the voice of her tormentor, Aliester C.

Vickie.

"No." She flailed her arms with all her strength, striking at the hands that held her.

"Vickie—stop it!"

Vickie looked up and saw Mitch Lisciotti bending over her. The smell of sulfur burned the air and she started. Smoke filled the darkness around them. Several flashlights shot beams of illumination through the church, and she knew that Garcia was gone. Above her, next to Mitch, knelt the woman who had helped her change into the robe. Sobbing tore the air bitterly.

"I don't understand," the woman in the pink dress wailed. "I don't understand what happened. She wasn't even burned."

Mitch was pale, and his face was filled with fear. "Are you okay?" he asked.

She was dead. She knew that now. The water had scalded her, but had done no physical damage. Only the freezing death inside her hurt. "No," she said.

"She wasn't even blistered," the woman said again, poring over Vickie's skin as if studying a scientific specimen.

"The ambulance is on its way," shouted a distant voice.

"Are you hurt?" Mitch asked again through the murmur of other voices. He helped her to sit up. The church seemed more like a cavernous mausoleum now. Vickie wanted to get away from this place. "I've got your clothes," Mitch whispered. "Can you walk?"

She nodded again.

He took her shoes from the bundle under his arm and set them on the floor. She pushed into them groggily, the wet robe heavy on her legs. She thought of the preacher's face, bursting and boiling, and hung to Mitch as he helped her to her feet.

"Easy does it," he said, steadying her, then turned to the woman in the pink dress. "I'm going to take her to the sanctuary to sit down."

"Is she all right? My husband—"

"She's all right. It's okay. We'll be sitting in the sanctuary." He walked Vickie off the platform, pushing through the dispersing crowd. Staring, crying . . .

"Please, let's go," Vickie whimpered.

"Yeah," he said, pulling her to the door.

37

Mitch's arm was firm around her waist as he led her into the lobby. But Vickie seemed unable to concentrate on the present, her mind replaying the horrors of her past again and again like a skipping record. Her father had been stolen from her, then her first baby. She would not lose this one.

Their steps echoed in the emptiness. Vickie moved in a daze. They stepped out the door onto the sidewalk. The streets were deserted tracks between the tall downtown buildings.

Dead.

"No," she murmured. She was insane, and so captivated that she no longer knew the real from the unreal. She was driven on only by her need for a baby.

As if in reply the baby kicked her hard, making her gasp.

She *did* want the baby. *She wanted it.* She wanted so badly to be a mother, *to be a woman.*

She plodded with Mitch through the shadows, feeling the wet weight of the choir robe. Motionless cars wobbled in her vision. The smell of reeking blood followed her.

Dead.

The muffled voices grew dim behind them, replaced by traffic and sirens. She looked up, and outlined by headlights, a figure was closing in. He was smiling, the teeth shiny above his jeans jacket and T-shirt. "No," Vickie whispered, blinking.

He was gone.

She closed her mouth, wanting to hide. She *was* crazy, too, and so tired. . . . Her will was crumbling, and the baby's rough movements inside her hurt worse than anything she'd ever imagined. She set her face, trying once more to close the door to her mind.

But she could not lock it.

She had no key.

"Vickie," Mitch urged. "Come on. Come on."

"Why?" she said, her legs no longer able to move. "Sarah was wrong. It *didn't* work. What can we do now?"

Handling her like a heavy bag, Mitch forced her to stand against him and then dragged her ahead, bearing her weight. "There's got to be a reason." He stopped, picked her up, and carried her between the parking spaces. When they reached his car, he set her down and leaned her against it. "I wanted to run, Vickie. I wanted to just leave you and run when the lights went off. I wanted to run *again.* But I couldn't this time. We can't just quit. If we do—if I let you give up, then I'll have to deal with *that* guilt." His face was open, pleading. "Sarah said we have to overcome our guilt to do better, and use the second chance it gives us."

He opened the car door. Farther away sirens grew louder, blasting the night's relative peace. Mitch was right, and more people were going to die like Sarah and Mother if she didn't stop it. She knew that. But— "D-death is still my savior," she whispered, admitting it. "Garcia was there. He came to me and he saved me from dying in that water, just like before."

The siren became louder.

"Get in," Mitch told her quietly, and she could taste the dread in his tone. "Come on, Vickie." He urged her into the front seat, and then went around to the driver's side and got in.

"Did you hear me?" she asked.

He started the car.

38

"And the bizarre reports are still growing," the radio announcer reported dryly. "It seems that everyday sanity has gone to hell in a handbasket at this hour. It is confirmed that Jim Whitten, a dead man who somehow returned to life in the greatest medical miracle of our time, jumped from the window of his room at the Observer Institute two hours ago. Dr. Don Fowler of the institute staff has stated that he saw Mr. Whitten leap from the fifth floor of the Coates Medical Building in what appeared to be a suicide attempt, but when Fowler and others hurried outside to give the man medical attention, Whitten was gone. Blood was found on the pavement and has been identified as Whitten's type, but a careful search of the institute's grounds has turned up no other sign of the missing man. Whitten must be assumed to be dead once more, or at least dying at this hour. Authorities are urgently requesting anyone who sees him or knows his whereabouts to call 911 immediately. In related news, yet another woman who was reported dead awakened moments later. It makes seven cases since the St. Paul hospital and Observer Institute's reports of Jim Whitten and an unidentified patient were released Thursday. The federal agents who took over the researches of that private laboratory have incarcerated all these other patients there, and unnamed observers state that these so-called living dead men and women appear to go into sudden violent rages. A federal spokesman has again stated a belief that this may be the result of some chemical and radiation testing the Chinese have not admitted to. The testing that the spokesman is referring to is that of a bomb exploded over the jet stream in the Pacific late last week. The bomb may have contained some kind of chemical reagent that stimulates the motor nerves of certain recently deceased human beings. As most of us know now, the jet stream has recently moved directly over the area of northern Oklahoma and the storms it's causing in this region may have resulted in undetected fallout."

Mitch Lisciotti trembled, staring out the windshield at the night. There had been no streetlamps for the past fifteen miles. Tree limbs rustled on either side of the gravel road. He was scared shitless, especially by the news of Whitten's escape. The dull pain of his broken hand on the steering wheel gnawed at the outskirts of his mind, overshadowed by Vickie's sharp breaths. He looked at her every thirty seconds or so, wanting badly each time to strike her awake, remembering too well what had happened the last time she slept. Even worse, he feared that every time she nodded off it might prove another's end. The radio announcer said that the number of these living dead was still growing, and according to Sarah's notes, that was the horror Vickie's sleep brought about. Shuddering, Mitch wondered how many of his fellow tenants might have died as Vickie slept in his apartment. "Vickie!" he muttered again.

She jerked her head up tiredly and blinked, slapping her hands against her cheeks. She ran one hand down over her stomach.

They had stopped at a gas station before leaving Tulsa, where she changed out of the wet choir robe and dressed in her shirt and jeans. On her return to the car, he'd told her of his intention to take her back to the deserted stadium where this had all begun. Vickie had said nothing at all, then closed her eyes as he drove. He'd jerked the steering wheel often to make the ride bumpy and keep her from nodding off. But her silence gave him a chance to go over what happened in the church.

The defeat of Sarah's plan did not destroy its validity, but proved that problem was more complex than he had thought. The one simple truth that was apparent was that he had never been able to overcome his guilt and the death hiding in him until his forced confrontation. It had taken his near-fatal meeting with the nightmare Tabitha only a dozen or so hours ago to open his eyes to what Sarah told him all along— that though he might have wronged her, he had not chosen death for her.

Mitch drove purposely over a pothole.

"Ouch." Vickie shifted beside him. "I *already* ache all over."

"Do you need to stop?"

"Before much longer. The call of nature, you know."

He gave a forced smile. "As long as it's not of supernature."

Vickie smiled and relaxed back into the seat.

Glad that Vickie was fully awake, Mitch kept an eye on the fuel needle as they looked for a gas station. Spindly, bare trees and flat farmland stretched off on both sides of the road.

"Don't worry," he teased without feeling, "the seats are vinyl. Drip-dry."

"Not funny." After a moment she yelled, "Rest stop!"

Halfway through a yawn he saw the roadside

gas station through the straggly branches ahead. A red neon sign sputtered its prices.

Mitch took a deep breath. "We'll stop to fill 'er up again and get something to eat, too, okay?"

She didn't answer immediately, then: "Okay."

He turned in.

"Just in time," Vickie cried.

He stopped at the slender, rusty gas pumps, then got out into the fresh country night and stretched his back. Vickie's door slammed and she hurried toward the building.

Mitch unhooked a gas nozzle and unscrewed the gas cap.

"Mitch." Vickie had stopped halfway to the building.

The alarm in her voice ripped fear back into his thoughts. "Wha—"

"This is it!"

Even with the ten-foot distance separating them he could not mistake the stunned recognition in Vickie's downturned open mouth. He dropped the gas nozzle and ran toward her. As she started to run, he grabbed one of Vickie's arms and jerked her hard, using that violence to forget his desire to escape. She had to see what was happening as he did now—as her own choice. "We agreed," he gasped. "You have to be here!" He held his damaged hand away from her feeble strikes. "You have to deny death!"

Only in confronting the truth could he, Vickie, or anyone be free of guilt or death's delusion. "We . . . we have to—"

"Goddammit, no!" she cried, shaking with tears. "I can *feel* that it won't work! It didn't work at the church!"

"We can't let the Klingons win!" Mitch shouted back, then blushed at the madness of his words. "Sarah knew it all along, Vickie, and I know because of Tabitha. I was inviting her to haunt me. I welcomed it because it relieved my guilt."

"No! I can't do it. I can't be here again."

"You *are* here." He felt the brisk spring wind on his cheeks. "You *must* be here." He laughed hysterically. "We choose our own hell, and it's so much nastier than fire and brimstone because it's what we think we want even if we really don't want it. God damn, it's so fucking simple—"

"Get me out of here!" Vickie screamed. Her movements were frenzied now, out of control. "I changed my mind because it won't work. We already tried."

He yanked her so close that their faces slapped together. "You're like me. You're still more afraid of life than you are of death!" The madness that had made him understand was strong, and he smiled with triumph, welcoming the single-mindedness of lunacy that held him up against his fear.

"No . . ." Her voice weakened and her struggles became feeble. "No."

The office door swung open and a heavyset man in a billed cap stepped out, his jowly face half-lit from the building's interior. "What the hell's going on?"

Mitch held her shuddering body close and waved his bandaged hand. "Sorry," he called. "Just getting some gas."

"The hell you say." The chunky redneck walked toward them. "You having some problems?"

"Nope," he said. He walked Vickie back to the car and picked up the nozzle, fit it into the opening. As he squeezed painfully on the grip with his broken hand, he met Vickie's eyes. "We've both hidden too damn long, and it's catching up to us. It caught up to *me* and I had to go through every painful memory all over again. But now I know who I am, and what I am, and there's nothing else I can do but what I'm trying to do now: to make up for it."

"I tried," she whispered.

He shut his eyes and almost cried at her voice. "You *have* to do it! The little train tried and tried, even when Humpty Dumpty fell off the wall—but you *can* put him back together again!"

"I can't."

He released the nozzle's handle, sniffing the stink of gasoline. He nodded at the man who was waiting for them several yards away, put back the nozzle, and screwed on the cap. "You have to," he said.

She looked up at him, her expression unreadable. "I know."

He pushed her at the office. "Now get inside and use the bathroom."

39

Vickie sat on the all too familiar floor, gazing into the open mouths of the empty lockers as she waited for Mitch to come back inside. She reached out to take the last potato chip crumbs from the sack on the blemished table, still starving after their meager slot-machine snack of sweet rolls and chips. Her eyes strayed around the home of her nightmares. The dust and cobwebs were undisturbed, the metal chair and tattered, stinking blankets in the same place, as if her encounter with Garcia had occurred only minutes before. Everything was the same.

Everything.

She could hardly breathe in the fear that had easily overcome her exhaustion. The horrors of the past and present were combined. She had let Mitch bring her back to Hell, and nothing could protect her. Not even Mitch in his sudden, disgusting, shivering confidence. He would not be able to do anything about it.

As if he had ever been able to, anyway.

"Vickie?"

The door creaked and she turned to face Mitch.

"Do you feel better?" he asked, running a hand nervously through his hair.

The chill of the baby permeated her; the pain of its quickening growth was becoming more severe. "It's okay. I feel better," she lied. It was as if the baby were responding to the place, as if the baby knew where they were. Pain stabbed her insides, cramping her intestines. She clenched her teeth, feeling bitterness. The worst part of it was that it was hers. The baby was hers! "You asked me to *trust* you . . ."

He held up a transistor radio, then licked his lips.

Vickie glared at him, trembling with the memories that lived all around her. "You acted concerned. You said you cared, and you asked me to trust you." She bit her lip. "You asked me to trust you, so I did." She shook her head. "And then you brought me here. There are dead here. They want life."

"You have to face this," Mitch said. He walked to one of the shack's murky windows and wiped his index finger through its thick, grimy coating. "This is the insane thing to do, Vickie." His eyes gleamed strangely. "That's how I know it's *right.* I see all my problems magnified in you, and it took death itself to make me reject death. I lived in that hell for a long time. I held Tabitha to me and I wouldn't let her go . . . until now." Mitch turned the radio on.

Heavy-metal music blasted out of the tinny speaker.

Vickie jerked up straight. Mitch was standing where Aliester C. had those terrible months ago. The song blasted the night's silence.

Mitch set the transister radio on the table. "This is all we can do. Don't you see? Sarah told me you can't run from the very thing you cling to. She said I could never be cured unless I wanted to be, and she was right." He moved closer, his voice raised over the sound of the music. "All any of us have is *our* choices. We have the choice between life and death. I thought that I killed Tabitha, but *she* did it. She alone held the ability to choose. Even Sarah had that choice!" As he crouched close beside her, his hand caressed her back with a sudden tenderness. He lowered his voice. "I'm afraid. But to be afraid, you have to have *hope,* Vickie. When you're dead, you have nothing and can only *want.* I came too close, and that's what I learned."

Vickie felt very, very tired. Frigid lifelessness coated her insides. Her very soul strove to deny his words, but she hoped, too. She had hoped to gain her father's life from death, and had prayed to death in that hope. She buried her face in the musty blankets.

Life.

The shadow waited.

The shadow. The shadow that had come to her baby, Samuel, in the nightmare. The shadow that had sacrificed his tiny, unborn life to death—by her own consent—a decade before his conception.

It sucked the dreams of life as they appeared in her soul, and it waited as she became filled with the dark souls of those whom she served guiltily and fearfully. Sarah had told her that her voluntary union with death merged the realities of life and death so tightly inside her that death had become her very life.

Vickie climbed to her feet, pulling free of Mitch's embrace. "You—you're crazy, Mitch! I mean it. *I mean it!*"

He stood, hands at his sides, looking at once determined and afraid. "I know I must be, because I called the radio station, Vickie, and requested a song. I'm challenging you to accept life in the face of death. And I'm inviting death to be here with us."

She screamed. "No! No! No!"

"It's no one you haven't met before," he said with a shiver. "I requested Aliester C.'s Seance song. I remember it from when I was younger. The album cover said you could bring back the dead by playing it . . . *and believing in it.* It . . . it was a big joke, then." He shook his head. "But the joke was on us. We need to stay here until this is over. We have to stay here."

". . . *you can never leave!*" sang the radio.

Mitch's figure seemed suddenly ominous, unstoppable in its insanity. "We have to stay until it's over."

She was more terrified of him than any of the nightmares made her. "Help me!" she pleaded.

"I am," he said.

"That was the Eagles, from their 1976 album *Hotel California,*" blasted in the golden-voiced announcer. "And now, a special request going out to the beyond from Mitch and Vickie, a weird twosome if my guess is right. See if you can guess this one, listeners, it's another golden oldie, a *live* performance if you want to call it that, and still sends lightning rods up my spine . . . or something like that."

Vickie's body was coated with sweat and her heart beat into her hollow soul. Mitch went to her, his body tense and his tongue clicking loudly.

"Seance . . . seance . . ." chanted a cacophony of voices, silenced by the sudden electric chord of a violent guitar. A harsh baritone voice blared out:

*"Ghosts and devils dance in the night . . .
    bringing us unearthly fright!
They come to us in our dreams . . . holding us
    close and . . . craving our screams!
They take our life and give us death . . . but we
    return as they do . . . throwing off our funeral
    wreath!"*

"Mitch, *stop it!*" Vickie pushed against him and tried to run for the door, but he had her. She scratched at his face, catching skin under her nails. The frenzied drumroll erupted into a cymbal crash. *"Stop it!"*

*"Come to us, dead spirits—now!
Take us from our Christian vow. . . .
Bring us your death and return—and how—"*

The cymbals clashed into the drum's rolling pace once more, tinny in the small speaker.

*"Come back from your shadowy grave . . . come,
    let us be your willing slave!
Death on earth, death's will over men! Show us
    how to steal . . . and sin—
Bring us back to life again!"*

The shack's windows ballooned, exploding in a shattering crash that shot slivers into the air like bullets. Mitch and Vickie ducked, covered their faces. Glass pelted the floor at their feet, and Vickie's ears popped in the freezing, tornadic wind that whined after. The wind knocked Mitch back into the lockers. They struggled to hold on to each other. She squealed, feeling the pimples of goose bumps rise on her forearms.

"Deny death, Vickie!" Mitch yelled. *"Now, Vickie—now!"*

The radio was on fire, bathed in rippling yellow flame. Black smoke billowed from it through the room.

"Death will be, but not for *free*," sang out a high, biting voice, free of the transistor's tinny speaker, but distant . . . outside. The voice was joined by a rattling, frenzied synthesizer.

The door had blown open in the wind, and a heavy luminescent haze was filling the room, obscuring the peeling walls.

Shapes took from outside the doorway among the overgrown bushes. The haze carried a bad earthy smell like burning tires, only worse. She gagged, knowing it was the stink of death. Her ragged fingernails dug into Mitch's shoulder.

Mitch pulled her up and dragged her forward, into the fog that stung her with its electricity and made her skin crawl. The synthesizer's blare raped the air, driving into her and the baby. It moved inside her as if it was dancing.

Dozens of shapes surrounded them outside the shack. They sang out. *"We're all babies in black, ready to thrill. Babies in black, dying to kill!"*

Vickie tried to push Mitch away, but the fingers of his undamaged hand squeezed deep into the meat of her arm, pulling her into the sounds. The baby's movement made it hard for her to breathe.

"You don't dress a baby in black until it's dead, and when it comes back to life it'll bite off your head!
We're the babies, can't you see?
We just want your blood to make us free!"

The mist brought tears to her eyes, and she *couldn't* see—didn't know how Mitch could see to keep dragging her on. The smell of death grew thick, driving up into her nostrils, burning her throat with its flames. She coughed desperately. Mitch coughed too. She could no longer see him through the mist and her tears, but his hand was firm and his steps forward slow and constant. The baby's dance had grown frenzied. It felt as though the baby was stomping her intestines into ground hamburger, clawing her unprotected organs in a fervency to be free of her body's prison.

"We want your blood to make us free!"

The fog separated into wispy streams, exposing an unlit stairway that led through from the back of the bleachers to the front. The steps were cracked, splintered. She didn't want to go. Behind her the voices screamed and the synthesizer splattered the air. Vickie took Mitch's hand in hers. As she held it tight it swelled, becoming huge and strong.

"Come on, baby-girl," Daddy said, standing beside her in place of Mitch. "There is no hope in death. But none of these souls accepted that. *They* never really believed in life. That's why you have to believe, Vickie. You know that death is not the end. There is choice in death. It comes in what you choose to accept, as your friend learned. The life after death doesn't have to be the horror you've seen, because if that's all there is . . ." He was tall, his voice was gentle and kind, and he smelled like home. "If there is no joy to life, then there is no purpose or hope, and if hope ends forever, then there is no point to *anything.*"

"Daddy!" She clutched him hard, pushing her face into his work shirt and inhaling his reality as his hands rubbed against her back. He *had* come back. "Daddy, I need you."

Wrapping her hand in his just the way she'd dreamed, she followed him up the shivering steps. Though the voices and music still blasted all around them, they were mere background to the sigh of Daddy's breath now. Even the baby's wrenching movements no longer frightened her. *Daddy* was leading her to the top of the stairs. She wanted him to take her away, to fly her far from this hell.

The stairway opened onto the bleacher's landing, and Daddy stopped. The plank benches below, around, and above them were filled by estatic, hollow screams, by long-haired teenagers in multicolored T-shirts, bell-bottom jeans, and miniskirts. They jumped up and down noiselessly, dancing like the baby inside her to the harsh melody from the football field below. On the fifty-yard line sat a wooden stage.

Garcia—*Aliester C.*—stood in its center, flanked on one side by psychedelic drums and a dwarf drummer. On the other side were two hunchbacked men with knife-ended guitars. A naked redheaded woman danced and strutted before them, straddle legged as she bent forward, poking a long machete up between her legs and then licking the spurting red liquid it brought forth. She moaned, *"Fuck off with life. Get fucked by death, 'cause fucking's what it's all about! Fucking makes me scream and shout! Rape the children and be real cool, then stab the babies with your tool. Life is hopeless, anyway."* She spat the foaming blood. *"So suck death's sperm and we can play!"*

Garcia clapped his hands briskly and loped to the woman's side. He reached down to take the dripping machete handle between her thighs and pulled it up without effort until it split her abdomen. She giggled hysterically.

"Come to death—bring death to wife," he chanted, raising the big blade to the cheers of the naked teenagers groping each other before the stage, *"Come down here, Vickie, to be our life! Fuck the Father, Son, and Holy Ghost to piss,"* he screeched, his urgent voice echoing through the stands. *"Then fuck Vickie for eternal bliss!"*

Vickie clutched at Daddy. He took his hand away and backed from her into the growing breeze.

"It's your decision, baby-girl," he said behind clenched teeth, pointing down at Garcia. "Go to him."

With uncertain feet she took a step forward, then looked back again. Daddy was gone. Mitch stood there instead, his wide eyes staring at the crowd that inched nearer as they danced and sang.

> *"We're babies in black, wanting to live.*
> *You have the life and you must give,*
> *Fill us with blood and make us dance*
> *Fill us with life and give us our chance!"*

Dripping blood, the red-haired, laughing woman jumped off the stage and floated up onto the bleachers in a greenish glow. It spilled all

over the destitute stadium. The jeering teenagers stilled as she passed. The bleeding woman
moved between them until she stood about six
feet from Vickie. The laughing woman blasted
her with cold, sweeping wind, jiggling her stark
naked body and reveling in the force. Her pale
face was lined with hatred. Vickie turned away,
remembering how this woman had taunted her
before, jeering as Garcia bled to death before
Vickie's shocked eyes. Vickie gasped for air. In
the fog that had grown up behind the woman, a
man in dark glasses and jeans jacket appeared. A
boy barely old enough to shave stepped forward, his arm shredded, dripping purple blood.
The mist turned into fire, flames burning over
the bleachers, and the boy's mouth drooled a
frothy slime. . . .

Vickie groaned, trying to push a scream
through empty lungs. There were more, more.
They all wore horrid, bloody faces—hungry
faces—and their hands clutched at each other,
tearing at each other with fingernails and teeth.
The fog bathed her in icy tingles.

"Vickie."

Aliester C. appeared directly in front of her.
Beside him was Jim Whitten, the minister she
had caused to die only hours ago in the baptistry. Their frenetic, empty convulsions were reflected in luminous, barren eyes.

Footsteps clomped down the bleachers toward her. Mitch grabbed her and forced her to look at Garcia. "Vickie," he cried over the crackling fire and the terrible moaning.

The faces of the teenagers had become the face of her dead baby, Samuel.

"Fuck the dead for eternal bliss—Fuck the Father and His ghost and Son . . . to piss!"

An oozing horror of a woman stepped forward from behind Garcia. The woman's head was close to bald, the few remaining yellow tangles hanging over dripping eye sockets. Fragments of brain dropped down onto her sunken, bloodless cheeks.

Vickie gagged, recognizing Sarah. Garcia came closer and stroked his fingers over Vickie's stomach, over the kicks of the baby. The baby's movements were frenzied, as if it was desperate to tear itself out of her belly.

"Mitchell," Sarah wheezed through a twisted, lipless mouth. Her face looked as if it had been crushed and then torn inside out. Sarah reached out with rubbery, limp fingers, the nails colored purple and half eaten away. *"Mitchell, believe—accept."* Her grating vocal chords whistled like steam from a kettle. *"We must all die. Let me at least live in death with you."* Her rotting face wrinkled and dripped.

"Mitch!" screamed another figure, back in the smoke and fire.

Mitch Lisciotti's mouth dropped open and he

staggered away from Vickie. Vickie knew the second woman was Tabitha. He struggled to the stairway against a hundred clawing teenagers.

Sarah's decomposing face touched Mitch.

"Vickie, please!" he cried, trying to force his way down the stairs. Fists pummeled into his back. *"Please,* Vickie!" Mitch sobbed painfully.

A hundred hands grabbed him and began pulling the flesh from his body. Vickie screamed as his blood splattered her own lips, making her taste dying, cold panic. The shapes of the teenagers were spreading red and yellow tongues of fire erupting all over the stadium, fed by the rushing winds. They still wore Samuel's baby face, and their agony tore at her heart. Words dissolved in her mouth, and she flinched from their reek of decay.

> *"You don't dress a baby in black until it's dead,*
> *and when it comes back to life it'll bite off your*
> *head!*
> *We're the babies, can't you see?*
> *We just want your blood to make us free!"*

Samuel. Her baby.

Her father.

Garcia's green-glowing face smiled, and he dropped his hands down to his jeans, unbuckling them slow. "It felt so good, didn't it, Vickie? It *always* feels so good. Every one of us can make you feel good forever and ever. We can make you feel like the woman you are! You're our mother and we want to suck on your tits until they're raw and bleeding and fuck your dry cunt until we're scraping your bones."

Garcia dropped his pants and jerked Vickie toward his rigid penis. "You *are* life, Vickie. Give us *our* life! Fuck off with life and fuck with our *death*—" He pushed her down on the bleachers, pulled her shirt open, and tore her bra free.

"Death into life," the red-haired woman screeched beside them, ripping her own yellowed flesh with an uncanny fingernail . . . deep.

"G-God—" cried Vickie, seeing the shining, red blood pour out over the woman's milky, bared bones and dripping intestines.

The screeching wind whipped at Vickie. The vertigo of frantic violence grew.

Garcia pulled her jeans down her legs, dragging her panties off with them. She closed her eyes. Ice froze her soul from inside. She hated it. *She hated it!*

But it was her baby.

Vickie choked, wanting Daddy to come back for her.

"D-Daddy," she cried.

But he could not be here. *He believed in life.*

She groped for sanity in the pelting wind as Garcia's hands spread her legs apart.

"I'm going to fuck your dry little cunt, Vickie, and split you up the middle so your life will make us all free forever . . . so we can fuck you every minute like the woman you want to be. And your new child will grow as big as the earth, and he'll fuck you too!"

His voice changed as he spoke, and Vickie looked up into the skinny, sweating face of Jim Whitten. Jim Whitten was naked, shaking with anticipation, and surrounded by the naked teenagers waiting for their opportunity. Whitten's short, skinny penis pulsed to enter her and dripped his excitement with a pink flow of gooey issue. His hand reached out above her to take the stained machete from the ghostwoman who was tittering lustily. Vickie screamed and heard an answering thunder rip the black sky. Green lightning exploded from horizon to horizon, turning the rippling flames covering the stands to green, and from the high, billowing clouds came a boiling rain.

Daddy.

But Daddy could not be here.

The rain drenched her and Vickie's lips tremored and she squirmed under the hot splashes drenching her arms and legs and dripping from Jim Whitten above her. The heat of it was life. Her life. She was alive and her father was dead. Jim Whitten began to inch inside her painfully. Her hips trembled. "In . . . the name of the Father, S-Son, and Holy . . ."

In the name of death.

She spit out a mouthful of water. *"In the name of Life!"* she screamed. Her voice cracked. *"The Father, the Son . . ."* She coughed and choked and felt her stomach tearing, ripped into burning pieces. She felt the warmth of Mitch's blood still on her lips. *"A-and the Holy Ghost!"* she cried, denying the blackness that dragged her down . . . *to Hell itself.*

40

"It's half past four in the morning now for all you that lost your watches here at KKOK in Stillwater, and I'm Dinty. I'm gonna try and keep you rockin' all night long. The tornado warning is over and the funnel cloud that dipped down an hour ago has disappeared and taken that nasty storm along with it, along with half of the old Eagle Stadium outside town, according to listeners' phone-in reports. That's where Aliester C. died several years ago, you know, so let's start off with this oldie and finish blowing that ol' rocker right back to where he belongs. This is 'Back to Hell,' by Aliester C."

She was in Hell. Vickie curled up under the heavy, rotten-smelling blanket, feeling feverish. The smell of sulfur and smoke was close around her. Something tugged at her. *She was in Hell.*

"I'm not even going to try to pick you up."

Vickie opened her eyes. The mist had partially dissipated. She lay on wet grass. She was naked.

Mitch smiled blankly, sitting with his radio among charred, shattered lumber that ran up to the remnants of the creaking bleachers. The sky above was clear and clammy in the gentle stirring of the air around her, and a bright ring circled the full moon. "I— Sorry, I'm tired. I'm just fucking *tired.*"

"M-Mitch?" She had seen him bleeding—she watched him dying.

"Yeah." He sighed, wiping his smudged face. *". . . back to Hell, where I belong . . . back to Hell to sing this song—"*

She stared back at him. "You're not dead."

Mitch rubbed his leg. His slacks were torn. "That's where they fucked up. Panic makes me too nutso to accept my own death. I guess I've just had too much experience being crazy." He shook his head grimly. "But that's a crock, too. I just about busted my leg. And I hurt my fucking hand again when the tornado slammed down and tore this fucking place apart. Hurt like hell." He stopped. "Uh, almost like hell. . . ."

". . . pain and lust is my desire—Hell is what I require—"

"But I saw you dying."

He shook his head more firmly. "The only

dead guy here is one of those assholes who attacked you, and there's no sign of anyone or anything else. It's that Jim Whitten guy, I think. There's a chunk of wood as big as a phone pole rammed right through his guts. I've been listening to the radio, too, and they said the other people who had come back to life went completely berserk about the same time that tornado hit us. No good explanations, but some spokesperson is trying to say the changing atmospheric conditions overdosed them with the supposed chemicals from that Chinese bomb. They just freaked out and started trying to kill any living human being who was near. The feds say they're sending all of them to a special security barracks in Lawton to continue observation under better-protected circumstances." A faint smile arched his mouth.

Vickie lay back with uncertain relief.

"Of course they'll never figure out what happened or *how* it happened, but I've got a feeling they're all going to be studying it for a long time."

"We know, though, Mitch, we saw—"

"We saw *nothing*, Vickie, and that's the honest truth. It's just like guilt, and it's only real if you believe in it. Life is the real meaning—*life and love*. I know that without a doubt now. I know that Death is all one big fucking lie. You saw death, so you saw nothing . . . and nothing can't be real." He grinned and gathered up her clothes that lay beside him. "I guess that's the logic of insanity. We're just damn lucky this happened to *us,* so we could figure it all out." He tossed her the clothes. "I saw *nothing* too."

She met his smile, remembering her daddy's short return and wondering if it had really been him—if somehow he had seen her need and come back to her through Mitch. Mitch turned his back, and she stood to dress. Her weight was wrong, all wrong. She dropped the blanket and looked down at herself in the bluish white moonlight, at the shape of her slender, curved body—her whole and barren body, no longer pregnant with death . . . or life.

"And since we want people to think that we're almost sane, Vickie," Mitch said, laughing, his back still turned, "we're going to act sane and not tell anyone about this, right? We'll keep our mutual understanding of insanity a secret— or maybe it's just our mutual *insanity.*"

"You're not crazy," she whispered, remembering her earlier accusation. She pulled on her wet clothes. "Okay," she said softly, "you can turn around."

He did turn, smiling broadly. She went to him, stepping between cracked beams, and took his arm. "Where is Jim Whitten?" she asked.

Pointing to a pile of larger wooden beams, he clucked his tongue, just once. Whitten's body was crushed between the sections of wood. She squeezed her eyes hard, her hand drifting down over her stomach.

She could never have a baby now. She choked out a sob and felt the tears of memory, of *all the memories*, the death of her innocent unborn son, Samuel, and all the rest of her life. "Oh, God." She began to weep, unable to stop the tears.

His arms were close around her. "Hey—you overcame it, Vickie. You chose life in spite of all the lies. *You chose Life!*"

Her hopes had been distorted and bent, but he spoke the truth. She forced herself to nod, trying to relax at the feel of his arm around her waist. "But—but I wish . . ."

He raised his eyebrows.

"I still wish I . . . could have a baby."

He rubbed his hand briskly over her back. "It's a helluva lot easier to just adopt."

The simpleness of his comment caught her, and she laughed with him. She laughed hard until they were both crying and fell against each other, hugging one another, holding together with everything they still had. She held him with gratitude, with caring, with that power flowing through her and filling the emptiness that had been. She had survived, and so had Mitch, and she had made it on her own, just like Daddy had wanted.

She *was* pregnant . . . *with real life*.